W9-CDG-494

THE WIFE'S SECRET

WITHDRAWN

ALSO BY KERRY WILKINSON

Down Among the Dead Men

No Place Like Home

Watched

Ten Birthdays

Two Sisters

The Girl Who Came Back

Last Night

*The Death and Life of Eleanor
   Parker*

THE JESSICA DANIEL SERIES

The Killer Inside (also known as
   Locked In)

Vigilante

The Woman in Black

Think of the Children

Playing with Fire

The Missing Dead (also known
   as *Thicker Than Water*)

Behind Closed Doors

Crossing the Line

Scarred for Life

For Richer, For Poorer

Nothing but Trouble

SHORT STORIES

January

February

March

April

THE ANDREW HUNTER SERIES

Something Wicked

Something Hidden

SILVER BLACKTHORN SERIES

Reckoning

Renegade

Resurgence

THE WIFE'S SECRET

KERRY WILKINSON

Bookouture

Published by Bookouture in 2018

An imprint of StoryFire Ltd.

Carmelite House
50 Victoria Embankment
London EC4Y 0DZ

www.bookouture.com

ISBN: 978-1-78681-707-5
eBook ISBN: 978-1-78681-706-8

PART ONE: EXODUS

ONE

SETH. NOW

They say you can't choose your family. That might be true, but you can certainly leave them off the guest list when you're getting married.

As for friends? Well, what counts as a friend? Raj is slumped against a wall in the corner, a best man in name only. A default choice, I suppose, because someone has to do it. You can't turn up to get married without another bloke in a matching suit at your side. It's not even about the tradition, it's someone with whom to make small talk while you're standing at the front next to the registrar, hoping your wife-to-be hasn't had second thoughts.

'Happiest day of your life,' he muttered as we stood together a few hours ago. He was spouting clichés, but it was true. Well, sort of. How can these things be measured? Has our wedding day been better than the time four of us bunked off school and went to Alton Towers? It should be, of course it should, but a moment in time from more than a decade ago can't be ranked against something so completely different. Will we laugh more than that time he put a football through a window by accident?

It's been good, though. Very Charley and me. More sparklers in the garden than flashy fireworks booming over Big Ben. Small. Concise. *Us*.

'She left you already, big man?'

The clap on my back sends me stumbling forward; more the boozy swirl than the force of Rafi's hand. If you can't get lashed on the day you get married, then when can you?

Rafi is Raj's brother. We're not even that close, but they come as a pair. Buy one Indian friend, get another free. There's only eleven months between them in age, so I've always pitied their poor mother. Five children in a little over four years? People have been given OBEs for less than that.

'I knew I should've got the prenup,' I laugh. It's the third or fourth time today I've used that line. Standard wedding-day joke. The girl behind the hotel's reception desk got the first take. Gets a laugh – or at least a forced smile – every time. That's despite me not owning anything of any particular value. Charley can have half my credit card debt and the mortgage if she wants. If we're marrying for money, then we've each made one hell of a mistake.

Rafi continues giggling through his nose. He's drunk as well. Not quite sleeping while standing up like his brother, but well on the way.

'How's Raj?' I ask.

We both look to the corner where my best man is proving to be anything but. He is using one hand to hold himself up, the other to cradle his empty pint glass. His eyes are closed but he's giggling to himself.

'He keeps popping outside for air,' Rafi says.

'Is air a cure for being drunk?'

'Ha! I found him in a bush five minutes ago. I think he'd fallen asleep. I had to drag him back in here. Good job the speeches are done.' He licks his lips and peers around the room. 'Where is the lovely bride?' he asks.

'Probably popped to the loo. It takes her ages to hitch that dress up. Alice had to help her out last time. I think it's a two- or three-person job.'

Even as I'm speaking, I spy Alice near the buffet. She made most of the food, so if anyone gets to enjoy it, it should be her.

'That's women, man,' Rafi says, still laughing. 'You're stuck now. Your whole life: one woman.'

Another thing people say when you tell them you're getting married – especially when you're still in your twenties. Charley's twenty-eight and I'm a year younger. A nudge and a wink. One woman, eh? Because, if it wasn't for Charley, I'd have females hurling themselves at me…

I laugh anyway. It's the thing to do. Everyone's a comedian when it comes to christenings, weddings and funerals. That's what having to get dressed up does to people. We're all so uncomfortable in our suits, dresses, control underwear and who knows what else that the only way to release tension is repeat the same jokes we've heard over and over.

Rafi stumbles away to check on his brother and I'm alone with my nearly finished pint. The room is slowly filling up, although no one can fail to notice that it's almost entirely people *I* know. A few faces from work, some old university pals, a couple of the lads from football. You hear 'reception-only', you think, 'free food', possibly even the chance that the first drink might be paid for by the happy couple. Bottles of wine on the table. Fingers crossed and all that. We've all been there.

From nowhere, it feels like I'm being sucked into a pit, a panicked second or two where I try to remember how much I've drunk. Is the floor spinning? The ceiling? Me? I've not had *that* much.

Then I realise I'm being pulled at by someone a lot smaller than me.

It's Charley's niece, Daisy. The curls in her blonde hair are beginning to fall out as her big moment as a first-time bridesmaid comes to an end. She's only five, still at that age where everything is a wonderful new experience and the world is a big place in which anything can happen. The time of unicorns and Santa, or Santa riding a unicorn.

It's her father who speaks: 'Any idea where Little C is?'

I have no idea why Charley's brother-in-law calls her this. Mason Renton is busy trying to keep his other child, seven-year-old Dillon, from doing knee skids on the dance floor. Me? I don't care. Go for it, kid. It's probably more fun than a first dance.

'I was just wondering that myself,' I tell him.

Mason has one hand on his son's shoulder and offers that weary gaze parents frequently give non-parents: *Bloody kids, huh? Be grateful it's not you.*

I actually quite like Mason and considered asking him to be my best man even though we don't know each other that well. I thought Charley would appreciate it. They've always been close. In the end, I suppose I figured it should be a friend.

'I'm going to get them up to bed,' he says.

Daisy lets go of my leg and scowls in disgust. As Mason heads for the door, both his children combine for a unified moan about bedtimes. I suspect Mason's true reasoning is that he wants a few quiet hours to himself in his room once the kids are asleep. It's been a long day for everyone.

As the door pops open, the spinning lights and booming music from the adjacent room pours through, and then it's gone again. We're in the smallest of the hotel's conference rooms, which is plenty enough for us. Charley and I are good at low-key.

There's another reception going on across the hall. One of those where the bride invites everyone she's ever met and it becomes a competitive sport. Five photographers and double-digit bridesmaids.

A 'my day'-thing.

I saw it in the groom's face earlier when we gave each other a nod and a half-smile near the toilets. There was no joking around then. He was wide-eyed, still in shock as if he'd seen an articulated lorry slam into the side of a Mini. *Christ, I've got a lifetime of this,* he was thinking.

I said as much to Charley afterwards. She smiled softly, the visual pat on the head. She's been quiet all day.

'Your better half around?'

A woman's voice. Weddings are a veritable *This Is Your Life* and Emily approaches from behind, drifting into my vision as if from nowhere. It's probably the booze. Her hair is sticking to her forehead and she's panting slightly. She's been doing all the running today, camera in hand. Trying to remember everyone's names and telling people to smile is a thankless task. I wouldn't want to do it. Some people act as if asking for a smile is like enquiring whether there's a spare kidney going. I guess that's what sisters are for. Older sisters in particular.

You can't choose your family and all that.

'I'm right here,' I say.

Emily tilts her head, one hand on hip. 'I asked for the *better* half, not the sloshed half.'

'She *was* here…' I reply. It's pretty clear Charley isn't around. There are a little more than thirty people in the room and none of them are in white. There's no competitive sport on this side of the hall, no fight to be centre of attention. If Charley was in the room, she'd be easy to spot.

'I'll check the toilets,' Emily says and then she's off again, scuttling across the dance floor and through the door, allowing the other party to infiltrate our space for a few more seconds.

Raj has stopped leaning on the wall and is now using his brother to prop himself up in the corner. Everyone else is doing their own thing, huddled in twos and threes, probably eyeing the three-tier cake, wondering when we'll finally get to the business end of the day.

Alice is still fussing over the buffet, lining up the canapés so that everything's perfectly OCD. She glances up and then quickly back down as I approach, talking to the orangey flatbread things. I can't even pronounce half the things she's made.

Her dark hair is pinned up with an array of clips. She was Charley's main bridesmaid, the only adult.

'Hungry?' she asks.

'I've got my eye on those mini éclair things.'

She bats at my fingers as I reach for one. 'Not until after the first dance.'

'Speaking of first dances, have you seen Charley?'

Alice steps back, looks up and scans the room. 'Toilet?'

'Isn't that a two-person job?'

She hums under her breath. 'Yeah… I'll call her.'

Alice performs some sort of magic trick, producing a phone out of thin air. I've never known how women manage it. Lads jam a wallet in a back pocket, phone in the front and that's that. Women's clothes don't really do pockets and yet they somehow find an array of places in which to hide their valuables.

Her thumb darts across the screen and then the phone is at Alice's ear. She pouts a lip, tilts her head and then shakes it. 'No answer.'

Emily picks that moment to push back through the door and shrug towards me. 'She's not in the toilet.'

The three of us stand together, peering around the corners of the room as if Charley, as if *my wife*, is hiding somewhere, white dress and all.

'Maybe she's gone for a lie-down?' Alice suggests.

'She never said.'

'Give me your room key and I'll go check. I'll check mine, too.'

I fumble into my pockets and hand the key card over. Charley and Alice shared a room last night, but now the honeymoon suite is supposed to be for us. Not the *main* honeymoon suite, of course. The 'my day' bride from across the hall has that. We're in the evening suite, whatever that means. It has its own living room and a four-poster bed, which is more than fancy enough.

Alice drifts away, leaving me and my sister next to the food. We stand awkwardly for a couple of seconds, neither knowing what to say to the other. This is how it should be with siblings, I think. Those huggy best friend brother-and-sister-types have always creeped me out.

'Have you checked on Mum recently?' she asks.

We both turn to the small table nearest the cake where our mother is sitting by herself. Emily and I had spoken about how we were going to keep an eye on her today, but it's been so crazy. Em's been busy taking photos while I've been, well, getting married.

'I'll go,' I say, sensing Em's sigh of relief.

Mum's got herself a small glass of sherry and is busy munching a packet of Polos from her bag. She's watching the room hawkishly, suspicious of people she doesn't know. I sit opposite and she jumps, squinting towards me as if we're strangers. She's squat, hunched into herself, wearing her Sunday best of a purple skirt with jacket. It's so big on her, like when a kid gets hand-me-downs from a big brother or sister. The sleeves flap on her skinny arms and the gold bracelet is rattling on her wrist, clinking on the table.

She glances up to me and, really, honestly, there's a moment where I hate myself so much.

It's hard to look at her.

Parents are supposed to be strong and wise. As a kid, you think they know everything, a fountain of knowledge for the wonder of the world around. It's only when you're older that you realise it's all one big bluff. They're making it up as they go along, terrified they might drop you on your head or something.

There was a time when my mother was strong and wise but that went in the years after Dad died.

'Seth?' she croaks, like it's a question. As if she's not entirely sure.

'Hi, Mum.'

'Who are all these people?' she asks.

'Mainly my friends. Some people from work. Some from the old days at school.'

She nods, but I don't think she really heard me.

'Where's your sister?'

I point to Emily who's over near the DJ. 'She's been taking photos all day, Mum. You remember?'

Her eyes widen as if it's all news to her and there's such a big part of me that wants to walk away. That horrible taunting voice deep down. Is this how I'll end up remembering her? Not the robust kick-arse woman who'd stomp into school to defend her bullied daughter. Not the laughing mother who buried us in sand at the seaside. That person's gone, leaving a body-snatcher in her place.

'Charley,' she says and there's a beautiful moment of clarity. 'You married Charley.' Her glassy stare focuses on me for only a second, but it's enough to bring back that flood of memories. Sometimes I wish she wouldn't have these flashes. It's only ever a cruel taunt, never more than a second or two.

'Have you seen her?' I ask.

There's a pause. A long pause. You get used to them with Mum. Sometimes it happens in the middle of a sentence. She'll start saying something, bringing up a TV programme she watched, something on the radio, or remembering the glimmer of an encounter from years ago. Then she'll stop herself mid-sentence and stare at the wall. Sometimes she'll pick up from where she left off; most times, that's it.

'She was in the hall,' Mum says.

'Charley?'

'In the hall.'

'When?'

'I was going to the toilet and she was by those nice French windows at the back. The ones with the lilies on the other side.'

I blink. She's never usually this clear. People and places blur into one. Forty years ago is now. She thinks I'm my father; she forgets Emily's name.

'When?'

'Not long ago.'

'Are you sure?'

'I remember her pink dress.'

I stare at her, but she's only got eyes for her Polos. She slurps on one and smacks her lips.

'Charley was wearing a white dress,' I say. 'We got married today, remember?'

There's a pause as she continues to suck the mint. 'Of course I remember!' She slaps the table. 'I *said* I saw her in the *white* dress.'

The viciousness is a recent thing. Sometimes she snaps at Em or me and it's hard to know what to do. It's not her fault her mind plays tricks, that sometimes she needs a coaxing, cajoling presence and other times that very thing infuriates her. Em gets it the worst, but then I always was the favourite. Dad once said that Mum would have kept having children until she had a boy. They only stopped at two because I came along.

'Sorry, I must have misheard,' I say, not that it matters because she's back to staring at the wall. 'Do you want anything?' I ask. 'Another drink? Some food?'

'Don't be so silly,' she scolds – and that's that. Like someone's pressed a reset button in her head. There's no point in asking about Charley again and this conversation is over.

Alice presses through the doors as I head towards them. We each stride into the corridor, moving away from the battering *thump-thump-thump* of the music across the hallway. Her face says it all.

'You've not found her?' I ask.

'She's nowhere,' Alice says. 'I checked the toilets upstairs and down. Your room, my room.' She hands back my key card. 'I even checked the car park. Tried calling her again but there was no answer. You'd have thought someone might notice the woman in the wedding dress.'

'Mum says she saw her by the French windows.'

They're a little way along the corridor, floor-to-ceiling doors that open out onto a small garden at the back of the hotel. It's where we had some of the wedding photos taken. I've never looked up why they're called windows and not doors.

We continue along the corridor until we're at the right spot. There's a separate mat scuffed with dirt on top of the carpet. As Mum said, there are lilies on the other side of the glass. Perhaps she was right about seeing Charley?

'Here?' Alice asks.

It's only a word, but I sense the hesitation behind it. My mother might have seen Charley here – but there is a stronger chance she either imagined it or confused herself. Alice and I stand together staring at the doors. They're closed, children's fingermarks all over the lower panes.

'Perhaps Charley wanted some air?' Alice says.

We head outside into the cool summer evening. The sun has dipped past the trees in the distance, but it'll still be light for a while yet. Tiles are arranged in a swirling circle underfoot, with a sundial in the middle and clipped grass outside that. There's a cut-through to a car park beyond.

'Char?'

Alice's voice is crisp against the silence. There's no reply, only the faint *thump-thump-thump* from inside.

We edge further outside and I head for the car park. It's a small gravelly area, probably where the staff leave their vehicles. All the guests park at the front.

'Charley?' I call.

Nothing.

At the back of the car park is a gap in the hedge and a gritty road that leads to who knows where. Other than that, it's green with hedges, overgrown fields and trees. Very *Escape to the Country*. Very British.

Charley's name is pinned at the top of my contacts list but it doesn't even ring when I try calling. I try three times back to back, waiting for the 'sorry, your call cannot be connected' message before hanging up.

Once more for luck. Except there is no luck and there is no answer.

It's my wedding day. *Our* wedding day – and yet my wife is gone.

TWO

Five in the morning.

I'm not sure quite what I expected from a wedding night but it definitely wasn't a pair of brothers sleeping top-to-tail in the marital bed. I consider taking a photo on my phone. Once Charley's back and explains how this is all some strange mix-up, we'll laugh at this.

Raj is still in the full suit: waistcoat, shoes and a handkerchief in the pocket. There's crusted dirt at the bottom of his trousers and a scuff along the back of his jacket. I have no idea how he got so filthy as he wasn't any help when I went out to the woods at the back of the hotel to look for Charley. I don't actually blame him for his state. He even asked if I minded him having 'a few drinks' earlier in the evening. No one expected the bride to disappear.

Rafi has his feet on the pillows. He's the bigger of the two brothers and has been snoring like a bear for most of the night. Despite the annoyance, there's a melodic hypnotism about the way his chest rises and falls, all accompanied by the type of noises more usually associated with a strangling. As I stand at the end of the bed and watch, he snorts, holds his breath and then gags on something before rolling onto his side and draping a hand across Raj's lower back.

What a shambles.

I check my phone again. No missed calls, no texts. Nothing. In the phone menu, Charley's name is at the top with a neat little (63) at the end. If she wasn't my wife and she wasn't missing, this would be classic stalker behaviour. I turn the (63) unanswered calls into (64) and then stare at the screen, willing something to happen. Nothing does, so I make it (65) before putting it back into my pocket.

The hotel's corridors are quiet as I mooch through them, taking the stairs instead of the lift. The other wedding party finished a couple of hours ago and even the stragglers have drifted back to their rooms or off home.

On the ground floor, the sign reads: 'Fire door, keep closed', but the door has been wedged open and a trio of empty wine bottles have been left on the floor, along with a condom wrapper. At least someone had a good night.

The girl on reception has been there all night. As she sees me approaching, she tugs the single earphone out and smiles apologetically. She's only late-teens or early-twenties, probably left with the shifts no one else wants.

'Any sign?' she asks.

I'm not sure if she's amused or bemused by the whole situation. If she's worked here for any length of time, she's probably seen more than her fair share of weird, but I doubt the hotel has ever lost a bride before.

I shake my head. 'I don't suppose anyone's reported anything…?'

'Sorry. The bride from the other wedding party came through here a couple of hours back, but that's it.'

She's giving me the closed-lip *I-don't-know-what-to-tell-you* smile, which is fair enough. She's been working all night and the least I can do is give her an hour or two of peace. Husbands and wives walk out on each other all the time, don't they? Admittedly, it's not usually a few hours after the ceremony, but she probably thinks we had some kind of drunken fall-out. There's usually a viral story or two like that each year. *Drunken bride arrested after glassing groom.*

Alice is on the first floor and opens her door after the quietest knock I could manage. Her face is full of hope that instantly fades when she sees me. 'No sign?' she asks.

'I was hoping you'd heard something…?'

She shakes her head but nods me into the room anyway. Her hair is down and she's changed out of her bridesmaid dress into fleecy bunny rabbit pyjamas.

'Did you get any sleep?' I ask.

'Twenty minutes or so. I thought I heard my phone ringing, but I must've imagined it.'

Alice plops herself down on one of the two double beds and I sit on the other. She fights a yawn and then points at the caked soil on the bottom of my trousers. 'What happened to you?'

'I went out to the woods at the back of the hotel in case Charley had gone for a wander and fallen into a hole or something. It's too dark to see anything, but if she is out there, then she's not answering.'

A yawn burns through me before I can even think about fighting it.

'You should get some sleep,' Alice says.

'The best man and his brother have the marital bed.'

'Oh…'

'The sun's on its way up, so I'm going to head back out. Should be a bit easier in the daylight. There might be footprints or something…'

We both sigh, knowing it's a load of old nonsense. Why on earth would anyone leave their own wedding reception to go for a wander through the woods; heels, dress and all? It's something to cling onto, though.

'She never said anything, did she?' I find myself asking. 'About not going through with it. Did she mention second thoughts?'

Alice turns to face me and she has the same apologetic smile that the girl on reception was wearing. 'She seemed nervous the night before – but that's normal, isn't it? Everyone's nervous before a wedding. *I* was, worrying about the food and all that. Hoping I didn't trip over my dress.'

'But she never mentioned not going through with it?'

'She *did* go through with it.'

It takes me a moment to realise that Alice is right. Charley and I *did* get married. We *are* married. It was only after that she disappeared.

'I don't understand what's happened.'

We sit in silence for a moment. The bag that contained Charley's dress is on the bed behind me, so are her regular clothes. There's a make-up bag that's hers on the side table. Her phone charger. If you were planning to leave, wouldn't you take a phone charger?

'Do you think we should call the police…?'

Alice's question might as well be my own.

'Isn't it twenty-four hours for missing people?' I reply.

'I think that's a myth. You're supposed to let them know as soon as you're certain there's a problem.'

And that's the thing. When I call the police, that'll be admitting that this *is* a problem and not a misunderstanding.

I push myself up from the bed and tell Alice I'm heading back outside. 'She might be stuck somewhere, unable to shout for help,' I say.

'Yeah…' She doesn't sounds convinced.

'Either that or someone took her.'

Alice is blank. 'Who?'

'I don't know. Someone.'

She bites her lip and then lets it go. I think she might say something, but then she glances away to the door. She's Charley's best friend, business partner and bridesmaid. Alice knows my wife as well as anyone.

'What?' I say.

She shakes her head. 'Nothing. I think I'm going to try to get a bit of sleep before checkout.'

Back in my room, Raj and Rafi have moved onto spooning, but I'm not sure who's getting the better end of the deal. Both are now upside down, feet on the pillows, with Raj snuggled into the back of his brother. I think about waking them to ask for help, but it would only ever be a waste of all our time. Charley isn't in the wooded area at the back of the hotel. She's not in the adjacent field, nor the gravelly car park. She's not in Alice's room and she's not in the evening suite.

I head to the window, where the sun is low in the sky, casting a moody orange glow across the perfectly still garden. Charley would love this view.

I think about calling 999 and then remember those news stories every year. There's always some bloke who dials the emergency number because his pizza's turned up late, or a woman who thinks she needs the police because the remote control's stopped working.

This isn't that bad, but is this an emergency? I hope not. A misunderstanding, I tell myself. It's a silly bit of confusion that'll all work itself out.

I find myself calling 101 anyway, waiting as the phone rings. It's nice to hear something other than a woman's voice telling me I can't be connected. I expect to end up on hold, or perhaps some dodgy lift music, but there's a click and then a woman asks for my name and wonders how she can help.

My mind is suddenly blank and then I hear myself stammering something about my wife going missing.

'How long has she been missing?' the voice asks.

'Since about eight o'clock last night. Maybe a little before. I'm not sure.'

'What's your wife's name?'

'Charley Willis. Well, Charley Chambers now, I guess.'

'Where did you last see her?'

'We were chatting to my sister at the reception.'

There is a short pause and then I realise I've somehow forgotten a large part of the story.

'At a wedding reception?' she asks.

'Yes, sorry. At *our* reception. We got married yesterday. We were waiting for people to arrive and then she disappeared.'

'Right…'

The pause is a little longer this time. I wonder if she's got a script and is frantically flipping through the options to where it reads 'wedding day change-of-mind'.

'Is your wife vulnerable?' she asks.

'How do you mean?'

'Does she have a history of self-harming or mental health problems? Anything like that?'

'No.' It's an instinctive answer; defensive, as if to say 'yes' would reflect badly on her or me.

The handler must pick up some uncertainty. 'Vulnerable could simply mean that she depends on somebody else…'

'I wouldn't say she's vulnerable but she is sort of… known.'

'In what way?'

'She's Charley now, but she was Charlotte Willis. Her parents were Paul and Annie Willis.'

'Oh.'

The hesitation is longer this time. It's still only a second or two, but I can sense the surprise. I know what she's thinking because I was thinking it when Charley first told me who she was. These are the types of pauses that become normal when you're marrying into a family dynasty.

The woman asks for Charley's age and description, then she wants to know where I am and where we live. She double-checks my phone number and says someone will visit this afternoon.

This is why Charley doesn't use the name Charlotte any longer, why she doesn't tell people her parents' names. Older people remember who she was and younger people have learnt it.

Charley is a horror story parents tell their children; an urban myth that's all too true.

And she's missing.

THREE

15 YEARS AGO

Police Sergeant Mike Heyman, Langton Constabulary

It's hard to believe they're sisters.

Charlotte is thirteen years old, hugging her legs to her chest, all elbows and knees. Martha is nine years older, a woman not a child. There are similarities beneath the surface – mainly the green eyes – but, while Martha's stare expectantly at me, Charlotte's are fixed only on the floor. Aside from that, though… Martha's hair is dyed black, loose around her shoulders; her sister's is light and clamped back in a ponytail. Charlotte is too young, but there is a hint of a tattoo sleeve peeping out from the bottom of Martha's top. She has one of those long pyramid earrings angled through her lobe and piercings through her nose, lip and eyebrow.

'I'm Charley's guardian now,' Martha says, showing off a stud in her tongue. She looks me in the eye and speaks confidently.

Charlotte doesn't flinch. It's no surprise. She's in shock. This isn't the type of thing anyone gets over with a finger-click, let alone a kid.

It's times like this where you think of the training. Words are hard to come by but we're all this poor girl has right now.

'Hi, Charlotte. My name's Mike,' I say. 'We can give you a bit more time if you want…?'

She looks up to me, blinks. 'Charley,' she says. 'It's Charley.'

Her voice falters.

'Sorry,' I reply.

Martha leans in, a hand on her sister's knee. 'We'll do this now,' she says. 'Right, Char? While it's fresh.'

There's a blink and then: 'Yes.'

I glance past the pair of them towards the house. It's typically big: detached, with a long driveway that snakes away from a quiet country lane. The middle of nowhere and now a real-life horror story.

Charlotte… *Charley* has refused to move from the lawn since the time we arrived. It's not the ideal place for an interview, but Martha is right about one thing – fresh in the memory is key. The longer we wait to talk, the more she might forget.

'What do you remember, Charley?' I ask.

She gulps and licks her lips. For a moment I don't think she's going to answer and then her sister squeezes her knee again.

'You're safe,' Martha says. 'I'm here. I'm not going anywhere.'

Charley nods slowly. 'I was in bed,' she croaks. 'I was asleep and then I woke up. I thought I heard a scream from downstairs.'

'Do you know what time this was?'

'It was dark… I don't remember. I don't think I looked at the clock.'

'That's fine,' I say, trying to be calm and assured. To pretend that I'm the grown-up here and that I don't feel sickened by everything that's happened. 'Do you know if it was a man's scream or a woman's?' I add.

'I think it was Mama's…*Mum's.*'

She corrects herself quickly but it feels like there's something there. She is staring at a spot on the floor, lost in the horror.

'What happened then?'

'I listened. I didn't know if I'd dreamt it. Like when you wake up and you're not sure if it's real.'

Charley stops for a breath. She angles herself closer to her sister, who puts an arm around her.

'There was another scream,' Charley adds. 'I think it was Mama again.' A breath and then: '*Mum* again.'

She hugs her knees tighter.

'Go on,' Martha whispers.

'Father presented this security thing on telly,' Charley adds. 'He was a bit funny about safety after that. He said that if I ever heard anything like that, if I thought someone was breaking in, I had to go into the wardrobe and hide. There's a hamper in there for dirty clothes. He said get behind it and stay still and quiet until he or Mama said it was safe.'

She's speaking slowly enough that it's easy to note down what she's saying. I pause at the end of her sentence. 'Mama' is a new one on me. Never heard any kid call their mum that. Even 'Father' is a bit odd. Not 'Dad' or 'Daddy'.

'So that's what you did?' I ask.

Charley nods.

'Did you hear anything while you were in the wardrobe?'

'Someone coming up the stairs.' She uncurls her legs and stretches them out. 'I think that's what I heard. I don't know. There are these little slits across the front of the wardrobe doors, but I couldn't hear everything properly. The bedroom door was shut.'

I wait, not wanting to ask the question. Even I hear the reluctance in my voice when the words appear: 'Were there any other screams?'

She shakes her head slowly and the reply is clear enough: 'No… I don't know. I don't think so.'

I've had witnesses go to pieces having seen far less than she has. There was a circuit judge who could barely tell me her name after a driver sped across a roundabout and embedded himself into a lamp post in front of her. A trained therapist simply stared at me after an armed robbery at a bank. It's impossible to judge who'll be a reliable witness and who'll be a gibbering wreck.

Charley's doing well. There are a few stutters, some hesitations, but she's composed, especially for a thirteen-year-old. There's a sense of a calm from the sister. It would usually be a non-starter to interview two witnesses together, but I don't think I'd get much out of the younger sibling without Martha.

'What happened then?' I ask.

'I waited.'

'Did you hear any other noises?'

'Not until my sister came in.'

'Nobody entered the bedroom until then…?'

'No.'

I turn to Martha, who hasn't stopped watching me. A thick streak of eyeliner has smudged into the rest of her make-up from where she's been rubbing her eyes.

'What time did you get here?' I ask.

'About half-two,' Martha replies. 'Maybe a little later. I'd been out in the city. Got a taxi back.'

That's good. There'll be a record of that somewhere. It will make the time easier to verify.

'Do you live here?' I ask.

'No, I've got a flat in Chalk Farm. You know that? Near Camden. I usually visit here on Saturdays.'

'It's a bit early.'

She shrugs. 'Sometimes it's not worth going home after a night out. I come here, get my head down for a few hours and then have lunch with the family.'

That explains the smeared make-up. She's been out all night. She yawns as if to emphasise the point.

'What happened when the taxi dropped you off?' I ask.

'I let myself in.'

'And what did you see?'

Martha has removed her arm from Charley's shoulders and they're sitting by themselves. 'I went into the kitchen to get a sandwich or something. Sometimes there's chicken in the fridge. The door to the living room was open and then…' She glances sideways momentarily to her sister. 'I'd rather not say… not here. Perhaps we can do this again later?'

With a nod, I let her know that's fine. It's not the older sister's statement I'm worried about.

I turn back to Charley: 'What happened when you heard your sister's voice?'

There's a brief pause in which Charley turns to her older sister and then gulps. 'Martha came upstairs calling my name. I heard her open the door and then I said I was in the wardrobe. She told me we were going to go out the front of the house and that the police were on the way. She told me not to go in the living room.'

Charley holds up her palms and I see it for the first time. The sun is starting to rise, sending a gloomy orange seeping through the clouds. Perhaps it's the light, but I don't think so. Despite my sixteen years in the job, I can't stop myself shivering. I don't think Charley notices, but Martha does. For a moment I wonder if she's going to press forward and put a hand on my knee. It was too uncomfortable to kneel and too intimidating to stand. I'm sitting on the lawn with the girls. In the end, Martha rocks back and offers an apologetic, humourless smile. It's like she's comforting me.

'I tried to stop her,' Martha says.

Charley's hands are stained a dark, crusty crimson.

'It won't come off,' she says and I shiver again. 'I tried washing them. I didn't mean to touch anything. I just… It was Mama.'

She tails off but she's said plenty.

Behind the girls, a pair of uniformed officers emerge from the house and they each take deep breaths. The younger one is a new recruit, only been in the job a couple of months and I can't believe she's seen anything like this. She stares off into nothingness as my friend Johnny pats her on the shoulder.

'I think someone's sorting you out with a place to stay,' I tell Martha while looking around for a person who might know what they're doing. 'We can figure out a lift.'

She nods and pushes herself up from the ground, offering a hand to her sister. 'Do you want a Maccy D's, or something?' she asks.

Charley shakes her head and clings onto Martha's arm, leaving a sticky red smudge. 'I just want to go.'

FOUR

SETH. NOW

It takes two knocks before Emily opens the door to her hotel room. She yawns her way through a 'morning' and the now-usual follow-up about whether Charley has reappeared.

I ask her how Mum is, but my sister's sigh says plenty, as does: 'We should have kept her off the sherry.'

There's no humour there – but this is how we talk about our mother. It's the only way to deal with it all.

Em edges into the hallway, pulling the door almost closed behind her. Her voice is a husky whisper: 'She forgot where she was when she woke up and started screaming about being kidnapped. She didn't recognise me.'

I squeeze the bridge of my nose, trying to make everything go away. I don't want to deal with this today. Em makes me feel even worse by folding her arms as if to emphasise that she's my mother, too.

'I called the police,' I say.

It might be the tiredness, but Em's eyes widen. 'What did they say?'

'Someone's coming over to the house this afternoon.'

'I can't believe nobody saw her leave. How can someone disappear in a wedding dress?'

'Mum said she saw Charley near the doors that lead into the back courtyard.'

A tilt of the head. *Really?* Em doesn't say the word, but I know what she's thinking. Mum says a lot of things.

'When I picked her up yesterday, she thought it was for a silver jubilee party,' Emily replies. 'She called me Evelyn. She thought I was her old best friend.'

'I know – but she was really clear for once. She mentioned the lilies at the back of the hotel. She wasn't making them up – they're actually there.'

Em peers off to the side. Neither of us want to argue. We've been here before. 'I spent a couple of hours going through your photos,' she says. 'I wondered if there might be something in them. Some stranger that no one knows…'

'And?'

A shrug. 'You both look very happy.'

Emily is not a professional photographer as such. She does IT at the local technology college, which means she's *really* good at turning things off and on again.

She does not like that joke.

Because she was a bit bored, Em took a photography class a year and a bit ago and set up her own blog. She got a booking from the local council to take pictures of their renovated wildlife reserve and has been trying to build on that ever since.

Better than turning things off and on for a living, I guess.

Charley is one of her biggest supporters. It was her idea to ask Emily to photograph our wedding in the first place. Em said she'd do it for free, but Charley insisted on paying the going rate.

'Do you want to come in and look at a few pics on my laptop?' she asks.

This is Emily's way of asking if I want a few minutes with Mum, to at least understand what she's dealt with all night.

We head into the darkness of her room. The curtains are pulled, with the only light coming from a tall dim lamp in the corner. Lights in hotel rooms are always a lottery. Wall switches bear little or no relation to what's being powered. Sometimes there are lights on the ceiling, other times it is a scattering of lamps that can't be switched off from the comfort of the bed. Don't even get me started on those ones that are plugged in next to the bed, taking up the only socket that could be used to charge a phone.

Mum is sitting in a chair close to the lamp, with a newspaper on the desk in front of her. She squints at Emily and me through the dim light and then turns back to the paper.

'Do you know a nine-letter word for a tipping point?' she asks. 'Blank-blank-r-blank-s-blank-blank-blank-blank.'

One of the doctors a few years ago suggested that doing a daily puzzle or two might help Mum with her concentration levels. It's odd how some things stick with her and others don't. She does a crossword every day, as well as an arrowword or two. She's good with language and can remember bits and pieces of pop culture from even the most recent of years. Band names and hit singles, she knows. Oscar winners are embedded; she remembers authors and books, Wimbledon champions and Premier League-winning managers.

But her own children?

Sometimes she looks at Emily and me as if she's never laid eyes on us before.

Not this morning. For now, she seems relatively aware.

'I'm not sure, Mum,' I reply.

She nods acceptingly and pulls at the curtain, allowing sunlight to flood into the room.

'It was a lovely ceremony,' she says. 'What a beautiful venue. The gardens, the flowers, the fountain. Emily was showing me some of the photos. At least one of my offspring is getting ready to give me some grandchildren…'

There's a smirk, not the viciousness from yesterday. This is teasing and Emily lets it go.

'How is Charley?' Mum asks.

I exchange a quick glance with Em, who has a *don't-ask-me* expression.

'She's having a rest,' I reply.

'I'm not surprised. It was a long day yesterday. Weddings always are. Getting ready in the morning, then the arrival and ceremony. Speeches, food, the dance. You just have to enjoy as much as you can. When your father and I got married, it was a register-office job. We didn't have the money. He looked lovely in that chocolate brown suit of his. All wide cuffs and collars. I'm sure I've told you about it…'

She has, and we've seen the faded photos, but it's surprising to hear her speaking with clarity.

Mum turns to me and, for that moment, I wonder if she's going to revert to thinking it's her wedding day again. 'I think there's a D on the end,' she says. 'A tipping point: Blank-blank-r-blank-s-blank-blank-blank-d.'

'Threshold?' Emily suggests.

Mum turns back to the paper and laughs. 'Threshold! That's it. Clever girl.'

She scratches the letters onto the page and then starts to tap the pen.

'Mum… do you remember seeing Charley yesterday?' I ask. 'You said she was in the hall…'

'By those French windows. I always wanted a set like that at the back of the house. but your father wasn't a fan. He said it would be too hot in the afternoons because of where the sun rose.'

She peers up, gazing through the window towards the gardens at the front of the hotel. The sun is higher now, the lush green lawn drenched with warmth. The fountain has been turned on and jets of water are spurting high into the air. Em and I exchange another look, asking silently if this is it.

'Do you remember what she was doing, Mum?'

'Who?'

'Charley. When you saw her in the hallway.'

There's a lengthy pause and then Mum turns back to the pair of us. She squints between Emily and me and takes a breath. It is already hard to picture her in any way other than how she is now. The wrinkles on her face are starting to crease into each other and I swear she's shorter than she used to be. There's a stutter when she speaks, a constant distantness.

It's horrible.

Of all the illnesses to afflict us, there can be little worse than dementia. A person's own mind betraying them has such a knock-on effect on everyone else. It's devastating when your own mother looks at you and asks who you are.

I will her to stay with us, if only for a couple more minutes.

'She looked lovely,' Mum says.

'I know. In her dress… her *white* dress.'

'Not too fancy. Not like some of the ones you see with frilly bits everywhere and trains that need half a dozen people to hold. Hers was perfect.'

There's a lump in my throat. From nowhere, I think I might cry. Charley looked every bit as wonderful as Mum has described.

'Where exactly was she, Mum?'

'By the French windows, I told you.'

'But was she walking past them, or going outside?'

Mum stops, thinks. I can almost see her mind ticking over. 'I'm not sure. She was just standing there.'

'Did she say anything?'

A grin: 'She said to tell you that she loves you.'

I blink, surprised. 'Those were her exact words?'

'Right. "Tell your son I love him".'

'Then what happened?'

'What?'

'What happened after that? Did she say that like it was a goodbye? Or was she simply being nice?'

Mum turns back to her crossword and frowns. 'Streamlined,' she says. 'Five letters, ends in K.'

'Mum…?'

She doesn't look up. 'What?'

'Do you remember what happened after that?'

'After what?'

'After you saw Charley in the corridor.'

She turns to the window, then me. She's biting her lip, drumming her pen absent-mindedly. 'Sleek,' she says. 'That means two down must be bedding.'

FIVE

Checkout is a morbid affair. Everyone from the other wedding party is traipsing past me with curious sideways stares. Word is obviously out that the other bride had second thoughts immediately after the ceremony. Some of them look on in sympathy, most with bemusement. A few are wearing that sideways smirk. I'll be all over their Facebook accounts within hours, if I'm not already. There's nothing comparable to another person's misery to get a load of likes.

The only upside is that the hotel is nice enough to have comfy sofas in the reception area. I guess that's the sign of a classy place. Comfy sofas means it's a potential wedding venue; a two-for-one sticky-floored restaurant on the side means it's probably one to miss.

I've got Raj on one side, Rafi on the other, with our bags at our feet. I should probably have left already, but seeing as I dragged friends and family out here for the ceremony, I figured it's only fair to say goodbye.

'You should've got some food in you,' Raj says with a hint of a slur.

'I've never seen a buffet like it,' Rafi adds. 'Raj was taking pictures.'

Raj has his phone in his hand. 'Well, I think I was,' he says. 'New phone. I don't know what I'm doing half the time. I took nearly ninety photos of my own shoes last Saturday. I only got the phone to take wedding pics.' He returns the device to his pocket and I sense him making eye contact with his brother behind my back. 'Sorry, man. I should've helped you look and all that.'

It's hard to know what to say. I don't blame him, so offer a shrug.

As we sit in silence, the other happy couple stride into reception to a string of claps and whoops from their guests. The bride is bleary-eyed and looks like she might have spent a good portion of her wedding night emptying her stomach. Her hair is a straggly mess, far from the pristine pictures of the day before. The groom is in long shorts, flip-flops and a football top.

'Marbs, baby!' he shouts, breaking into a frog-like jig where he bounces from leg to leg. 'We're going to Marbella, a la-la-la; a la-la-la.'

Some of the other blokes join in until the bride whacks her new husband in the chest. 'Will you keep it down? My head's bloody banging.'

'I told you not to down those Jäger shots.'

'I'm not the one who was weeing in the bath at four a.m.'

'I'm surprised you noticed with your head down the bog.'

There are a series of awkward looks between the assembled guests as the newly married couple bicker their way into the car park. A couple of the bridesmaids trail behind, dragging a set of suitcases.

It would be funny, but then I realise their wedding is still more of a success than mine. At least the happy couple know where each other is.

Rafi is fidgeting and I sense another glance between the brothers. 'We kinda have to get off…' Raj says.

'Family meal,' Rafi adds. 'Mum goes ballistic if we're not all there by twelve.'

We all stand and shake hands. What else is there to do?

'Sorry about… well…' Raj tails off.

'It's fine.'

'Let me know when Charley gets home. It's probably a misunderstanding or something...'

It's at the point where I'm not sure what sort of misunderstanding could lead to a bride disappearing on the night of her wedding. It's not like Charley could've forgotten which hotel everything was happening at.

Rafi apologises, too – and then I'm saying sorry to them. I don't even know what we're all apologising for, but we're British and that's what we do. The brothers head out the front door muttering to themselves, leaving me standing in the centre of reception.

It's all very upmarket: vases, big bunches of flowers, pillars for the sake of pillars, rugs. Lots of rugs. They're everywhere.

Emily and Mum arrive together, but Em is keen to get her back to the care home. That sounds awful, but it's so hard spending a whole day with our mother. It's rewarding and devastating all at the same time. After a few hours, there's an emotional tiredness that trumps anything physical. As if every waking moment is on edge in case Mum says something offensive or hurtful. A constant battle to hang onto an already frayed temper.

'I'll email you over some photos later,' Emily says. She can't even force a smile.

'Where are we going?' Mum jabs a finger towards me, shouting loudly. 'You! Where are we going?'

'We're taking you home, Mum,' Emily says.

'I don't want to go there. Not with you.'

Emily manages to usher her out through the doors as I help with the bags. The last I see of them is Em helping Mum into the passenger seat of her car and then being hit in the head when she tries to clip in the seat belt.

'Sorry,' I say, but I'm not sure Emily hears. With a scuff of tyre on gravel, they're on their way.

Before I can head back inside, Mason is making his way down the steps, Daisy and Dillon scrambling around his feet as they wheel out their suitcases. Daisy's is pink and fluffy, in the shape of a piglet. Dillon's is some sort of robot.

'Where's Auntie Charley?' Daisy asks. She's one of those kids who has no shyness around adults. Everything's an upfront question: *Why this? What's going on with that?* She'll be some sort of superstar scientist one day. Question everything, believe nobody, treat authority like the joke it is.

There's an awkward moment in which Charley's brother-in-law catches my eye with a silent apology. He doesn't know what lie to tell or, perhaps, whether to lie at all.

'She's had to go,' I say. 'She did tell me to thank you for being her bridesmaid, though. Everyone thought you looked wonderful yesterday.'

Daisy examines me with those big green eyes that run in her family. There's a hint of Charley in them.

'Can we go?' Dillon moans, taking a couple of stomping steps towards the car park.

'Where has she gone?' Daisy asks.

'She's probably gone for a rest,' Mason says quickly. He shrugs behind his children's backs, but we're not kidding little Daisy.

'Why would she need a rest?' Daisy asks. 'It's morning.'

'Sometimes adults need to rest during the day,' her father says.

Daisy shakes her head. 'I want to say goodbye...'

'I'm sure she wants to say goodbye as well,' I say. 'Um...'

Mason has no idea how to explain everything and neither do I. Luckily, Dillon is kicking up enough of a fuss that Mason manages to shuffle them off towards the car park without either of us needing to give a better explanation.

He mouths a 'sorry', but again I find myself shrugging.

I give Alice some help in loading the leftover food into her van and then she kisses me on both cheeks, says sorry and then disappears. That's my family, Charley's family and each of our best friends all gone.

Not me.

There's a new woman on the reception desk when I head back inside. Older, more of an authority type, who punctuates the word 'Sir' with a smile that has a distinct 'go away' vibe. I ask if the manager's in yet and she squints at me as if I've asked for her first-born.

'Is there a problem?' she says.

'I'd rather talk to the manager, if that's okay…'

Her expression tells me that it's very much *not* okay, but she punches a number into her phone anyway and then mumbles something into the handset before smiling extra sweetly and telling me it'll be a couple of minutes.

The manager is one of those bounding enthusiastic types. All short hair and sharp suit. The type who enjoys team-bonding sessions and writes long emails for all members of staff. He already knows who I am and ushers me into a back office that's filled with coats, a pair of cluttered desks, a microwave and a kettle.

'I'm sorry about everything that's happened,' he says and we're back to apologising to one another.

'I was hoping you could help me,' I say.

'I'd love to.'

'Could you possibly let me look at the security footage from last night?'

A shake of the head. Not that keen to help, after all. 'I'm afraid that's out of the question,' he says. 'We have many guests staying with us and we have to abide by confidentiality laws.'

It sounds suspiciously like he's making it up.

'Are you married?' I ask.

'No… but I'm not sure what that—'

'I am. I got married yesterday afternoon, but my wife disappeared a few hours after the ceremony. All I'm asking is if I can see whether she walked out of the front door. I know there are cameras out front and more in the car park. If she went out that way, then at least I'll know.'

The manager purses his lips and then clucks his tongue. He clicks his fingers and then pistols a single finger towards me. 'You've got it, pal.'

He leads me through the hotel corridors, past a pair of cleaning carts and the toilets until we reach an unmarked door. He pushes a key card into the lock and then holds the door open for us to head inside.

It's barely bigger than a cupboard, but the wall is a mass of monitors, with a bank of whirring computers stacked on the other side. There's only just enough room for the pair of us to squeeze inside, not enough space to sit.

The manager asks me about the time and then jabs a few buttons on a keyboard before loading the footage onto the monitor in front of us. Most of the CCTV that turns up on the web or in police appeals is grainy and near useless – but this is high-definition and clear. There is one camera pointing directly at the steps in front of the hotel, two more covering the car park and another at the front gate.

He scrolls through the timestamps of the camera covering the front steps, making an hour skip through in a couple of minutes.

People head outside for smoke breaks, while guests arrive for both evening receptions. The concierge helps someone lug a giant gift inside, the other groom nips out for a cigarette. A teenage couple leave together and then make a beeline for the bushes on the other side of the fountain.

No Charley.

'Are there any cameras at the back?' I ask.

'It wasn't considered cost-effective.'

'What's out there?'

'A small photo garden and staff parking.'

'What about the land beyond that? The woods and that lane.'

The manager clicks away from the footage and the screen goes blank. 'Those woods are general land – nothing to do with us – and the track leads to a country road. We use it for service deliveries mainly, plus staff get in and out that way.' He waits for a few seconds and then adds: 'I'm sorry I can't be more helpful.'

'If she didn't leave through the front door, is it only that back door she could've gone through?'

A nod. 'There are fire exits. Anyone could've left and then gone out on the service lane.'

'Can you show me the footage of her arriving on Friday afternoon? She was with her friend, Alice. They checked in together. I think it was about four o'clock.'

'Any reason?'

I sigh, shake my head. 'I guess I just want to see her.'

SIX

15 YEARS AGO

Charley Willis, 13 years old

'Where's the farm?'

Martha is busy paying the driver but then clambers out of the black cab onto the pavement. 'What?' she asks.

'I thought you lived on a farm?'

There's a long row of three-storey houses on the side of a wide pavement, a bumper-to-bumper line of parked cars and then a park on the other side of the road.

The taxi zips off into the distance as Martha wrestles my bag onto the pavement.

'Why did you think I lived on a farm?'

'You always said you lived in Chalk Farm.'

'This *is* Chalk Farm,' Martha says. 'It's not a farm, it's an area of London.'

I turn in a circle, bemused at the whole thing. Why call it a farm if it's not? Why did I spend so many years thinking my sister lived on a farm?

Martha pulls my bag onto her shoulder. 'Let's get inside in case there are any paps about.'

'Paps?'

'Men with cameras. Scum of the earth.'

Martha digs a key out of her jacket and heads down a set of concrete steps to a basement I hadn't noticed. The front door is hidden in an alcove barely noticeable from the street. She twists and turns the key, muttering a bad word under her breath before finally shouldering her way inside.

'Sorry for the mess,' Martha says.

It doesn't take long to see what she's talking about. Mama and Father always kept everything spotlessly clean – or the cleaner did – but Martha doesn't care about any of that. The door leads directly into her kitchen and there is a stack of pans in the sink. A half loaf of bread has been abandoned on the side and has started to crust with mould.

It's been two days since I sat on the grass talking to that police officer. In the end, they put us in some sort of 'sheltered accommodation', as they called it. Somewhere safe until they said we could come here. I think a lot of it was down to Martha. She was always arguing with someone in the other place, telling them we should be allowed to come here. It's the first time I've been to her flat, the first time I've been to London. I only saw bits and pieces from the back of the cab, but that was enough for now. So many people. Cyclists, skateboarders, pedestrians, people in suits, people in shorts, bright red buses, jet black taxis, cars everywhere. It was making me dizzy.

Martha leads me through the kitchen into a dim hallway. There are three doors and she nudges open the first with her foot. 'This is your room,' she says. 'Well, it's my room technically, but I'll take the couch. Don't worry about it.'

My sister drops my bag onto the bed and then crouches to pick up a pair of boxer shorts. Definitely not hers. She frowns at them and then throws them into the overflowing bin in the corner.

'Who do they belong to?' I ask.

'Don't worry about it. I'll clean up in here properly in a bit. New sheets and all that.'

The dresser is cluttered with all sort of random junk, including a long, thick glass tube. It's like a chimney with an extra pipe off to the side.

'What do you do with that?' I ask.

Martha snatches it away. 'Don't worry about it.'

'Is it a bong?'

She stares at me: 'How do you know about bongs?'

'Someone at school was talking about them.'

'You're too young for that stuff. I'm gonna need a proper clear-out in here…' She looks up. 'Do you want to go and watch TV or something in the other room? I might have to go out to get bin bags.'

Martha shrugs off the tatty cardigan she's been wearing. It's like something Mum would throw out, but it suits my sister. Because she hasn't lived at home in a long time – and because Mum would argue about it – this is the first time I've ever seen the full extent of Martha's arm tattoo. It stretches all the way from her shoulder to her wrist, a long vine of ivy intermingling with various symbols and letters.

'Did it hurt?' I ask.

Martha bites her lip piercing and grins: 'What d'you reckon?'

'Mum reckoned you were doing it to embarrass her and Dad.'

There is the merest glimmer of a smile. 'Yeah, well. Mum reckoned a lot of things…'

Martha twists so I can see the tattoos a little better.

'How long did it take?' I ask.

'About nineteen hours in total. My mate Xavier did the first bit a couple of years ago – you remember that? He's been adding to it ever since.' She points at a swirl a little below her elbow and then I realise it's not a swirl at all. It's a letter C. 'That one's for you,' she says.

I reach out and take her arm, running my fingers across the smooth skin. There's no bump at all.

'Why'd you get it?' I ask.

'Because you're my sister, Char. Because this is one fu— frigged-up world and sisters have to look out for each other.'

I let the grin creep across me.

'"Frigged" is not a bad word,' Martha says. 'Besides, even if it was, you can say what you want now you live here.'

She holds the door open and leads me into the living room. There's a TV on a scratched cabinet, a sofa with foam spilling from the sides and a cream carpet that's peppered with inky brown stains. It smells a bit funny, almost fruity.

'Coffee,' Martha says, nudging a toe towards one of the stains.

There's another bong on the window ledge and Martha scoops that up, leaving the room and then returning empty-handed.

'I don't want to leave you alone, but I've got to go to the shops,' she says. 'I need bin bags to clean up this mess, plus there's no food in the fridge. It's better to leave you here than take you with me in case there is a pap out there.' She pauses breathlessly and then adds: 'Is there anything you want me to bring back?'

'Carrots…?'

Martha has a hand on her hip and tilts her head sideways. '*Carrots?*'

'Or peas.'

'You're thirteen years old, Char. Peas and carrots? Nobody likes vegetables – not even adults. People only eat them because they think they should. You can have whatever you want. Ben and Jerry's? Chocolate gateau? Jaffa Cakes? Don't give me all that peas and carrots nonsense.'

She's smiling, but there's something else there. It sounds like she's annoyed with me.

'Anything you want,' she adds.

'I don't know.'

'But you like ice cream, right?'

'I guess.'

'I'm sure I can find something.'

She has one hand on the door, but then steps back into the room. 'Char…'

'What?'

'You're going to have to be careful about telling people your name. It won't be long before someone finds out where I live. Our faces are going to be on TV, in the papers, the magazines.' She bites her lip. 'Maybe not yours. There are laws about under-sixteens. I'll have to look it up – but people will know who I am. We could do without getting any hassle from the neighbours. If anyone knocks on the door, ignore them. I've got my key and can let myself in.' There's a metallic cluck as Martha plays with her tongue piercing. 'I'll pick you up a phone,' she says.

'Mum said I'm too young for a phone of my own.'

'Yeah, but you're here now and I want to know you're safe. I'll get you one like mine. You can play games and all sorts. I'll get enough food so we can bunk down for a couple of days and not have to go out. Hopefully everyone will leave us alone.'

Another break, another tongue clink.

'Do you need any more clothes? Underwear? Anything like that?'

I think of my room back at home. The wardrobe full of dresses, smart skirts and tops. The high socks, the shiny shoes. Mum always wanted me to look my best. *'How can you feel good inside if you don't look good outside?'* she'd say.

'You can't ever go back there,' Martha whispers. She's read my mind.

'Oh.'

'You know why, don't you? They'll say you can, but you can't. This is a new start, Char. You and me.'

She smiles, but it's sad and distant, as if there's something she wants to add but she doesn't know the words.

'How about I just get you a few basics,' she says. 'That'll get us through the week, then, when everything goes a bit quiet, we can go shopping properly. You can pick out your own clothes.'

'Okay.'

Martha nods, then steps out of the room. She bobs back and forth, but then disappears along the hallway. She does something in her bedroom and then calls out 'see you soon' before heading out the door.

I slouch onto the sofa, sitting and listening for a few moments. There is the faintest sound of traffic, but it is otherwise quiet. This is the type of silence Mum or Dad constantly wanted. It's strange that the three of us lived in that big house where they could never seem to get it – and yet, here, in this small one-bedroom basement, everything is still.

There's a part of me that wants to go hunting through Martha's stuff before she gets back. The boxer shorts and bongs hint at so much more and yet I'm not sure I want to know. Martha had her life before what happened to Mum and Dad, and I had mine. Now it has all changed and we're here together.

There is one thing, though.

During our time in the sheltered accommodation, I was never alone. If Martha wasn't with me, then the family support officer was. If I went to the toilet, someone would sit outside. They said it was 'standard procedure', but I'm not stupid. Not *that* stupid anyway. It was protection. I heard the whispers late at night. They talked about 'the killer' and whether he was out there.

I was allowed to watch television, but it was always on someone else's terms. Either a limited set of channels, or one of the movies they had there. I could never choose myself.

I do now, hunting to find the 24-hour-news channel and waiting for the adverts to finish. I wonder whether what happened to Mum and Dad is news at all. Whether I'm featured, or if Martha is on there. Perhaps we're a small snippet buried below everything else that's going on? There's always bombs going off somewhere, always men in suits babbling on about the who has the most money. That's surely more important?

Except it's not.

This is what they were trying to hide from me. Perhaps she's done it on purpose by going out, but Martha has left me free to watch what I want.

My parents are the first story. A woman is staring seriously towards the camera, with pictures of Mum and Dad in the little box over her shoulder.

'The hunt goes on for the intruder who killed Paul and Annie Willis in the early hours of Saturday. Police say they are following a number of leads, including reports of a suspicious red vehicle spotted in the area. Paul Willis was the host of such consumer shows as *Today, Tonight* and *Ripped Off*, while wife Annie is a bestselling author and frequent lifestyle contributor to *Good Morning Britain*. Bryan Manion reports.'

The screen changes to images of my dad from television. He's young, probably in his twenties, wearing a cape and top hat. He's presenting some sort of talent show with singers and dancers. The reporter says he was a fixture on British television for almost thirty years. Then it's Mum's turn. She's thin and fit, dressed in skin-tight Lycra and stretched out into a yoga pose. It's hard to judge her age, but she has a bob of tightly curled hair. I'm not sure I ever saw her looking like this.

The reporter is stony-faced, standing outside our house with a microphone, the police tape and car behind him.

And then he makes me shiver.

'Police confirmed last night that the Willis's youngest child, Charlotte, who is just thirteen, was present when the attack took place, adding that she was hiding upstairs as the horror went on below.'

It sounds like another person. *Charlotte* Willis, not Charley. Another me. Another life. Charlotte Willis is a thirteen-year-old child, Charley is me.

The screen cuts back to the woman in the studio, who has someone I vaguely recognise sitting next to her. The caption says it's another television presenter, someone from Father's past. They used to work on the talent show together, but it was before I was born.

'It's such a loss,' the man begins – but this is all enough for me. It's time to change the channel.

SEVEN

SETH. NOW

Never join the neighbourhood watch scheme. That should be one of the first things you're told when you buy a house. For some reason, people believe having a sticker in their window makes them less likely to get burgled. Either that, or that sticker is the only thing that will persuade a neighbour to call the police if someone is acting suspiciously.

In truth, people will call the police anyway and burglars couldn't give a toss about some sticker. The neighbourhood watch scheme is simply an excuse for nosey sods to get away with being nosey sods.

I barely have a foot out of the car before Mr Cass from next door is bursting out of his front door. It's not like I think everything's about me, but he must've been sitting at his window all morning waiting for me to get home. He's been living in the same house for seemingly all of eternity and is the head of the neighbourhood watch scheme. There's every chance that's by default as nobody else wants to do it.

He's pleasant enough, I suppose. A retired widower in his early sixties. I can hear Charley in my mind telling me to be nice. *He's lonely*, she'd say. *He wants someone to talk to.* That's the thing with Charley. She makes you want to be a better person. She cares about others. Perhaps someone could believe she left me – but Alice? Little Daisy with all her questions? Dillon? She loves those kids and I can't believe she'd abandon them.

Mr Cass is all smiles: 'How are the newly-weds?' He looks towards the car, where it's clear there's no Charley.

'Not bad,' I say, hoping to end the conversation early. I grab my bag from the back seat, but he's still waiting on the pavement.

'Where is Charley?' he asks.

'She wasn't feeling well.'

He eyes me up and down and it's only then I remember I'm still wearing my wedding suit. I've been in it all night, all morning. The legs are crusted with dirt and the suit is crumpled like a teenager's school shirt come the end of the week.

'Aaaah, one of *those* nights...' Mr Cass chuckles to himself. That *if-only-I-was-your-age* laugh that old people have. There must be an age where you learn that. 'Bit too much champagne...?' he continues.

'Something like that.'

'Well, I hope she's feeling better soon. When's the honeymoon?'

'We're not having one – not yet anyway. Charley was talking about opening a second shop and then we were going to go travelling next year.'

There's a short pause as I realise I'm talking in the past tense.

Mr Cass rocks back on his heels, either not noticing, or moving on. 'Aaaah, that's all the rage nowadays. My grandson's off travelling at the moment. He was in Peru the last I heard.'

He smiles awkwardly and I can hear Charley again. *The poor fella's a little lonely.*

Bloody hell, it should be lovely that he's been waiting around for us to get home. If Charley was here, she'd have really appreciated it.

We stand awkwardly, neither quite knowing what to say. Mr Cass eventually takes a step back towards his house. 'Well, if you need anything, you know where I am.'

'Thank you,' I reply. 'And thanks for the card. It was lovely of you.'

He smiles and then we each head our separate ways.

As soon as I'm inside and the door is locked, I drop my bag. 'Charley? Char? Are you here?'

My voice echoes around the house, bouncing off the walls and returning back to me.

No answer.

'Char? You here, hun?'

Even though there's no reply, I check the downstairs rooms anyway and then head upstairs. The bathroom is empty, as is the spare room. One room left – our bedroom. I pull down the handle slowly, holding my breath, the last hope. Except she's not inside either.

She's not here.

I head for the nightstand next to the bed, pulling out all my socks and dropping them on the floor. There's a hidden compartment in the middle drawer and I lift it out, revealing our passports, birth certificates and a couple of other documents. It's where we'll put our marriage certificate when we get it… assuming it still means something now.

Charley's passport is still there. I thumb through the pages, eyeing the holographic photo that doesn't look much like her. She is dead-eyed, her greasy fringe slightly askew. She doesn't even wear her hair like that any longer and there's never an occasion where she'd be so emotionless.

I return everything to the drawer, put my socks back in and then head to the wardrobe. It takes up the entire wall opposite our bed and is plenty more than we need. All of my clothes are shoved to the right side, hers to the left. As far as I can tell, everything she owns is still hanging here. There are dresses, tops, a couple of suits, summer clothes, winter wear. Below are her shoes. She only has a few pairs, not like some of the lunatics you read about. One pair of big heels, one smaller, a pair of Converse, some walking boots, some leather knee boots, running shoes – and that's it. Nothing missing that I notice. If she was planning to leave, surely there would be a sign?

Her purse and driving licence were left in the room she'd been sharing with Alice; her passport, clothes and shoes are all at home. Where could she be going without any of that?

The kicker is in the living room.

There is a framed photo of Dillon and Daisy together when they all went trick or treating last year. Dillon is Iron Man; Daisy is that girl from *Frozen*. Charley dressed as Rey from *Star Wars*, lightsabre and all. She took them around the estate as they harassed the locals for all manner of sweets and chocolate. There's no way she'd leave the photo behind. She loves that picture and she loves those kids.

There's the other photo, too. The one of her and Martha. Charley is seventeen or eighteen, which would make Martha somewhere in her late-twenties. They look nothing like each other – Martha with her dark hair, sleeve of tattoos and paperclip drawer of piercings; Charley blonde and fresh-faced. It's only the eyes they share.

They're at a party somewhere, perhaps a nightclub. They're both a little bleary-eyed, but their smiles… Even now, after everything from last night and this morning, it's hard not to grin when I look at the picture. This is happiness: two sisters who've been through it all together and come out the other side.

She wouldn't have left this either. There's no digital version of the picture – Charley told me Martha had to buy the original from the nightclub photographer. If she's left this, then it can only be because she's planning on coming home… or she never planned to leave in the first place.

I head back upstairs and, for the first time since we moved in together, I go through the drawers on Charley's side of the bed. I'm not sure what I'm looking for, but there's jewellery, underwear and socks. The usual stuff. Nothing hidden underneath and no secret valuables compartment on her side.

Except there is.

It's well hidden, wrapped into a pair of socks, but there's a small brown tub with a white lid. A pocket of small tablets rattle around inside and after googling the name on the label, I find out they're antidepressants.

I wonder why she never told me.

They're only available by prescription, so she must have been to the doctor at some point. We haven't talked an awful lot about what happened when she was thirteen and the aftermath. I suppose I always assumed she'd have gone through therapy of some nature, perhaps a programme of medication. Nothing to be ashamed of.

Is this a throwback to that?

I really wish she'd said something.

If she needs her medicine, then she's without that, too, wherever she is.

Back downstairs, I unfold the laptop and turn it on. There's only eight per cent battery, which is entirely my fault. The cable isn't long enough, so I end up sitting on the floor underneath the window, cradling the device. I load the browser window and go to the webmail shortcut. I know Charley's email address but not her password. We're not one of those snooper, let's-share-everything couples.

Is this a step too far?

Charley doesn't do social media, there are too many ghosts in her past to want to be found easily, so it's only email. Perhaps there's a clue? An explanation of why she disappeared?

I type her email address into the box and then click into the password field.

Would her password be something to do with me? Martha? Her niece and nephew?

I type 'DaisyDillon' into the box and press enter.

Red letters: 'That password is incorrect.'

Of course it is. There'll be numbers in there somewhere. Perhaps the years they were born… but would the digits go between the names? After the names?

Do I want to do this at all?

We're not that sort of couple. We have a life together, but we do our own things, too. She has the shop, she spends time with Alice. She visits Mason and the children. I have my own work friends, I play football on Wednesday nights, sometimes I have to travel for a course. We don't do jealousy, we don't play games.

I close the browser window and then flip the laptop lid down. I rest my head against the window sill and close my eyes. I need to get out of this suit, to force myself to sleep. It's been thirty hours or so since I last had any meaningful time with my eyes closed. Perhaps a few hours of rest will help me think of something, some reason, why all this is happening.

There's a perfectly good bed upstairs, even the sofa in front of me, but the wall feels comfortable for now. It's fine for a quick nap in any case.

Just a quick nap…

Then the doorbell rings.

EIGHT

15 YEARS AGO

Ian Hendry: Chief news correspondent, Langton Chronicle

'Oi, Hendo, y'big bender. How's it going?'

I turn into the biggest of man-hugs, not knowing who's squeezing the life out of me until the bear of a man lets go.

'Bloody hell, how long has it been?' the man says.

I let out a long, deep gasp and recognise my assailant more by size than any facial features. Jack has put on a good few stone since we were at university together. He's six-foot and plenty, the width of two men.

'Twenty years…?' I try.

'Christ, it is, isn't it? What a bunch of old bastards we are.'

The people around us are starting to shuffle away, partly because of Jack's immense size but largely, I suspect, for other reasons, such as taste and decency.

'We should probably keep the bender talk to a minimum,' I say, lowering my voice.

Jack grins and then his face falls. He turns in a semicircle, almost wiping out a cameraman at his side. It's only a swift bit of ducking that saves the man from losing an ear.

'Yeah, sorry. Forgot where I was for a minute.' He pauses. 'Good to see ya, though. Twenty years? Bloody hell. I thought we'd all be unemployed by now, replaced by some kids copying and pasting off the internet.'

'Don't joke,' I tell him.

'Yeah, right… I know. They just announced a load more lay-offs at our place. I don't know why they even bother to call it news nowadays.' He waves a hand up to the steepling, beautiful church that soars above us. 'This on your patch, then?'

I nod. 'Not much happens here, if I'm honest. A wedding each week, that sort of thing. You get used to it.'

Jack lets out a low whistle. 'They don't build 'em like that any more.'

He shuffles in closer and then bears down over me. I think he's trying to whisper but it's still loud enough for everyone around us to hear.

'Do you know if the kids are going to be here?' he asks.

'That's what everyone's saying.'

He whistles again. 'Poor sods. That little girl…'

I press up against the stone wall that rings the church. It's where the police have jammed all the media – written, TV and radio. There are half a dozen satellite trucks parked along the road, annoying all the locals; then all the celebrity newsreaders have shown up for a day in the countryside. They're in a line on the other side of the road, each doing solemn pieces to camera with the church in the background. All very 'Candle In The Wind'.

'I didn't know you were covering the patch where the Willis lot lived,' Jack breathes. 'You must've had one hell of a week.'

'Something like that,' I reply.

He's not wrong. His badge tells me he's working for one of the papers on the south coast. There's no connection from there to Paul or Annie Willis, but that's not stopped journalists from the rest of the country showing up. The nation's first family and all that. Nobody mentions that neither Paul nor Annie had been on television in the past eighteen months. The TV channels had effectively pensioned them off, but that doesn't fit the narrative of tragic loss. If there's one thing we do well as an industry, it's rank hypocrisy.

'D'you know if that's all three kids?' Jack adds.

'I don't think anyone knows. I've heard rumours, but I guess we'll find out.'

Everyone is eagerly straining over the wall, staring along the road towards the row of police cars. There's a nervous anticipation after the week and a half of non-stop speculation and drip-drip-drip of police leaks. This is the first time that something is actually happening: real, concrete news.

'What's your job for the day?' Jack asks.

'People-watch. I'm supposed to be keeping an eye on the mourners, counting the flower bouquets, that sort of thing. You?'

'Atmosphere piece. We've got an eight-page memorial pull-out in tomorrow's edition. Gotta fill it with something.'

We catch each other's eye and share that *really?* look. All that training, all this experience and this is what it's come to. Neither of us wants to be here. It's a funeral, for crying out loud. What is there to say that hasn't already been said? This is the full stop to the endless narrative that's been going on for twelve days.

'You know who I blame?' Jack's in my ear again, talking too loudly. 'The public,' he adds. 'They lap all this up. It's a funeral and they're broadcasting it live on Sky News. A bloody funeral!' He nods across the road. 'Look over there. Celebs trying to get their faces on TV again. They've probably never met Paul or Annie. I reckon half this lot are only here because they're hoping the killer turns up.'

There are a couple of huffs from the surrounding reporters, but nobody bothers to speak up. He's probably right. News-wise, what better time for the killer to show himself? Or herself, I suppose. It's not as if the police have given up much information.

Before anyone can say anything else, there's a collective intake of breath. A police car cruises past, followed by a people carrier with tinted windows. Both glide to a stop outside the church gates and then a man in a black suit hops out of the driver's seat of the people carrier. He strides around the vehicle and slides open the door at the back.

If this was a film premiere, everybody would be talking at once, trying to attract the actor or actress's attention. It's a strange, sombre atmosphere. Like five o'clock on a Sunday morning in a city centre when there's a silent anticipation in the air.

Martha is the first out of the car; the most well-known of the Willis children. She found the bodies and called the police. If she wasn't so forceful at telling them to do one, she'd be a tabloid darling. Her black hair is straight and down, her tattoos covered with a long-sleeved dress. The red-tops love a famous young woman who looks like she might have a filthy mouth on her. For the broadsheets, she's a potential wild child. Everyone in the media has heard the stories of multiple boyfriends and drug-taking in nightclub toilets. No one will dare print it, of course. Not yet. Give it a couple of weeks until after the funeral and then it'll be open season. I wonder if she knows what's coming. Or if she cares.

There's a gentle rumbling undercurrent of murmurs and whispers from the crowd. It's not just celebrities and newsreaders across the road; the village has come out, too. That's not to mention everyone else who could be bothered to drive out to the sticks. It's a wall of black over there, like an elderly goth convention. Some just want to get on the telly or wallow in other people's grief.

Not that I'm innocent in all this, of course. We've all got bills to pay.

'We love you, Martha!'

The call comes anonymously from the crowd, but Martha doesn't acknowledge it. She reaches back into the car and helps her sister onto the road. There's a gasp from the assembled mass that's so deep it creates a moment as if it has forged its own gust of wind.

This is what everyone's been waiting for.

Nobody has seen little Charlotte in the twelve days since everything happened. There was one photo released to the press: Charlotte with her parents from three years ago. They'd done a magazine article for one of the Saturday pull-outs and she is sitting in the middle, hair in pigtails, looking tiny. A happy family of three.

She's in a knee-length black dress now, her golden blonde hair loose around her shoulders. The sisters look nothing like each other. Charlotte is prim and correct, while Martha arches forward, as if ready to snarl for the cameras. The elder sister whispers something to the younger and then they step away into the open, hand in hand.

Charlotte stares past us, up towards the church, blinking towards the sun. This will be the photo that everyone wants for tomorrow.

The girl who lived.

There's nothing quite like a bloodbath survivor to sell a few papers or get the ratings up.

The sisters have already taken half a dozen steps towards the church when the final sibling emerges from the car.

Liam Willis is the eldest, two years older than Martha and eleven years above Charlotte. He's completely different again; taller than Martha without the looks with which both girls have been blessed. One of his eyes is narrower than the other, his nose is squat like a boxer's and there's something not quite right with his mouth. It hangs lower on one side than the other and he's chipped a front tooth. He gives a small wave towards the elderly goths, nods and then jogs to catch up to his sisters.

Nobody knows an awful lot about him. He was born at the height of his parents' fame and is in few of the cuttings from the various magazine shoots his parents have done.

A pair of police officers quickly follow behind the trio. They all make their way along the crumbling paved path towards the church. Everyone turns to watch, but it's only Liam who glances back over his shoulder to acknowledge those who've turned out. A few moments later and they're gone.

There were no tears in the end. I think that's what people were hoping for, especially from Charlotte. If it cries, it flies, and all that. The picture editors that haven't yet been made redundant will be annoyed. That's what happens when you become public property: you're not allowed to be upset on the inside, it's got to be open and in front of the country.

Still, there's time yet. Thirteen is a little young. There are a few flimsy barely enforced laws about this type of thing. Someone will throw half a million at Charlotte in a few years' time to make a documentary or sell her story. Perhaps they'll get her to write a book? More hardbacks to clutter up the shelves at Christmas. Everyone likes a good bit of misery on Boxing Day.

And Martha? Glamour shoot by the end of the summer, I reckon. That'll be stage one, followed by 'my shame' a couple of weeks later when the toilet drug pictures finally sell. Build 'em up and then batter them down.

These kids might think this is the end. Get the funeral over with and then start to rebuild. They don't know the half of it. They belong to the nation now. Those people across the road haven't driven halfway across the country and holed up in a B&B overnight for nothing. Some of them were here at three in the morning to get a prime spot.

No.

They want their pound of flesh. They want sordid details. Blood, gore and melancholy. This is *our* massacre, don't you know.

This is the beginning.

I hope those poor kids are ready for it.

NINE

SETH. NOW

It isn't Charley at the front door. It's hard to hide my disappointment as Alice smiles weakly at me.

'No news?' she asks.

Alice is already stepping into the house even though I've not technically invited her in. It's fine... or it would be at any other time. She's usually here for Charley – either for shop talk or friend talk. It feels odd with it being just us.

'Nothing,' I reply.

Alice is carrying Charley's bags from the hotel. There is one with the clothes she was wearing on Friday, as well as the empty flattened oversized bag that contained her wedding dress.

Everything is suddenly beginning to feel very final. All the bags and clothes we took to the hotel are back at the house. It's all here except for Charley herself.

Alice closes the door behind her and follows me along the hall into the living room. She places the bags at the back of the room and waves away the offer of tea. I didn't want one myself, but it's what you do, isn't it? Guest comes over, you offer tea. That's what separates us from the animals.

'I've been calling her all morning,' Alice says, plopping onto the recliner. 'It doesn't even ring.'

I hold up my phone. 'Ninety-one unconnected calls.'

She looks at hers. 'Thirty-seven.'

I win.

Charley says that some customers think she and Alice are sisters and it's not hard to see why. They share the same style of loose dresses and sandals, that floaty hippyish look that only some women can pull off successfully. When it doesn't work, it's more overdose-in-a-bush chic. Alice is wearing a one-piece long blue dress, her legs curled under herself. There is still the hint of wave to her hair from the ceremony.

'Do you think we should call Liam?' she asks.

'Her brother…?'

I know who he is, of course… it's just he's never mentioned.

Alice shrugs. 'Has she talked about him much to you?'

'You've known her longer than me.'

'True, but she's only mentioned his name once or twice – and that's because she said you guys were visiting him.'

I nod. 'It was a few months ago. I don't think they'd spoken in ten years or so. Something ridiculous. He contacted her out of the blue, saying his wife had given birth to twins a few months before. She didn't even know he was married. They live thirty miles or so away, down the M3 and off at Basingstoke.'

'Did you go?'

'On a Sunday just after Easter. They've got this big four-bedroom detached new-build.'

Alice is nodding along and I wonder how much of this she knows, if anything. Everyone knows a person who shares too much. That walking disaster who dumps everything that ever happens to them on Facebook, or with a friend, oftentimes both. The one who lurches from one drama to the next, oblivious to the fact that divulging every morsel of their life to the viewing public is probably why their existence is perpetual chaos.

Charley is not one of those people. She's the opposite, internalising almost everything and revealing little. It's no surprise given what happened to her. Alice is her best friend and yet I doubt they share too much.

Alice shakes her head, more puzzled than annoyed. 'She never said anything about twins.'

'She loves Daisy and Dillon so much that I think the idea of having two more nieces out there trumped anything that might have happened before.'

A pause. We're both thinking it. Alice says it.

'What *did* happen between her and Liam?'

'I have no idea. I assumed they fell out in the way families do. She didn't want to talk and I never asked. No point in bringing it all back up again, not after what they went through.'

This is the problem with knowing someone in the public eye. Even when you *really* know them. When you live together, sleep together, when you get married, there's always that tiny seed of doubt that festers because of what you've seen or read. Who is the real person and who's the media concoction?

Alice nods. She knows this, too. 'What happened at Liam's?'

'Not much, I guess. We went in and there are these two gorgeous little girls. I know they're twins, obviously; I know it sounds stupid, but they're identical. They were even smiling at the same time. These two babbling little girls, Skye and Jasmine. I thought Charley was going to cry. She and Liam's wife, Helen, had a good long chat in the living room about giving birth and that sort of thing. You know what Charley's like around new people, but she wasn't fazed at all. It was like they were old friends.'

'What about Liam?'

'He hardly said a word. They barely acknowledged each other. It's not like I was adding much to the conversation; we were both letting our other halves talk.'

Alice offers her hands up. 'So perhaps Helen knows something about all this?'

'I'm not even sure how to contact her… or Liam.'

Her brow ripples and Alice sits silently, waiting for the explanation.

'We've not been back,' I add. 'After about half an hour in the living room, Liam asked if he could have a word with Charley. They disappeared out of the room for ten minutes or so. When she came back, Charley said we were going. She said goodbye to Helen and the girls and that was that. She was really quiet on the drive home. I asked a week or so later if we should add Liam and his family to the wedding guest list, but she said no.'

Alice stares at me, then blinks. She doesn't need to say it because I already know. It does sound odd – but only because neither of us know the context of why Charley and her brother didn't speak for so long.

Her attention flickers to the window and then she stands. I follow her gaze to the police car that has just pulled up outside.

TEN

15 YEARS AGO

Grant Westlake: Wills and probate solicitor

It's only a matter of time, I suppose. David Willis has been striding back and forth close to the windows for fifteen minutes now. His wife is statuesque in the corner chair, watching her husband and not the rest of what's going on in the office. It's hard to know which of the two might blow first.

David's the obvious one, of course. All that pent-up rage on show as he bounds across the same patch of carpet. I find myself hoping his shoes are clean. Christina has enough work to do as it is.

Sometimes, it's the silent types that go first. Minutes of saying nothing, hours, and then *boom*, the volcano erupts.

Paul Willis has been in the news for weeks now and I'd seen him on television before that, of course. He was my client and a familiar face. This is the first time I've met his brother. The thinning grey hair is the same, the height and composure is there… it's just David is like a dodgy waxwork version. Not quite the real thing. A pound-shop imitation.

I glance in David's direction once more and then finish my little speech. '…All I'm here to do is to read the will and then ensure the wishes are adhered to. That's it. I'm not here to make any actual decisions.'

I've finished my bit and now it's their turn to chip in. The gasps and small interruptions were one thing, but now the truth is known. At least I've got a big desk in front of me for protection. My office feels uncomfortably full. David and his wife at the back, Liam leaning on a bookcase off to one side, Martha resting on the door and little Charlotte sitting cross-legged on the floor in the far corner. She's peeping around the chair she's chosen not to use.

'So that's it, then?' Liam says. He claps his hands together and turns to the rest of the family. 'I get a little over a million quid?'

'And a third of the house,' I add.

'What's that worth?'

'I have no idea. You'll have to decide among yourselves what you want to do.'

'How d'you mean?'

'One of you might choose to live in it. If that's the case, perhaps the other two will want to have their share bought out? Perhaps you can come to a private arrangement about who lives there and if any money changes hands? I'm only here to execute your parents' wishes – and that says the house is divided equally among the three of you. What you do next is up to you.'

Liam is nodding along. I don't know what his financial state was before, but if his shabby jeans give any indication, then he certainly wasn't rolling in it. He's now a rich young man.

Neither of the daughters have said a word. Charlotte is hugging her knees to her chest. Her stare hasn't left me since I started speaking. I wondered if there was a glimmer of disbelief when I said that the three children were to share everything equally. It's no surprise, of course. How can a thirteen-year-old comprehend that amount of money? I can't fathom that she'll ever go back to that house, not after what everyone's saying about it. The house of death; the Willis bloodbath. Who'd want to live there? Let alone if you'd been hiding upstairs as everything happened below.

David Willis has finally stopped striding. He spins and jabs a finger in my direction. 'Now, look here,' he begins, theatrically, voice raised. There's a vein close to his ear that's been throbbing for a couple of minutes and I wonder if it might actually burst. Poor old Christina. Can't expect her to clean it up if it does. 'I don't care what it says,' David shouts. 'I don't care. You hear me? I had a verbal agreement with my brother that goes back years. *Years!* Paul said he'd look after my kids if anything were ever to happen to him. There were witnesses.'

His wife is nodding along in agreement.

'Not only that, I *GAVE* him the deposit for that house. They'd never own it in the first place if I hadn't put up half the money. He never paid it back and I never asked because he said he'd look after my kids if and when it came to it.'

David is snorting through his nose, a bull ready to charge. Typically, it is me who has to wave the red flag.

'I'm not sure what you'd like me to say. It isn't down to me to make judgement about the content of the will. The will says the money, estate and house is to be split in three equal parts between Liam Willis, Martha Willis and Charlotte Willis. The only mention of you is that you should be given access to the video library to pick and choose whatever you want. If you so desire, the entire thing is yours.'

That's definitely done it. There's practically steam hooting out of David's ears. His cheeks have flared red and there are flecks of saliva on his bottom lip. 'Videos?' he shouts. '*Videos?* Do you know what videos are worth? Nothing. You can't give them away. Even the tips won't take them nowadays. Who wants *videos?*' He flashes an arm in Charlotte's direction. 'She's thirteen. *Thirteen!* What's a thirteen-year-old going to do with that sort of money? Waste it all on Barbies while my kids are denied what's rightfully theirs?'

I open my mouth to explain everything once again, but I don't get a word out before the older sister turns. They say she's the wild child, not that she appears to care what anyone thinks of her. She's wearing a vest even though it's cool today, showing off that full arm of tattoos. Not my thing and, personally, I couldn't care less, but it riles some. There are men with cameras outside and I wonder if she's done it for their benefit. Not for the attention as such, more to annoy people.

She steps towards him, stone-cold. Although she's shorter than her uncle, for all the world, I'd swear she was taller. She's somehow looking down on him, even though she's actually looking up.

'If you *ever* point at my sister like that again, I will rip your finger off.'

Her uncle takes a small step backwards.

'If your kids want money,' she adds frostily, 'how about they get a job?'

I'd be cowering away under that stare, but David is too far in now. No point in blowing a gasket if you're going to wilt under the first challenge, especially when your wife is watching on. He doesn't dare wag a finger, though.

The uncle pushes himself higher onto the tips of his toes. 'Oh, *you're* one to talk,' he sneers. 'Slumming it in some London hole, shagging your way round Camden, from what I hear.'

Martha smiles, eyes narrow. She sticks out the tip of her tongue and bites it. 'Go on,' she starts. 'Say that again.'

There's a part of me that wants to let it play out. The little corner of consciousness that makes a person slow down when there's an accident on the other side of the road.

'Now, now,' I say, and I hear my father talking. Bloody hell, we're so British. 'I do not want this in my office. This ends now.'

This is nothing new, of course. After a death, everyone is all lovey-dovey until the money has to be split, then it's like the storming of the trenches.

Martha moves first, not exactly *backing* down but at least motioning away from her uncle. Nobody else has shifted through-out the confrontation.

'Look,' David says with a modicum of conciliation about him, 'even if the will splits everything in the way it does, there is no way I'm letting the house sale go through on top. I *gave* my brother part of the deposit. I've got paperwork for it all. I've got lawyers, too. You can keep your money and I'll tie everything up in so much red tape that the house will never be sold. Either that, or we can come to some sort of arrangement…'

He leaves it hanging there. Not quite conciliatory, I suppose, more a polite threat. His wife is nodding along once more. Go Team David.

'You're not having my money,' Liam says matter-of-factly. 'No way. Do what you want with the house, but they left that money to me and that's that.'

Martha opens her mouth to speak, but Charlotte stuns everyone. 'I don't care,' she says softly. Everyone has stopped to look down at her. She's so small on the floor, still hugging her knees tight. 'I don't want their money,' she adds.

That's enough for David. He claps his hands together. 'There you go then! That's that solved. We can take that share and split it among the nephews and nieces. You can then do whatever you want with the house.'

'No.'

Martha speaks firmly, bristling with authority that belies the fact she's only twenty-two.

'What?' David replies. 'You heard her. She doesn't want it.'

'She's thirteen,' Martha says. 'She'll get that money when she's old enough. If she wants to give it away then, it's up to her. She's not making this decision now.'

David turns to his wife for assurance. There's a microscopic nod and then he pumps himself up once more. 'What about *my* kids?'

Martha steps towards him once more. 'Perhaps they can find some parents who earn their *own* money and don't spend their lives scrounging and moaning?'

When a kettle boils on a stove, there's always that little rattle when it's nearly ready. A little shunt to let everyone know the water is almost done. David's eyebrow is twitching and he's close to popping. That vein is bulging so monumentally that I can almost see the blobs of blood flowing through.

It's hard not to like Martha. Perhaps it's me, my age, that dirty-old-man thing which is hard to pretend isn't there. I don't know why people call it that. There's the insult factor, of course, but what do they expect? For the most part, if a man is attracted to women, that doesn't go away simply because they hit a certain age. At one point, it's considered healthy and normal, a year or three later and you're a dirty old man.

Even with that, it's not as if I have a thing for her in that way. There's something fundamentally appealing about a young person who couldn't care less about who he or she stands up to. Not attractive in a physical sense, more an admiration thing.

David is bobbing on the tips of his toes, apparently unsure of where to go from here. Martha has already dared him once to insult her and I can't see him taking her up on the offer.

In a flash, he lunges for the door, pausing for a second to jab a finger in my direction again. 'You've not heard the last of this,' he bellows. His wife storms past him and then he slams the door. Or tries to. It catches on the carpet and inches slowly into place, making a gentle click rather than the ferocious bang.

There's a moment of silence, but the tension is still there until Liam levers himself away from the bookcase. He peers around the room and takes a breath. 'That went better than I thought,' he says.

ELEVEN

SETH. NOW

It's always the husband, isn't it?

That's the way the story goes. Get married, wife has an unfortunate tumble off a cliff or something… It's like the dodgy marriage jokes, another of those clichés. I can't remember the stats, but when a person is killed, it's almost always by someone they know. Ditto if someone goes missing in suspicious circumstances.

There are two police officers. The man is in uniform, the woman in a pale grey suit. Suit means CID – a detective – but I'm not sure if that's a good or bad thing. It means they're either taking this seriously and will do what they can to find Charley… or they think I've bumped her off somewhere.

PC No Hair has, well, no hair. I forgot his proper name as soon as he told me. He's one of those who starts going bald at twenty-odd and then shaves it off to give nature a jump-start. He's not said anything, but his colleague has the steely glare of a woman who looks like she's seen a few things in her time. DS Stanley is late-forties or early fifties, carved from granite with grey eyes.

I have to remind myself that I *didn't* do anything wrong. That I was with people through the reception anyway. I feel guilty for no reason other than that I haven't had many dealings with the police. I'm not even old enough to be at where it feels right nodding to a police officer if I see one on the street. When you've lived enough of your life that a polite nod to a member of the Old Bill is perfectly friendly and acceptable. There must be an age where it suddenly clicks into place. Forty-something, I reckon – and I'm not thirty yet.

'Did you have any sort of argument in the days leading up to Ms Willis's disappearance?' It's DS Stanley who's doing the talking.

I let the name slip go. It's *Chambers* now, not Willis. Perhaps the officer said it on purpose, wondering how I'd react. DS Stanley is being polite, but I know there's suspicion under there. I can imagine that tone dipping into something that would strip paint from a wall.

I shake my head. 'Nothing. I didn't see her much on Friday because she went to the hotel with Alice. I didn't check in until Saturday.'

'But all was fine before that?'

'Right.'

'And Alice is the young woman who left as we arrived…?'

'Exactly. They run a sandwich shop in town, named Martha's. Alice was the main bridesmaid.'

DS Stanley mutters something to PC No Hair, who asks for Alice's details. He notes everything down and then turns back to his colleague.

'Are there any other friends who might be able to shed light on what's happened…?' she asks.

'Charley doesn't have a lot of friends. She's a very private person. She spends some time at her brother-in-law's and babysits her nephew and niece now and then. Other than that, it's mainly Alice.'

DS Stanley looks up and I'm locked in her stare. 'What about family?'

That's the question, isn't it? What *about* family? It's what Charley's entire life has revolved around. It's never *her*, it's about her mum and dad. The family.

'She doesn't get along with her brother,' I say.

'And he is…?'

'Liam. He wasn't at the wedding – her choice. He's married with twin girls. We visited a couple of months ago, but they've not been in contact since.'

The detective nods. 'Any particular reason why they don't get on?'

A shrug. 'Family stuff, I guess.'

I wonder if she's going to follow it up. It's not much of an answer, but it's the best I have. She makes a note on her own pad and then looks up once more.

'And the brother-in-law…?'

'Mason Renton. He was at the wedding with his kids. There's Dillon, who's seven, and Daisy, who's five. Daisy was the second bridesmaid. Charley loves those kids. There's no way she'd have left without saying goodbye…'

I stop myself from blurting out any stupid theories. Not yet, anyway. Time and a place and all that.

The detective writes something else on her pad and then purses her lips into an O. There's an obvious question, of course – Martha – but she doesn't ask. She'd already know the answer.

'Can you think of any reason why Ms Willis…' she stops herself, flips a page, 'sorry, why Mrs *Chambers* might choose to take off?'

'I wish I did.'

'Any clues she was unhappy?'

'I found antidepressants in her things upstairs. There's a prescription, so they're from a doctor.'

'Did you know she was depressed?'

'I'm not sure…' I look between the officers, hoping for some understanding. 'I mean… I don't know if she *was* depressed. We never talked about it.'

The pen scratches onto the pad again. Both are writing this time. This hardly makes me sound like a loving, devoted husband.

'Do you know anywhere she might have gone?'

'Only the shop. Alice said she'd been there but it's all locked up.'

'What about her parents' house?'

It's a direct question that leaves me gasping in surprise.

'I'd not even thought about it.'

'Have you ever been? It's, what, fifteen miles away? Twenty?'

'Why would we?'

The detective nods, acceptingly. Perhaps she's annoyed at herself for letting it slip that she knows plenty about Charley – or at least thinks she does. She knows what's been printed about my wife, she doesn't know the person.

'Just to confirm,' she adds, 'you and Mrs Chambers live here?'

'Right.'

'How long have you lived together?'

'She moved in with me about a year ago. A little over. She was living in a flat in town before that.'

I give the details to PC No Hair, who writes everything down.

'Have you noticed anything missing?' the detective asks.

'No – her passport's still upstairs, so are her clothes. Alice returned the bag she'd taken to the hotel, including the one that had her wedding dress inside.' I point to the Halloween photo of Charley with Dillon and Daisy, alongside the one of Charley and Martha. 'She wouldn't have left those,' I add. 'The one of her with her sister is the only copy she has. She takes those photos on weekend breaks.'

The detective pushes herself up and crosses the room, picking up the two pictures and looking at them. Perhaps it's the shield crumbling, but she smiles.

'Cute kids,' she says.

I try to reply but the words stick. This is Charley at her best. The Charley with whom I fell in love. I *wanted* to marry her, for us to grow old together. I thought that's what she wanted, too – but now she's gone. Did she walk away, or…

I blink away the thought. 'Sometimes Charley will babysit on an evening,' I say. 'Other times, we'll take them out somewhere on a weekend to give Mason a break.'

The detective nods along before returning the pictures to the side and then retakes her seat. She flips a page of her notebook and then names the hotel at which we got married.

'Who chose for the wedding to be there?' she asks.

'It was a joint decision. We visited a few places. Charley wanted something away from town in case anyone got word. She didn't want anyone from a magazine popping up.'

'Do you get much of that?'

I shake my head. 'Hardly ever… well, never, in fact. We've only been together for two years and I've never been photographed by a paper or magazine. She's careful, after everything that happened. Sometimes one of her dad's shows will get repeated on cable, or some clip of her mum is shared on YouTube. One of the yoga ones, y'know?'

The detective nods along.

'Charley doesn't use the internet much because of all that. People put comments on forums, or wherever, and she doesn't want to see it. She'll do some shopping on Amazon, that sort of thing. She's got email – but that's it.'

I pause, but the detective doesn't say anything. She's waiting for the rest.

'I've thought about pointing out that a lot of time has passed,' I say, 'that nobody's bothered who we are, but she grew up with all this. Sometimes she'll see someone with a phone or camera when we're at the beach or a park, that sort of thing. She'll turn her back, thinking they're after her – but it's just some guy or girl taking a selfie.'

The police officers exchange a brief glance before DS Stanley continues.

'So you got married at a hotel in the countryside…?'

'Right. Charley only wanted a small ceremony, which was fine by me. There were only twenty-one people there and that includes the registrar, the best man and two bridesmaids.'

I find the guest list on my phone and then pass on the details to the constable.

DS Stanley takes a long breath, flipping through the pages of her notebook before peering up again.

'You say you met two years ago?'

'Right.'

'When did you get engaged?'

'About a year back when she moved in.'

'So you never knew the sister…?'

The detective leaves it hanging there. She knows what she's asked.

'No,' I say.

'And you've not experienced the so-called Willis Curse…?'

There is an awkward silence. Both officers are watching me as I try not to squirm. I've not heard those two words together in a long time. It was a phrase from the news, something other people would say or write.

'I, um…'

She bats a hand. 'Sorry, I was thinking out loud.'

The detective bites her lip and, before I know it, I'm filling the silence.

'Other people have called it that,' I say, aware of how defensive it sounds.

'I know. I'm sorry.'

'Charley hated it. She said it wasn't true.'

'Of course.'

The detective pauses again, but this time I don't fill the gap.

'What do you do?' she asks eventually.

'I'm a vet. I work at Poor Paws in town.'

'How long have you been there?'

Time to count on the fingers. 'About four years.'

That goes onto the pad and then it's back to Charley.

'How did you meet?' she asks.

'At Martha's… the sandwich shop she runs with Alice. I went in for breakfast and, well… that was that, I guess.'

'That was two years ago…?'

'Right.'

She gives the sort of nod people do when they're not entirely sure if they approve. All a bit quick and that. Meet, move in, get married. Two years.

'Charley likes gardening,' I add, although I'm immediately unsure why. I suppose I want to talk about her. 'She took it up when she moved in. I'd let the back garden get a bit overgrown, but she cleaned it up and planted vegetables out there. Peas and carrots, mainly.'

DS Stanley is drumming her pen, then she snaps her pad closed. 'I have to ask… but it's common knowledge that Mrs Chambers inherited a large sum of money…' She glances upwards, indicating the house. There's no need to say it, because it's obvious. This is not quite a million-pound mansion.

'She gave the money away,' I reply. 'Before I met her. She said she used a bit to set up her shop, but that's it.'

'Who did she give it to?'

'She said there's a lump sum in accounts for when Dillon and Daisy turn eighteen – plus she has cousins on her dad's side. I'm pretty sure they got something.' I shrug. 'I don't know any of that for sure. It was before I met her. The only money we talk about is what she makes from the shop and my salary. We're like any other couple.'

The detective nods, but I'm not sure she fully accepts it. Who'd give away a million quid? There's all the interest that would've accrued over time as well.

'Charley's not that fussed about money,' I add.

'That seems clear.'

We talk about them needing a photo to show in case someone recognises her. I tell the officers that my sister took all the pictures at the wedding. If they contact her, she should be able to provide the most recent image possible, one that shows the dress as well. That's what Charley left in, after all.

The detective runs through the order of the day; the ceremony and the reception. She clarifies the last time I saw Charley and I tell her that my mother might've been the last person to see her. She nods with understanding when I talk about Mum's dementia and there's a second or two in which we definitely comprehend one another.

I explain that I'm off work for a week, supposedly to enjoy the post-marriage glow.

'No honeymoon?' she asks.

'We were going to save up and go travelling next year,' I reply. 'Charley was talking about opening a second shop first. Alice would manage one, she'd take the other.'

'Business going well, then?'

'You can check with Alice – but I guess so.'

I stop, breathe in through my nose and then tears feel close. I've been holding it together well, stoic and all that. That's what my dad would say. He didn't really do tears. Stiff upper lip. The British way. It's how I was brought up.

'It's what I don't understand,' I say, the words catching in my throat. 'She had plans for the future. *We* had plans. Why would you talk about all that and then disappear?'

Both officers start to stand. Their lips are tight, revealing nothing.

'Someone must've taken her,' I add, the thought suddenly clear as I jump up. I'm babbling, thoughts of keeping wild conspiracies to myself long gone.

'Why do you say that?' the detective asks.

I stare at her, mouth open. 'It's just… why else would she go?'

TWELVE

13 YEARS AGO

Charley Willis, 15 years old

'Listen to this one,' I say, looking up to make sure I have Martha's attention and then turning back to the laptop screen. '"Annie Willis changed my life. I started doing her exercises just after giving birth to my first child. Ten years on, and four children later, I'm still doing them every day".'

Martha frowns towards me but says nothing. I know she disapproves of me reading the tributes. It's been two years but people haven't forgotten. Martha is flicking through the mail, muttering with annoyance as she dumps half the stack into the bin.

'Junk,' she says.

'Do you want to hear another?' I ask.

She looks to me, biting her tongue in the way she does. They say you bite your tongue to prevent yourself saying something you don't mean – but it's a literal thing with my sister. She lets the bauble piercing poke between her front teeth and jiggles it back and forth.

Instead of replying, Martha holds up the letter she's just opened. 'Another one from the solicitor,' she says. 'Uncle David's still blocking the house sale.'

'I don't care about that stupid house. Let him do what he wants.'

'That's not the point, Char. It's not about the money. We earned that and there's no way I'm giving in to that arsehole.'

'That's Uncle Arsehole to you.'

Martha's seriousness slips. She smiles and then laughs, dispatching the letter into the bin. '*Uncle* Arsehole,' she repeats. 'I wish I'd thought of that. I'm using it next time.'

'I've got copyright on it.'

'I'm still using it.' We both grin and then she jumps up off the sofa. 'Come on, forget this – we're going out.'

'Where?'

'Somewhere fun.'

She pulls me up from the chair and drags me into the bedroom before opening the wardrobe and shunting all my stuff to the side so that hers is in the middle.

'I reckon you can pass for eighteen,' she says.

'Where are we going?'

She pulls a dress from the rack, one of the few she owns that isn't black. She holds it up against me, taking a half-step back and eyeing me up and down. It's green and short, above my knee. Nothing like what Mama would let me wear.

'I reckon that'll do,' she says. 'You can borrow a pair of my boots, bit of eye make-up and you'll be done.'

I take the dress from her and hold it at arm's length. There's a slim vertical triangle down the front and a built-in bra I'm not sure I'll fill.

'Padding,' Martha says, reading my mind as she always seems to do and then handing me a pair of gel-like chicken fillet blobs.

'Where are we going?'

She sighs, then smiles and throws her hands up. 'We're going to have fun, Char. To a pub or two, maybe a club. We're going to dance and have a drink or two.'

'Mama always said—'

'Forget her!' Martha bites her tongue again and then lowers her voice. 'And stop calling her "Mama". It's weird. Call her Mum if you have to – but you don't have to. She was a hypocrite.'

We stare at each other and I'm old enough to know this has been brewing. I've been pushing it: reading those tributes, wanting Martha's opinion even though I already know it.

'Let's go,' Martha says.

'What if I don't get in?'

'You'll get in – you're a girl.'

'What does that matter?

'You'll learn – but girls can do what they want if they're pretty. Clubs at fifteen, easy-peasy. I used to do it all the time. If anyone asks, your name is…' She wafts a hand around, thinking. 'What do you want your name to be?'

'Angel.'

'That sounds like a stripper's name.'

'…Which means I'm definitely eighteen.'

She nods towards me. 'True. You're Angel and I'm Bliss.'

'*Bliss?*

Martha shrugs: 'I was trying to think of another stripper name.'

'Angel and Bliss, we could *so* be strippers.'

'We definitely couldn't – but the doormen won't know that.' She waves me over to the mirror. 'Come on, let's do this.'

Mama used to take hours to get ready before going out. Some of my earliest memories are sitting at the bottom of the stairs as Father paced up and down the hallway bellowing for her to hurry up.

Perhaps because of that, Martha has got getting ready down to sprint form. In barely twenty minutes, she's swiped eyeliner onto my lids, lengthened my lashes with mascara, sorted herself out and we're both dressed. It helps that we're the same size for everything.

Ten minutes after that and we're toddling along the high street, laughing about nothing and everything. The hooker cards in the phone boxes are hilarious, so is the clearly drunk bloke who's sleeping in a shopping trolley. It's good to be outside. I've not seen a lot of the city since moving here. I barely went out at all in the first six months and only sporadically since. It feels exciting to be an adult.

I only start to feel nervous when I see the pub on the corner. There are two men in suits and dark bomber jackets standing outside the main door. Both are wearing earpieces, with little or no hair.

Martha barely flinches; if anything, she ups her pace.

Her boots are awkward to walk in, even though the heel is low, I have to quick-step to catch-up. I'm alongside her as we get to the bottom step.

'Evening, ladies,' the taller of the bouncers says.

'Hi,' Martha replies.

And that's it. We push through the doors and then we're inside. A couple near the door turn to look at us but quickly spin away. Nobody else pays us the slightest bit of attention.

Martha strides to the bar confidently, perching on a stool and patting the one next to her. I slot in and then she nods to the other side of the bar.

'What do you want?'

There is an array of bottles in the fridges. Some are easy to read – the ones with cider written on the label, the brown bottles of Budweiser or the green Carlsberg. The rest is a rainbow of colour.

'I don't know what anything is.'

'You like strawberries, right?'

'Yes.'

'Good!'

I can see the barman looking sideways at Martha as he finishes with another customer and then he sidesteps towards us. He looks Mediterranean, all dark skin and thick hair, but his accent is local.

'Evening, ladies. What can I do you for?'

'Two strawberry Smirnoffs,' Martha says.

He doesn't ask for ID, barely even acknowledges me as he turns and crouches to open the fridge. It might be on purpose… heck, it's *definitely* on purpose, but he shunts his arse high towards us. He's wearing incredibly tight trousers and I'm surprised he can bend that far.

Martha pays and he gives her a wink, then we're off towards the corner, bottles and straws in hand.

'Easy as that,' she says.

It's a cosy alcove, all soft seats and sticky tables. There's a television high on the wall showing music videos and a pair of fruit machines next to the sign for the toilets. We sit and then I start to read the label on the back of the bottle.

'Don't do that,' Martha scolds with a smile.

'Why?'

'Because it's all sugar. Stop spoiling the fun.'

I guzzle a mouthful and swallow.

'What do you reckon?' she asks.

'Tastes like strawberries.'

'Yeah – but best not drink too many of those.'

I have another sip and then relax back into the seat. It feels good to be doing something I shouldn't. There was a locked drinks cabinet at the house and I dread to think how Mama or Father would have reacted if they'd found me in it.

'Someone's watching us,' I say, nudging Martha's leg and nodding towards a man at the bar. He's what Mama would've called a 'typical student'. Skinny, with big waxy hair, a bristly beard and a bit of a slouch about him. 'He knows who we are,' I add, trying to hide the urgency.

'He doesn't.'

'How do you know?'

Martha smirks, laughs slightly and nudges me with her elbow. 'Because we're girls with our legs out, Char. He has no idea who we are, he's only seeing the flesh.'

I glance down at my legs as if to confirm they are actually there and, by the time I look up again, the studenty type is on his way over, one hand in pocket, the other cupping a pint of tumescent orange cider.

'All right, girls,' he says.

I'm not sure what to say, but Martha gets in first. 'We're definitely all right, thanks.'

I have no idea how she does it, but she makes something that could be friendly sound like a definitive 'get lost'.

The student doesn't take the hint, twirling around a chair and sitting on it so that his legs are splayed either side of the back.

'I've not seen you in here before,' he adds, looking from Martha to me.

'No, you haven't,' Martha replies.

'What's your names?'

He's still looking at me but Martha answers. 'Look, mate. I'm sure you're very nice. You like animals, you're kind to your mum, you do the cooking in your flat, you had a gap year in Tanzania, or whatever, and you're a fan of philosophy. Good for you. Now, can you practise a bit of pissing off that way.' She bats a hand towards the fruit machines but he doesn't move.

He's speaking only to me: 'Do you always let your mate talk for you?'

'Sister,' I reply. 'She's my sister, not my mate.'

'Do you always let your *sister* talk for you?'

'No… but, well, it'd be great if you could practise a bit of pissing off that way.' I point in the same direction Martha had and we sit waiting until he spins the chair back around, mutters something about it being 'our loss' and then shows that he's actually not a bad pisser-offer after all.

Martha ditches the straw and has a long swig from the bottle. 'That was pretty good,' she says.

'The drink?'

'You. Not in my league, obviously, but you're learning.'

I have a small sip of my own drink through the straw. The first swig was full of sweetness but that's wearing off and I can taste the bitter tang beyond.

'It gets better,' Martha says.

'What does?'

'Alcohol. You were sheltered at Mum and Dad's. This is what normal teenagers do.'

'Did you?'

It's rare that Martha's off guard. I know she has a softer side she doesn't show very often, but there's a moment where she squirms and then she can't look at me directly.

'Sort of,' she says after a moment. 'Don't worry about it. We're here now.'

She presses back into her seat, mouth of the bottle at her lips, and then she nods towards a man in a suit standing next to the cash machine by the door.

'What's his story?' she asks.

'How d'you mean?'

'This is the best game, Char. Pick a person and figure out their story.'

'How do you do that?'

She hums to herself, has another swig from the bottle. Hers is three-quarters gone but mine is largely full.

'Definitely married,' she says. 'Maybe separated.'

'How do you know that?'

'He's, what, forty-odd? Most people that age are married or divorced – plus he's fat. Most singles are trying to *not* be single so they keep themselves in shape. People let themselves go when they're attached.'

The man turns and stuffs a handful of cash into his pocket, then heads to the bar.

'On the pull,' Martha added. 'He's gone straight to the end of the bar where that girl's serving.'

It's true. He's leaning across the bar, gut pressed into the wood, stretching a twenty-pound note across to the blonde barmaid who's got an Australian accent and is probably only twenty or twenty-one.

He calls her 'love' and she smiles through it. Even I can tell it's fake. Once the man's got his drink, he gives her a 'Cheers, darling,' and then turns to take in the rest of the bar. I watch him sweep across the group of lads by the quiz machine and then focus in on a pair of women sitting in the opposite corner to us.

'I'm going city worker,' Martha says. 'He's separated and possibly been made redundant recently.'

'Why'd you say that?'

'His sort only come out here to pick up a bit of rough.'

It sounds ominously as if she knows that too well, but I don't say anything.

Martha nods towards the barman. 'Your turn,' she says.

'Um…'

He notices Martha's attention and winks at her once more but doesn't get a chance to say or do anything else because a group of lads pile through the front door and head straight for the bar.

'He's got a nice bum,' I say.

Martha laughs, raises her bottle. 'That's not speculation, Angel dear. That's fact.'

'Single.'

'Perhaps.'

'He's not gay.'

Another laugh. 'You're picking the obvious stuff here, sis. Let me help: he's a dancer during the day. Blokes don't get legs like that from standing behind a bar all night. Maybe an instructor, something like that. He's got a date tattooed on his wrist from eight years ago, so he's definitely a father. Probably a daughter, I reckon. Wouldn't surprise me if he's got a wife and kid in Portugal or Greece, somewhere like that. Probably shags a different girl every couple of nights. He'll either live upstairs or somewhere nearby. Minimum wage.' She puffs out a breath. 'Scar on his forehead means he was probably a handful at some point. Street kid, something like that. Knows how to take care of himself. Probably not someone to mess with.'

Martha downs the rest of her drink in one.

'I'm getting another,' she says, 'you can have one for every two of mine.'

I watch as she squeezes her way through the pack of lads. They each turn in sequence, apparently not realising someone's wriggled between them until Martha emerges at the bar. She grins at the bartender, leaning forward so that her chest is angled towards him. It doesn't take much for her to get his attention and order another bottle. Seconds later and she's back with me.

'That's how you do it,' she says. 'You witnessed a masterclass there.'

Martha instantly downs a third of her drink and then drags me over to the pool table, where she slaps three pound coins on the edge.

'You ever play before?' she asks.

'No.'

'Just hit the white ball into the other balls. You'll pick it up.'

And I do... sort of. The table is too big and I struggle to stretch – plus it's not always clear what's a spot and what's a stripe. I win anyway, though I suspect Martha lets me. It doesn't matter though because it's fun. I surprise myself at how much we laugh.

Then we're off to the other side of the bar because karaoke is starting up. Martha grabs the microphone first and sings a song I've never heard. 'Sings' is a loose term. She shouts most of it, but nobody seems to care.

When everyone's bored of karaoke, the music is turned up and the chairs are cleared. One half of the pub has become a dance floor and so we dance and we drink. I can't keep up with Martha's two-for-one ratio, but it doesn't matter. I don't know how long passes before Martha pulls me close. She's sweating and the make-up around one of her eyes is running onto her cheek.

'This is life!' she shouts, throwing her arms up.

I copy what she's doing, or at least try. It's all arms and legs and I have no real clue.

'Go with it,' she shouts, and so I do.

The ceiling is starting to spin and sweat is pouring from my forehead. My mouth is aching because I've laughed so much.

Time passes and the dance floor has thinned. Someone's clearing glasses on the far side of the pub and Martha finishes her final drink before dragging me towards the doors and wrapping her arms around me. She smells of sweat and strawberries.

'I love you,' she says.

Everything's hazy, a grainy grey mask directly in front of my eyes. 'Thank you,' I reply.

'For what?'

'You know.'

Martha pulls me tight, hugging me into her neck and squeezing.

THIRTEEN

SETH. NOW

I don't even realise I've fallen asleep until my phone starts to ring. At first I think it's a dream, some annoying buzzing bee chasing me along a trail, then I blink into the living room and realise my phone is flashing. It's five in the morning.

Emily's name is on the screen and my first thought is that something's happened to Mum. This is the call we've each been dreading…

'Em?' I say.

'Have you seen it?' she asks.

'Seen what?'

'Someone's leaked the story about you and Charley. You're all over the *Daily Mail*.'

It takes a few seconds for it to sink in. So much for what I told the police about never having a problem with the media… Emily apologises for calling so early but rationalises that she thought I'd want to know. That's true enough.

I thank her and then hang up, flopping back onto the sofa once more. There are four empty bottles of Stella on the floor near my feet and I vaguely recall flicking through the television channels at what was either late last night or early this morning. It's hard to remember.

'Charley?'

My throat is gravelly as I call her name. It stings and I hurry through to the kitchen, where I down half a pint of water in one.

Back in the living room, there are the remains of a half-eaten frozen pizza. Chicken and pineapple. Charley's favourite. The roof of my mouth is stinging slightly and it suddenly makes sense: there's nothing on the planet hotter than the cheese on a pizza. It's like someone has liquidised the sun and served it on a doughy base with tomato sauce.

As well as Emily's call, there are six texts on my phone. One from Alice, two from Emily, two from Raj and one from Mason. All are along the same line: Any sign of Charley? Hope you're well. Call if you need.

Thanks but no thanks… at least for now.

It's embarrassing, more than anything. What can I say to people? No, I don't know where she is? No, we didn't argue? Yes, I hope she comes back?

I can't keep having the same conversation.

And now I'm on the bloody internet. In the papers.

I pluck the laptop from the spot under the window where it's been charging all night. I remembered to turn the plug on, which is one thing, and the battery tells me it's at 100 per cent.

There's a photo of some teenager in a bikini at the top that must surely scrape decency laws, but I skim past that to the second story on the sidebar of shame.

Emily is right. They're using that old photo of Charley they used to print all the time. She was eighteen or nineteen, walking along a high street in London in a tight green dress that doesn't look like her at all. As well as those photos of her at the funeral, this is how the nation knows her. Green dress Charlotte: the slightly slutty Willis daughter who isn't the wild child.

Has the Willis Curse Struck Again?

I stare at the headline for a few moments. The sentence makes sense, the words all in the right order, and yet… I can't quite believe they've written it. This is exactly why Charley was so wary of people she didn't know, why she didn't like cameras. It's probably why she asked Emily to photograph our wedding. With anyone else, she'd have worried about someone leaking a picture.

The photo at the top of the actual story leaves me open-mouthed. The three stages of Charley. The eight-year-old in a staged magazine shoot with her parents; the thirteen-year-old at her Mum and Dad's funeral, the late-teen on the streets of London. The most recent picture is at least nine years out of date. A spectre of the past. This isn't *my* Charley. This is a stranger.

I can't read it, not properly, but I find myself scanning the page.

'…Charlotte thought she'd found happiness with local vet, Seth Chambers…'
'…Charlotte left the spotlight to move closer to her parents' old house…'
'…The latest mystery follows in the footsteps of what some have dubbed, "The Willis Curse"…'
'…The killer of Paul and Annie Willis has never been found…'
'…The Willis family misery was compounded four years ago, when…'

There are a few instances of 'sources said', but no actual names. Most of it is speculation; some of it an outright lie. I know for a fact Charley didn't move here to be closer to her parents' old house in Langton. She did so to attend a catering management course outside London.

I perhaps wouldn't mind so much if the article had been written as an attempt to find out what happened – but the fact Charley is missing is only mentioned once near the top. It says she 'disappeared shortly after her wedding to Mr Chambers'. No number to call in case somebody sees her, no appeal for her to contact home, hardly anything other than going over events that happened more than a decade ago.

My hand is actually trembling as I click away from the page. If Charley sees this, it's going to break her. She's built a life in this town, trying to escape what happened to her as a teenager, and now this.

I make it missed call numbers (104) and (105) but there is no answer.

Who could have leaked it? Not Emily and not Alice. It wouldn't be Mason, he has more than enough on his own plate with Daisy and Dillon – plus it's not the type of thing he'd do. So Raj? Would he really do that for a few quid? I've known him for twenty years. We first became friends because we ended up sitting together for registration at school. In the period between, we've been close and not so much. We went our separate ways to university and then started playing Wednesday-night football together when we moved back. I can't believe it's him. Rafi? Maybe – but the piece is so uninformed it's hard to shoulder the fact it could be anyone I know.

It must be the police. Perhaps not even the officers who visited the house, someone who works at the station who noticed Charley's name and thought he or she could make a few quid.

My phone is in my hand when it starts to ring, making me jump. It's quarter past five in the morning. The number is unknown – but it starts with 07, so must be a mobile.

I allow myself to believe it is Charley on a borrowed phone. She's stranded somewhere and needs help. Or she's seen the story and is calling to let me know how and why this is all a misunderstanding.

It's a man's voice: 'Mr Chambers…?'

'Who is this?'

'My name's Richard Kingston and I'm a freelance journalist. I figured I'd get in before the big boys to ask if you fancy telling your side of the story…?'

It might be the hour of the day but it takes me a moment to take it all in.

'What side?' I ask.

'I gather your wife disappeared on Saturday evening. The whole Willis Curse thing.'

'Stop calling it that.'

There is a short pause, a gulp perhaps. 'I'm sorry, Mr Chambers. No offence intended, but I thought perhaps—'

I hang up. Stare at the screen until it goes dark. I think about turning it off – but what if Charley actually does call? I could try only answering numbers I recognise, but what happens if Charley is in trouble and calls from somebody else's number?

The phone starts to ring again, the same number. I cancel the call and then click through the options to block the number. That's one thing, at least. I can leave my phone on and block anyone I want.

The sun is on its way up and I slept with the curtains open, meaning the living room is now doused with a foggy orange. Day two of no Charley.

Is this what it's going to be like? You hear people saying it's the not knowing that really affects a person. If there's a death, you can start the process of grieving; without that, you're left hoping – and it's the hope that gets you in the end.

Not a death. I push the thought away. She isn't dead.

A flicker of movement from the far end of the front garden has me on my feet. A pair of cars are parked on the road directly outside in a spot that would usually be clear. Two blokes are shuffling around, both wearing shirts and ties. Another man in a jacket clinks open my gate and heads along the path towards my front door.

I freeze, waiting… and then the bell rings. Whoever it is knocks at the same time. I'm barely in the hallway when the letter box is opened from the outside and a voice calls through.

'Hello? Mr Chambers? I saw you from the road and figured I'd introduce myself.'

I can only see his eyes, the door obscuring the rest of his features. His voice is muffled.

'Can we talk?' he adds. 'Perhaps you can let me in? Or we can go out for coffee somewhere? Perhaps some breakfast? I saw this diner place on the way over…'

We look at each other for a moment or two and then I turn and close the door to the hallway, heading upstairs to the back bedroom and closing that door, too.

Charley's pillow smells of her. I think about burying my face in it, but then realise I'm being ridiculous, a walking cliché. Give it a rest.

Whoever knocked on the door is still there, still calling through the letter box for me.

I sit up on the bed and wonder what he thinks is the best that can happen. I'll be so impressed by him shouting through the small flap at the front of my house that I'll let him take me on a first date to his 'diner place' and tell him everything about my life? Tell him whatever he wants to know about my missing wife? I can't believe that's how it works.

My phone rings again, a different 07 number this time, probably one of that lot outside. I press to answer: 'Please stop calling,' I say, 'I need the line to be clear in case my wife calls.'

There's a cough and then a nervous mumble. 'Is that Seth?'

'Who's this?'

'It's Liam, Charley's brother. We met a few months ago, if you remember?'

I'm so stunned that it takes me a second or two to gasp that I do remember.

'I know it's early,' he adds, 'but I saw the story online about Charlotte. I was hoping we could talk.'

FOURTEEN

12 YEARS AGO

Charley Willis, 16 years old

Martha is leaning on the door that separates the living room from the kitchen as she practically wrenches the landline phone cord out of the wall.

'Tell David to talk to me now or I'm coming round.' She stops for a second to let the other person speak and then growls: 'No, *you* listen. Put him on right now. I don't care if he's busy.'

Martha starts to say something else and then stops, taking the phone away from her ear and then staring at it.

'That cow hung up,' she mutters, before slamming the receiver back onto the cradle. A piece of plastic flies off across the floor, landing next to the leg of the stool on which I'm sitting.

She doesn't seem to notice, stepping away from the door, breathing heavily, eyes blazing. I'm not sure I've ever seen her this angry. Her fists are balled, top lip snarled. She glances past me to the kitchen table and the Sunday magazine article that has prompted the outbreak of fury.

Uncle David is on the left-hand page, standing tall, side-on and breathing in to try to stop his belly sagging. The headline reads: 'FAMILY FORTUNE', with a picture of Mum and Dad underneath. Mum's in her yoga outfit, probably how most people remember her, with Dad in a smart suit presenting some game show.

The pull-quotes are the kickers.

'Everyone thinks they had the perfect marriage but it was a lie'
'Paul and Annie weren't what everyone thought'

Martha looks from the magazine to the phone and back again. She's biting her tongue, the stud poking through her teeth.

'Get your coat,' she says firmly.

After three years of living together in her basement flat, I know there's a time and a place to argue with my sister. I've proven a few times that this can be the place – but this is most definitely *not* the time.

I do as I'm told and, five minutes later, we're in the car. There's no map, but Martha knows where she's going. She gets us out of London without a word, though each gear change sees the stick being thundered into place. *Wham!* Take that, third gear. *Oof!* Up yours, fourth.

Although she's not talking directly to me, Martha is mumbling under her breath to herself.

The city becomes the suburbs becomes the country. Wide roads become narrower. Low walls become high, overgrown hedges. It's been a while since we were out in the country. The city has become my home with its tall buildings and so many, many people. It's easy to be anonymous among visitors from countries who have no idea who you are. Some might shy away from groups speaking foreign languages; I find myself mingling among them. Safety in numbers and all that.

Almost an hour has passed when Martha eases onto the brake and slaloms her car sideways into a parking space on the side of the road. We're at the edge of a small village that is, for the most part, in the middle of nowhere. A typical one pub, one shop, one postbox place.

Uncle David's house is an old stone cottage with crumbling dark tiles on top. It's on the end of a long row of similar properties, all with neat gardens and hanging baskets at the front.

Martha doesn't wait for me as she heaves the driver's door open and barrels along the short path before hurling herself at Uncle David's front door. She thumps it with the side of her fist, sending an echo spiralling along the deserted street.

She barely gives anyone a chance to answer before rattling her fist onto the wood once more. I'm out of the car, leaning against the gatepost at the end of the path, close enough to hear and see everything; far enough away to be out of the firing line.

It's Uncle David who opens the door.

Aside from the photo in the magazine, this is the first time I've seen him since that day in the solicitor's office. He looks like he's spent most of that time eating, given how much weight he's piled on. At one time, he looked a little like Dad, but not any more. He's grown an extra chin and the skin on his cheeks are starting to overhang.

David tries to get the first word in but barely gets through: 'Will you—' before Martha shouts over him.

'What right do you have?' she says. 'What *right* do you *think* you have to talk about our family like that?'

David has both hands up, trying to cool the situation, but when Martha's raging, the last thing anyone should do is tell her to calm down. It's like emptying a bucket of water onto a pan fire.

'It's my family, too,' David replies, though his attempted defiance is belied by the hesitation in his voice.

'She's sixteen,' Martha hisses. Her voice is calmer, but it's steely calm, which, if anything, is scarier than when she shouts. '*Sixteen*. Do you know what she's been through?'

'I realise what—'

'It happened *three* years ago – and here you are bringing everything back up again.' She pauses. 'How much did they pay you?'

'That's none of your business.'

'It really is if it's me and my family you're going to be talking about.'

There's a click and then some woman pokes her head around the front door of the adjacent house. She looks from me to Martha to Uncle David. 'Everything all right?' she asks.

'Everything's fine, Jean.'

The woman doesn't seem convinced. She focuses back on me again, eyes widening with recognition. She waits for a moment, wondering if there's any chance she can get a front row seat, before deciding there's no way she can pull this off. Reluctantly, she closes her front door once more.

'You're causing a scene,' David hisses.

'You're the one that sold us out,' Martha replies.

Our uncle steps out of the house and looks both ways along the street. 'Do you want to come in and talk about this?'

Martha shakes her head, smiles. 'Oh, so now you want to do things in private?'

'Will you stop?' He looks both ways again. 'This is *my* home, Martha. Do you really think this is what your father would want?'

'Do you think he'd want you blabbing about our business to the papers?'

David throws both hands up. 'There's no talking to you, is there? I tried to tell you this back with that solicitor three years ago. My lawyer has been sending letters, but no one ever replies. You could've avoided all this if you only listened.'

Martha takes a step away the house, checking I've not moved. She's nodding. 'Oh, so it's back to the will again, is it? This is how we know you and Dad were brothers – it all goes back to the money. What is it with the men in this family? Liam's the same. Money-money-money.'

'What about you?' he replies sharply.

'What about me?'

'It's not like you turned your share down. You're a millionaire. Did you forget? And yet what have you done with your blessing? Nothing. You're still living in some London hole, still drinking your Mum and Dad's hard work.' He points past Martha towards me. 'Sixteen, you say? You sure?'

Martha takes another step towards me, away from the house. The implication is clear. 'Didn't I tell you what would happen if you ever pointed towards my sister again?'

Three years ago, I wasn't sure what to say. It was all too much, all too soon. This time I step forward, cupping a hand onto Martha's lower back. I don't know what she might do.

'Hey,' I whisper. 'Let's go home.'

Martha turns to me and then back to our uncle. I can see the anger draining as she takes one more step back. There's a gap of a metre or so between her and Uncle David now. No man's land between the trenches.

'This better not happen again,' Martha says, with a hint of demented calm. 'If I ever see your name in the media talking about my family, you'll regret it.'

'Go home, Martha.'

'I know a few of your secrets, remember. That time in Soho with the red-haired woman. What was her name? Sasha? Just a friend, was she…?'

David's eyebrows rocket up into his hairline and he spins to look behind. The door is most of the way closed and there's no one there. He speaks through clenched teeth: 'Don't you *dare* come here and threaten me.'

'You don't scare me, old man. You're a limp-dicked, bitter wet fart. The runt of a piss-poor litter. You think you're important just because your brother used to be on TV.'

One more step back. Her eyes are locked to David's and this time it is Martha who's pointing.

'Go on,' she says, 'run to the papers. Tell them whatever you want and see what happens. You might be my father's brother – but I'm my mother's daughter and if you ever knew anything about our parents, you'll know *exactly* what that means.'

FIFTEEN

SETH. NOW

As the morning has progressed, the number of reporters on the path outside my house has steadily increased. The bloke who was shouting through my letter box has disappeared back among his colleagues and nobody else has bothered trying to do anything other than hang around.

That's why it's a surprise when, a little after ten, there's another knock on the door. I'm at the back of the living room, in a spot where nobody outside can see me but where I still have a view of what's going on. I wonder if they know something I don't. It feels as if they're waiting for something, either that or starting some sort of siege, hanging on until I cave and head outside.

'It's Emily,' a voice shouts through the letter box.

I hurry to the front door and hide behind it as I unlock and swing it inwards. Emily blusters inside, laden with bags for life. It may be a time of crisis, but if you think mine is the sort of family that spends errant pennies on a plastic carrier bag then you have another think coming.

Emily bundles into the kitchen and then drops the bags, wringing her hands as I lock the front door.

'I didn't expect this,' she says. 'I was going to park out front like normal, but there's a long row of cars. I had to double around, park over the back and then lumber everything here.'

'What have you brought?'

Emily starts unpacking the bags. 'Pizza, bread, milk, Cadbury's Caramels. The essentials.'

'Chocolate is an essential?'

She frowns at me. 'Sometimes I wonder if one of us is adopted.'

We both grin, but it's all too brief. This back and forth is who we are. Even now, with everything that's going on, it's there.

A second or two later and I remember why Emily's here with bags full of shopping.

'No word?' she asks.

'Nothing.'

She nods towards the front of the house. 'Do you think we should call the police about that lot?'

'Are they breaking any laws? They're on the pavement.'

Emily opens the fridge and starts to unload the shopping. 'I don't know. If there's not a law against it, there should be. Public… hanging around or something.'

'If hanging around is a crime, then I'd have been in jail before I turned fourteen.'

My sister doesn't reply, but she continues to unpack the bags until everything is in a cupboard or the fridge. After that, she fills the kettle, flicks it on and then takes a pair of mugs from the rack. She drops a teabag in each – we're not made of money but we're not savages either – and then gets her phone out and starts to jab at the screen. I sit through it all, suddenly feeling the exhaustion.

'Thank you,' I say.

'Whatever. Next time I'm in need, you're doing the Tesco run.'

'Deal.'

Emily rests against the counter as the kettle starts to hum quietly in the corner. It's stainless steel, part of a matching set with the toaster, both chosen by Charley because my old plastic ones were 'too scummy' for her tastes. Mine too, if I'm honest – but I was too lazy to replace them. Toaster and kettle shopping is what you do when you know you're in a committed relationship.

'How was Mum?' I ask.

Emily glances away from her phone towards me and then back to the device.

'Oh,' I say. 'Like that.'

'Yes. Like that.' She sighs. 'She thought *she'd* got married this weekend. Kept wondering where Dad was. She got annoyed with one of the nurses and then started shouting. She thought I was one of the porters.'

I squeeze my eyes closed and listen to the fizz of the kettle. 'Sorry, Em…'

Emily shakes her head. This is far from the first time something like this has happened and it won't be the last.

Out of nowhere, Emily slaps her hand on the counter. 'Oh, for God's sake. Look at this.' She shunts her phone towards me in disgust. It takes a second or two for me to realise what's in the photo. It a side-on image of Emily with shopping bags and my house in the background.

'One of that lot out there must've taken it,' she says. 'I can't believe it's online already. Did you see the caption?'

I scroll up and there it is: 'Mystery blonde is shoulder to cry on'.

'This isn't anything to do with me,' she says, 'now some dickhead thinks I'm shagging my own brother – and he's told the world.'

I scroll up and down the page, but there's no way round it. It's only on the bloke's own social media account for now, but that's how these things start. Next thing you know, you've gone viral and some basement-dweller in a far-flung country you've never heard of is saying how much he hates your very existence.

'I'll go out,' I say. 'I'll tell them who you are and what's going on. All they want is a statement of some sort.'

'Don't. Let them print what they want – and then we'll show them up for the idiots they are. If you go out, you'll only make it worse. They'll get a picture of you blinking and claim you're drunk or something. Next thing you know, they'll be calling you a dog rapist on the front page.'

I reel back a little. 'Dog rapist?'

She grins. 'Well, maybe not that. I was thinking of the vet thing. Either way, don't go out there.'

The kettle clicks off and Emily pours hot water into both mugs. She uses a teaspoon to squeeze every last morsel of orangey liquid out of each teabag and then catapults both into the sink. After that, it's a splash of milk and a quick stir, followed by two sugars each and a stir for luck

That's how the Chambers family do cups of tea.

Emily passes me one, even though I'd not asked for it, and then heads into the living room. She immediately spies the empty beer bottles I've not cleared up.

'You're a cliché already,' she says.

'Piss off, Em.'

She bites her lip but smirks through it. 'Sorry.'

Emily slumps onto the couch and slips a coaster into place on the side table. They're very much Charley's, not mine. Tea mug rings were a Chambers tradition in the old house before Dad died.

'Life's too short for bloody coasters,' he used to say and, I guess, for him it was.

I miss him so much.

'Charley's brother called me,' I say.

'Liam?'

I've never told Emily his name – but people know. It's hard not to. Charley, Martha and Liam are all listed on their parents' Wikipedia pages, for crying out loud.

'I thought he was out of the picture?' she adds.

'Me too – but he wants to meet.'

'What did you say?'

'I said I'd think about it.'

'Did he mention if he knew anything about Charley going missing?'

'Nothing specific, just asked if I had an hour free today to meet.'

'Why don't you go see him? Can't do any harm.'

I breathe in the fumes of the tea but don't drink. 'I don't want to leave in case Charley comes home.'

'I can wait in. Rifle through your stuff, look for pornos under the mattress.' She winks. 'Like the old days at Mum and Dad's house.'

It's hard not to smile. As brother and sister, we're not touchy-feely, huggy-wuggy, but we've always been good at taking the proverbial.

Before I can reply, a flash of movement at the end of the path catches my eye. The assembled journalists have parted like the Red Sea to reveal fluorescent orange stripes on the side of a marked police car on the far side of the road.

I stand, watching as a suited officer emerges and starts to pace along the path to my house. Em is on her feet, too – and rests a hand on my shoulder. Perhaps we are touchy-feely after all.

'This is it, isn't it?' I gulp. 'They've found a body.'

Emily says nothing.

SIXTEEN

11 YEARS AGO

Charley Willis, 17 years old

Martha pauses at the front door, hands on hips. She peers around the kitchen once more and sees what I see. No more grimy plates on the side. No mugs full of mould in the window sill. It's clean now. Liveable. The taps are even sparkling, like they do in the adverts.

'You're actually leaving, aren't you?' I say.

'What do you think all the boxes were about?' She wears a thin smile but there's no humour there. 'Do you want me to stay?' she asks.

'No.'

'I will if you want. I'll tell Mason we can put this back a month or three. Maybe four.'

'You've just had him lug all your stuff out to the van.'

'Yeah but he fancies the arse off me. I'll get him to lug it all back.'

Martha grins but she's already sobbing. I try to remember whether I've seen her cry before. Definitely not after what happened with Mum and Dad. Perhaps when she was younger and living at home, during one of the blazing rows with Mum before she left? I can't remember. I was too young.

She dabs the corner of her eyes with her sleeve and tries to blink away the tears. 'Look at the state of me,' she says.

'I think the tears make you about ten per cent sluttier.'

Martha gasps a giggle. 'Only ten per cent?'

'Maybe twenty. You need to smear the eyeliner a bit more.'

Before I can say anything else, Martha wrenches me towards her and squeezes the living hell out of my lungs.

'I bloody love you,' she whispers.

'I love you, too.'

She lets me go and then takes a small step backwards. It's not quite enough to take her outside, but she's nearly there.

'I'm going to keep the flat,' she says. Again.

'I know. You've told me.'

'You can stay here as long as you want.'

'I will. Doesn't get better than rent-free. Are you going to pay the bills, too?'

'Don't push it.'

Another half-step backwards and Martha is on the threshold. Mason appears behind her, sweating from all the fetching and carrying. He's all rugged and stubbly; big arms and thighs, quite the rugger bugger. Martha's type.

'How are you, Little C?' he asks.

'Lonely!' I fake wail into my hands. 'I can't believe she's leaving me for you! I'm so abandoned.'

I peep through my fingers to find an unamused sister and a slightly confused sister's boyfriend.

'Do you need anything else doing?' he asks.

'Bit of wiring, the bathroom tap keeps dripping. I think the previous owner is a bit of a you-know-what. She had lads over all the time, but they never did anything about it.'

Martha slaps me on the shoulder. 'You lying little cow!'

We both grin, but it's probably too close to the bone for Mason. He bobs awkwardly and then says he'll see Martha in the van. She waits for him to go and then takes one final step backwards. She's fully outside.

'I'm gonna go now,' she says.

'So you keep saying.'

She smiles sadly. It's been a whirlwind few months. I guess it was always going to be when it came to Martha and someone she actually liked. It started with her stopping out for a night or two, then a couple of nights at a time, then weekends. Now she's moving across the city to live with Mason. She was never the slow-and-steady type.

I'm so over the bloody moon for her, I can't even put it into words.

'I'm really going to go now,' she says.

I gulp and, from nowhere, I'm crying too. Martha reaches out and holds me as we sob onto each other's shoulder. It might be seconds, maybe minutes, but we cry until we stop. That's what it is: a moment where it feels like we're done. One chapter finished, here's to the next.

'Thank you,' I say.

'You are very welcome.'

'We're still gonna have girls' nights out, yeah?'

Her features harden. 'You're seventeen, Char.' Then she cracks a smile. 'Of course we are!'

'I think your husband's waiting.'

She turns to the street. 'He's not my husband.'

'Yeah, but he will be.'

She bites her tongue and then beams. 'You're damned right he will be.' Martha moves to the first stone step. 'This is me leaving,' she says.

'It's not me, it's you.'

The second step: 'I'll call you when I get there.'

'It's only half-hour away.'

Step three: 'Northern line to District; head east. No excuses. I got you an Oyster card.'

'You'll get sick of me.'

Number four: 'We'll do the pubs out there next week. Just you and me.'

'Sounds good.'

Step five: 'Mason does nights every weekend in three, so you can stay over if you want.'

'I want the big bed.'

Martha is by the gate now. I can't see her feet and am staring up at the upper half of her body. She arches backwards and peers along to the street towards Mason's van.

'I've got to go,' she says.

'I know.'

'I love you.'

'I know.'

She grins wickedly. It's so unlike her, but there's a skip and a jump and then she's gone.

I wait in the bunker bit outside the kitchen window, staring upwards, wondering if she'll return. We've been talking about this for weeks, but I guess I wasn't sure it would actually happen.

'I love you, too,' I whisper – but it's only the dying pot plant on the lower step that hears.

I close the door, lock it, and head through to the living room. I've spent days, weeks, by myself in this place and yet it was always Martha's. She was always going to come home at some point, but now she has another home.

I'm wondering what to do with myself when there's a knock on the door.

I spring up from the sofa instinctively. Martha's forgotten something, which means we get to say goodbye all over again!

I race through the flat back to the door, unlocking it and swinging it open in one free movement.

Except it's not Martha.

It's Liam. He's tanned, wearing a loose T-shirt and ripped jeans, as usual.

'Jeeeeeeeesus,' he says. 'You've grown up, Charlotte. Man alive.' He holds a palm out at waist height. 'Last time I saw you, you were down there.'

'What are you doing here?'

He holds his hands up. 'We're brother and sister. I don't need a reason, do I?'

Liam steps towards the door and I find myself moving backwards, letting him in.

'Were you waiting for Martha to leave?' I ask.

'Martha?' He speaks as if he's never heard the name before.

'She only left two minutes ago. There's no way you turned up by chance. You must've been watching from over the road or something…?'

He shrugs as if it doesn't matter and then leads me through the flat into the living room, plopping himself onto the sofa in my spot.

I don't particularly want to sit next to him, so that leaves me with the lounger. Martha's seat.

'How have you been holding up?' he asks.

I crane my neck, ostrich-style. 'You've been gone for four years, Liam. Four years! I've not seen you since they read the will. Nobody knew you were in California until Martha got the postcard.'

Liam is nodding along. 'Oh, so you did get it? I wondered if you had.'

He tails off. One postcard in four years and now he's here as if this is all normal.

'I was doing the whole Hollywood thing,' he adds.

'What's the Hollywood thing?'

He flicks away a strand of hair that isn't there, preens towards the mirror on the wall at my side. 'Oh, y'know. Going to auditions, trying out for adverts, that sort of thing.'

Liam speaks as if this is the most normal thing in the world. I don't want to be mean, but I've seen Hollywood movies. I've watched American television shows. I've muted the adverts and changed the channel. I have no idea what his acting skills are like, but I *do* know my brother doesn't have the chiselled features to be a professional actor.

'Don't you have to be good-looking?' I ask.

I make it sound as innocent as I can: head-in-the sky, thirteen-year-old Charlotte, not Charley.

He eyes me suspiciously and it feels good to see him squirm. Four years! We thought he might be dead, or snorting his million quid on an island somewhere.

'What are you saying?' he asks.

'Nothing, I just don't know how it works. Did you get much work?'

It's barely there, but he shakes his head, dismissing the question. 'I'm back now.' A momentary pause and then: 'So… what's been going on?'

'You want me to sum up four years into a couple of sentences?'

He shrugs. It's not as if he cares. 'Have you been living with Martha this whole time?'

'She's my legal guardian. We did all the paperwork.'

'So she's like Mum?'

I stare at him and wonder if this is his dig back at me. 'She's *nothing* like Mum.'

He allows himself a hint of a smirk. 'Who's her fella? I never thought she was the settling-down type.'

We look to each other, but the passive aggressiveness is becoming too much. Liam scratches his crotch and shrugs as if to say he doesn't care about the answer anyway.

'Do you think he's still out there?' Liam asks.

'Who?'

Another shrug. 'Y'know. Whoever broke into the house that night…'

For a while after it happened, I thought about Mum, Dad and that house all the time. It felt like every minute. Even when I was talking about something else, it would be at the back of my mind. It was the first thing I'd think about each morning, the last thing before I drifted off to sleep. When I awoke in the early hours, it'd be right there, front and centre.

It's been four years and things have changed over time. Sometimes I would wake up and think of Martha, or the things we'd done the night before. I'd think of the games we'd play to evade photographers, or plot complicated routes so that we could get around without being followed. Either that, or I'd come up with new nicknames for the blokes with cameras. I'd plan what to have for dinner, read about people and things other than my parents.

And then there was one Saturday last summer where I realised I'd gone the whole day without thinking of Mum, Dad or that house. Martha had got us tickets to an event in Hyde Park. It was mainly music, but there were a couple of comedians, too. We each wore wigs and she had to cover her tattoos, but, other than that, it was a day in the park. We spent most of the time laughing and dancing.

That's been the pattern ever since. Remembering what happened is the exception now, not the norm.

Liam's question almost makes me feel like I've been punched. There's a moment in which it's hard to breathe.

'Why do you think it's a he?' I manage.

He blinks. 'It's always a bloke. You don't hear of women going around, breaking into houses and so on.'

So on. That is one way to sum things up.

'Is that why you're here, Liam?' I turn away from him. 'It's been four years.'

'That's what I'm saying: four years and he's still out there. Aren't you worried?'

'I wasn't until you came here and brought it all up again.'

'Did you get police protection, or anything? I saw it sometimes out in LA – the big celebs have their own security. You don't see it when they're being photographed because these huge blokes are behind the cameras. If anyone makes a wrong move, they're on them.'

'I don't want to talk about this.'

Being brother and sister can be a strange thing. If you make friends with a person, that's a conscious choice. You do it because you have something in common with them, you enjoy the same things, you can make each other's lives better. With family, there's no option. Liam and I have never been a part of one another's life. He is eleven years older than me and, even in my earliest memories, he had already left home. I don't know the type of things in which he's interested. He's nothing to do with me and yet I allowed him into my flat because we're related.

'You turn eighteen soon, don't you?'

He makes the question sound perfectly innocent, as if he's considering what I might want for a present. There's no way I'm that easily fooled.

'Vouchers,' I reply, playing him at his own game.

'What?'

'You can get me vouchers if you want. I've got my eye on a pair of boots.'

He tilts his head, cottoning on to the fact that he's been rumbled. 'You'll be able to buy anything you want…'

'I guess that's true.'

He waits and I know that everything Martha's told me about my brother is correct. It really must be a thing about the men in this family. The money gene.

'So… do you have any plans for it…?'

Liam speaks as if we're discussing what to have for tea. All innocent and friendly.

'Not really,' I reply. 'I'm happy here for now. Martha says I can stay and that she doesn't want to sell. She's not bothered, either. It's not like I need a lot of things.'

He blinks, apparently surprised. 'Oh… well I guess I was wondering if you can help your brother out. You'd be helping yourself, too.'

He waits, looking for a reaction, but I give him none.

'I have an investment opportunity,' he adds. 'A friend back in the States. He runs a vitamin supply company. It's all protein shakes and health food out there. It's massive. You can make a fortune…'

I play dumb: 'I don't understand what you're asking me.'

'You'll get your money back three times over.'

'What money?'

'A hundred grand or so. The exchange rate changes all the time, but it'll be something like that.'

'I give you one hundred thousand and you give me back three hundred thousand?'

He takes the question as some sort of confirmation that I'm interested, sitting up straighter, angling towards me and becoming more animated with his hands. 'Exactly. It's guaranteed money. You can't lose.'

'How long do I have to wait to get the three-hundred?'

'Six months, maybe? My mate says they're waiting to go public. When that happens, everything will sky-rocket. It's going to be massive. If you wait longer, you could make ten times what you put in.'

I suck on my lips, making it look as if I'm thinking about it. I'm not, and never will be, any sort of financial expert – but even I can tell that this is nonsense.

'So…' Liam coos.

'So, what?'

'What do you reckon?'

I shake my head. 'I'm all right.'

He throws both hands up. 'But this is easy money.'

I shrug. 'So what? I'm already inheriting more than I will ever spend. What am I going to do with more?'

Liam stares at me as if I'm a creature he's never seen. As if he's in the jungle and he's stumbled across a brand-new colour that mankind has never experienced. He doesn't have the words.

'I… er… what…?' he stumbles.

'I don't want to make more money. I don't care.'

'But what do you mean it's more than you'll ever spend? It's only, what, a million and a half with interest…?'

'What am I going to do with all that? Buy a house? Go on holiday? I'd rather find something I like doing and do that.'

He reels back and gasps: 'You want to get a… *job*?'

He makes the final word sound like an insult.

I shrug. 'Maybe. I don't need to decide yet. I missed a bit of school, but I'm trying to catch up online. I'll be a year or two older than most, but I might look into doing a course somewhere, or going to uni. We'll see. There's no rush.'

His eyes are on stalks, but then he sees another opportunity. 'But if you're not bothered, why not give a bit of money to me? If you treble the investment, all the better; if not, then you weren't going to spend it anyway…?'

'I thought I was "guaranteed" to triple my money?'

'You are… it's just…' He tails off and seems unable to comprehend that I'm going to leave the money sitting.

'C'mon, sis…' he says.

I'm annoyed now. The passive aggression is simply aggression. I'm not Martha and I'm sure as hell not my mother – but it's still there.

'"*Sis*"? Are you joking? We've not seen each other in four years. You sent one postcard – to Martha – and never mentioned me.'

'I was busy!'

'Didn't you get your own money? Everything was split three ways. If you need a hundred thousand, use your own share.'

He glares at me with a mixture of fury and disgust. 'You're not going to help, are you?'

'No.'

Liam leaps up from the chair, arching towards me, sneering. 'Y'know… Mum always said you were the bitch of the family and now I see why.'

He doesn't wait for a reply, charging out of the room, through the kitchen and slamming the front door on his way out. By the time I get to the kitchen window, he's already up the steps and gone.

'Nice to see you, too,' I tell the empty room.

SEVENTEEN

SETH. NOW

The police have not found a body.

That's made clear to me as soon as I open the door. 'It's not bad news,' the officer says. She asks to come in and then introduces herself as a family liaison officer, adding, 'Call me Fiona.'

She's far more mumsy than the granite-faced detective who was asking all the questions yesterday. Fiona gives off the air of a social worker, all whimsy and soft looks.

I lead her into the living room and introduce my sister, giving Fiona the lounger and sitting next to Emily on the sofa.

'I'm sorry if I worried you,' Fiona says. 'Liaison officers are usually only assigned in cases of bereavement' – she nods towards the front window and the journalists beyond – 'but we figured this was a special case, especially with the attention.'

'What does a family liaison officer do?' I ask. 'Liaise with families, I guess.'

'Precisely that. I'm the link between you and the police. With all the inquiries and attention, there's a lot of ground to cover. Any developments will be relayed to you through me and if there are any questions you have, anything that springs to mind that you might want to pass on to the investigating team, I'm here for that, too.'

'Does this mean there's news…?'

I know I'm being hopeful and expect a shake of the head, but Fiona looks between the two of us, silently confirming that I don't mind Emily overhearing anything. 'There are no obvious signs of your wife in or around the hotel grounds,' she says. 'A team who'll examine the site more forensically will be there today, but it's an incredibly contaminated scene. Staff arrive and leave via the back of the building, plus – as you know – guests can enter and exit via the corridor. We are doing what we can.'

The media leak is definitely bad in many ways – but if it's achieved something then it's that the police know they're in the spotlight now. Every day without a progress report on what happened to Charley will be another day of questions for them.

'Charley's brother called me,' I say.

'Is that unusual?'

'As far as I know, Charley's only seen him once in the past ten years or so.'

Fiona sits up straighter. 'Did he say what he wanted?'

'He wants to meet… Do you think that's a good idea?'

The officer seems surprised at being asked, stumbling over a reply. 'I… well, I'm not sure. It's up to you. I can't imagine it would do any harm.'

I poke a thumb towards the window. 'I can't really leave in my car. They'll follow and I don't think Liam was asking for a meeting with the media sitting on the next table.'

Emily starts to dig into her bag. 'Take my car,' she says. 'Go out the back and then follow the lane. I'm on the next street over.'

'What if someone sees me leaving? They'll follow your car.'

Emily lays her keys on the side next to her mug. 'I dunno, wear a mask or something.'

'I might be able to help with that,' Fiona says. 'That's another thing I was going to bring up. Someone probably needs to talk to the media, if only to tell them you have nothing to say. An official "no comment" is better than speculation. I was going to say that you could do it, or I could – but perhaps if I'm out front telling them you want some privacy…'

EIGHTEEN

I'll be honest: I had the *Mission: Impossible* music in my head as I ran along the lane at the back of my house. I risked a glance towards the media on the pavement and then sprinted towards the parallel road and Emily's car. Charley would have found it funny and called me an idiot or something. Who knows what neighbourhood watch think of the whole thing.

When she drives, Emily sits underneath the steering wheel of her car, practically in the footwell. I have no idea how she can see anything with all the dangly crap hanging from the mirror. I shunt the chair back to get inside and pull away without being followed.

It's not long before I'm on the M3, following it until the junction Liam suggested and getting off at the service station. Rows of lorries are parked diagonally off to the side, but it's generally quiet. I'm assuming Monday is not prime time for getting off the motorway to grab a Yorkie.

Liam is sitting on one of the high tables at the front of Burger King. There's a crumpled fast-food wrapper at his side and he's busy scanning everyone entering the building. He holds up a hand when he spots me and lifts the peak of his San Francisco baseball cap before taking it off. We shake hands, but it's awkward. Neither of us know one another and, at least from my point of view, he's someone my wife doesn't much care for.

He's unshaven, wearing tracksuit bottoms with a rip in one of the knees and a dark T-shirt. I know I spent an entire day in my wedding suit and have hardly slept, but I'm pretty sure that, of the two of us, Liam is the one most people would peg as the person who slept in a bush most recently.

'Been here long?' I ask, unsure what to say.

'Five minutes. I set off as soon as you called back. Saw the news this morning. I can't believe it.'

'That Charley left?'

Liam nods. 'Right – that's the problem with this family. Endless drama. Even when you think you're out, you get dragged back sooner or later. Them lot never forget who you are.'

'Journalists?'

'Right.'

'I suppose this is my first experience of anything like this. They pretty much left Charley alone…'

Liam nods along, though I'm not sure he's listening. He leans in and lowers his voice to a conspiratorial whisper. 'I thought I might be able to help.'

'Do you know where she might've gone?'

A shake of the head. 'I know someone from the old days with Mum and Dad. She's called a publicist, but, really, she's there to get people off your back. She knows what they want.'

'Oh…' I sit back on the stool and it's hard to hide the disappointment.

'What's up?' he asks.

'I thought you might have some idea what happened to Charley.'

Liam seems oblivious to why I might have thought that. 'Nah, man. I've only seen her once in years. You were there. Why would I know where she is?'

'Precisely – that's why I thought it might be important when you called.'

His nose crinkles as he chews his lips, not getting it. 'Look, I know it might not sound like much, but this publicist goes way back with Mum and Dad.'

I wish I'd bought a drink or food, if only to give myself a moment or two to think of something to say. It really does sound like Liam is trying to help but he has no idea how to go about it.

'Was there anywhere Charley used to go as a kid?' I ask. 'A hiding place? A favourite spot? Anything like that?'

He shakes his head. 'I was at boarding school and then moved out by the time Charlotte was old enough to be anything more than a baby.'

I knew there were eleven years between them – but only because of the Wikipedia page. It's not something Charley and I have ever discussed. That portion of her life is off limits to everyone. I've never brought it up and neither has she. I'm curious, of course, but where to even begin? '*You remember when your parents died, what was it like in the wardrobe?*' I've always figured that if she wanted to tell me about it, then she would. She talks about Martha and her time in London and I suppose that, in many ways, she's had two lives. There is Charlotte up until she was thirteen and then Charley afterwards.

'That must've been weird for you,' I say.

Liam nods – but it's not like before when I wasn't sure he was listening. He's paying attention, agreeing. Remembering.

'By the time she was ten, you were already an adult,' I add. 'You could've had your own kids but your parents had one of their own.'

He continues nodding. 'Right… like you say… weird.'

'Is that why you and Charley don't really talk?'

Liam has been staring towards the doors at the front, but he blinks and then he's focused on me again. 'It's the Willis women,' he says.

'What is?'

'It's probably hormones or something. You must know…?' He holds his hands out as if it's obvious.

'I don't know what you mean,' I say.

'They do mad things. Disappear on wedding days. All sorts. Mum used to have her moments and you must've heard about the wild child…?'

I have, of course. Long before I knew Charley, I knew who Martha was. I'd seen the photos of her falling out of nightclubs with a skinny rake of a boyfriend in tow. I can't remember if it was before or after what happened with the parents. Before or after she became Charley's guardian. It might have been a bit of both. Charley says they used to go out – but I don't remember her being in any of the papers in such a state.

Besides, Charley says it was never like that. It was all a mask that Martha wore. She embraced the wild-child thing because she thought it would annoy their mother. Under everything, Martha was sweet: a loving wife and mother.

'Martha?' I ask. 'What about her?' I have to force away the shiver that's licking my spine. This feels important.

'You must know what they think happened with the wild child and Mum and Dad's house…? Now it's Charlotte's turn. Must be an age thing.'

I think of what happened with Martha. There's no way the same could've happened with Charley. No way.

'She's never lost it with me,' I say. 'She likes the peace and quiet. She chooses to stay in almost every night and when we go out, it's usually for walks.'

Liam grins. 'If you say so, man. You know her better than me.'

He leaves it there, but I'm not sure what to think. What with people talking about the 'Willis Curse' and now Liam talking about the 'Willis women', it's disturbingly ominous.

'It was Charlotte's decision to stop speaking to me,' Liam says. 'She went off with Martha – and Martha never liked me. She turned her against me. After a while I stopped trying to contact them both. No point if they don't want to hear from you, is there?' He glances up, catches my eye. 'I always wondered if it was because the killer is still out there.'

'What do you mean?'

Liam picks up the burger wrapper and launches it towards a nearby bin. He misses. 'You know they never caught the guy, don't you?'

'But why would that stop her talking to you?'

'That's what I'm saying – it's the Willis women. They think differently to you and me. They do weird things.'

It's oddly unconvincing and yet there's a part of me that thinks Liam really believes it. He's saying something that would be implausible to most people and yet he speaks with such conviction that it's not worth questioning.

'I got back in contact when the twins were born,' Liam says. 'I know Charlotte dotes on the other two…' he swirls his hand.

'Dillon and Daisy,' I say.

'Right – them two. I figured she might want to meet her new nieces.'

I already know that bit… except that's not the only thing that happened on the Sunday we drove over to Liam's house.

'Did you argue that day?' I ask.

'When?'

'We came to your house and we were in the living room. Charley was playing with the twins, chatting to Helen and everything was fine. I couldn't work out why you'd spent so long not talking. Then you both left the room to talk about something and, the next thing I know, we're heading home.'

Liam gazes off towards the arcade, where a pair of lads have plastic sub-machine guns mounted on their shoulders and are busy blazing away at some digitised war zone. That's the benefit of British service stations over American ones, I guess. The kids over here only carry plastic automatic weapons.

'I don't remember,' Liam says. 'I said you guys could come back any time, but that was the last I heard from her. I didn't even know about the wedding date until I saw it online this morning. Figured she didn't want to see me.'

The not remembering bit is an obvious lie, but I'm not sure about the rest of it. I can't quite get a grasp on who Liam is or what he wants. He never quite makes full eye contact and doesn't stop fidgeting. Charley didn't want to tell me whatever they talked about and neither does Liam. If I couldn't get my fiancée to talk, then it's a bit of a cheek to push a stranger.

This damned family.

I don't want to think that and, if I'm honest, I probably don't. Not really – but Liam is convincing when he talks about the Willis women. Everyone knows the whispers about Martha. As for Charley's mother? I can imagine how a TV star and 'lifestyle guru' could perhaps be a little diva-like. There were hints in an old article written by Peter Willis's brother that the adults were career-orientated.

But Charley? She's different… isn't she?

Except she's now been gone for nearly two full days.

Liam passes me a Post-it note on which he's written the name 'PAMELA' and a phone number. 'Call her,' he urges. 'She knows you might phone. She's good.'

I figure there's no harm in having the option, so pocket the note and then we shake hands. It's Liam who instigates it.

'Perhaps after all this, we can go for a beer?' he says.

We pass through the doors onto the car park and he motions towards a crusty 4x4 in the front row.

'That'd be good actually,' I reply, meaning it. 'I'm sure Charley would like to see the twins again.'

Liam unlocks his vehicle and then places a hand on my shoulder. 'Sounds good – but first we need to get her back.'

NINETEEN

5 YEARS AGO

Charley Willis, 23 years old

'Look at the state of this place!' Martha flaps a hand towards the sofa. *Her* sofa, I guess. '*Cushions?* Since when did you get cushions?'

'Couple of weeks ago,' I reply, 'figured I'd smarten the place up.'

My sister is in the doorway, doing the hands-on-hips thing she does when she's getting all motherly. 'You've not got a boyfriend on the go, have you? Not without telling me?'

'I've not got a boyfriend on the go.'

She points towards the vase on the TV unit. 'So what's with all the feng shui?'

'I figured I'd redecorate. I've lived here for ten years and never bought anything new.'

'I don't like it.'

'That, dear sister, is because you're an old fart.'

She gasps with mock outrage. 'That's it, line crossed, I'm evicting you.'

'You can't evict me. Who else are you going to text at three in the morning when you can't sleep?'

'Good point.'

Martha flops onto the sofa and digs around behind her back, pulling out one of the cushions and launching it onto the lounger. She pats the spot next to her and I slot in at her side.

'I've been looking forward to this for weeks,' she says.

She places her phone very deliberately on the side table, face-up.

'Like the old days,' she adds.

'Not quite.'

'What do you mean?'

I laugh and point to the phone. 'You're going to call home, aren't you?'

She bites her tongue. Even though the large ear piercing has gone, along with the one through her septum, the tongue stud remains. 'No.'

I've had doorstop sellers who sound more convincing.

'You know your husband's looking after them, don't you?' I add.

Martha nudges me with her elbow. 'Aww, Charley, hun. You should come over more. Daisy's only six weeks old. She's so itty-bitty. I swear I saw her smiling the other day.'

'What about Dillon?'

'Terrible twos… no, *terror*-ble twos. I wish they could stay tiny.' She nudges me again. 'Anyway, sister time. You and me: Angel and Bliss, like the good ol' days.'

She reaches into the shopping bag she brought and pulls out a bottle of sparkling wine. There's no proper cork in the top, it's one of those plastic screwy things and Martha pops it off. The topper smashes into the ceiling and she shrieks a delighted yelp. She's giddy already.

I pass over two plastic flutes – they've been in the flat longer than me – and she starts to pour.

'What else have you brought?' I ask.

Martha finishes filling both glasses and then puts the bottle on the side table. She pulls a separate bag onto her lap and starts to sort through it. 'Wotsits, Monster Munch, Jaffa Cakes, giant Fruit & Nut. The essentials.'

'How is a massive Fruit & Nut bar considered an essential?'

She passes me the tube of Jaffa Cakes. 'You've never had a child, have you?'

'I've lived with someone who acts like one.'

Martha grins and rips apart the multi-pack of Monster Munch. She digs out one of the spicy ones and starts to eat.

'I've missed this,' she says.

'Monster Munch?'

She rests her head against mine. '*This*.'

Martha's shopping haul is quite the artery-clogger. As well as everything she mentioned, there are Peperamis, sausage rolls, plus Ben & Jerry's in the freezer.

'What movie do you want to watch?' she asks. 'I was thinking *Se7en*. Or *Reservoir Dogs*? I swear I've been watching the Pixar catalogue on repeat for the past two years. I need something that isn't a cartoon. I'm at the point where Nemo can get stuffed. Dory, too.'

This is the moment I've been dreading, or at least worrying about.

'You know what's on TV tonight, don't you…?'

Martha stops chewing. She sucks the mashed-up crisp from her teeth and then twists so that we're facing each other.

'You *are* joking?' she says.

'It's the tenth anniversary. I thought…'

Martha has mellowed beyond all recognition since getting married. After Daisy came along, she's even softer. There's still that steel to her, though, and I can only imagine how she'd react if anyone ever threatened her kids.

I almost flinch from her stare. A hint of the old Martha. Wild child Martha.

'Of everyone, aren't you the last person who'd want to watch it?' she asks.

'I know… it's just… I guess I'm interested in what people are going to say.'

'It's only some tenth-anniversary memorial cash-in rubbish. It'll be the same old people saying the same things about Mum and Dad. "Aren't they brilliant" and all that. We've heard it before.'

'Liam's going to be on it.'

Her eyebrows twitch, wondering if I'm making some sort of joke.

'I think it's because we said no,' I add. 'When that producer was emailing me, she said that if I wasn't interested that they'd have to go looking for other family. I thought it was some lame-ass threat to get me to say yes – but his name is in the TV guide.'

This is definitely the first Martha's heard of it.

'I can't believe he said yes.' She stops, downs her entire glass in one go. 'That sonofa ¾ You know he's done it for money, don't you?'

'Shall we watch?'

Martha is biting her tongue again, but there's a level of aggression about it this time, as if she's trying to hurt herself.

'Have you got his phone number?' she asks.

'Let's just watch. No point in phoning him up to abuse him before we know what he's going to say.'

Martha reaches for the bottle of wine and pours herself another glass. From the merriment and laughter of a few minutes ago, the mood is now dark.

'Put it on,' she says.

The only sound for the next few minutes are the adverts from the television and the noise of Martha eating. She rattles through the bag of Monster Munch and is halfway through a packet of Wotsits when the show begins.

She was right, of course. It *is* a rubbish memorial cash-in. The same old faces trying to cling to any degree of their fame by banging on about how much our parents gave to the entertainment industry. There are a few newer celebs. No one important, no one that famous. The *Celebrity Big Brother* sorts or red-carpet clinger-onners talking about how they grew up watching my father on TV, or how they used to do yoga with Mum in the mornings. At least the older ones knew my parents; some of this new lot are younger than me.

Martha and I don't really talk as we watch. She scoffs at a few instances, but there isn't a lot to say.

There are clips of Dad presenting a variety show in his early career, then a game show. A woman wins a car and she heads straight for Dad, wrapping her arms around him. After that, he's telling jokes for a Christmas special of someone else's programme. It's smiles. Everyone's happy.

Mum's segment shows the yoga poses that she apparently 'popularised to the nation' and then it moves onto her cookbooks. There's a clip of her creating some sort of 'kick-start' breakfast bar.

Martha snorts. 'That is such bollocks,' she says. 'I know for a fact that she came home after that demo and ate two Mars bars. She used to keep a secret chocolate stash around the house – there was all sorts in there. I found it a few times and nicked everything. She couldn't accuse me because Dad would hit the roof if he knew she was eating all that crap.'

The Fruit & Nut bar suddenly doesn't seem so funny.

After yet another advert break, we're finally back – and then Liam is on screen. The make-up team have done an incredible job scrubbing him up into something passable. He's in a suit that must have been provided. The shirt is tucked at the waist, making him look slimmer than he is. His hair isn't the usual shabby mess; it's been styled sleekly to the side and his facial hair looks more like it's supposed to be there.

There's a live audience and they cheer as he waves. It's weird. Seriously weird.

The female presenter is wearing some sparkly thing – glitter and tits, as Martha used to say. She waffles on about Liam being the eldest child, skimming across the existence of Martha and me – which is fine by us. That done, she asks Liam what it was like to grow up 'as the son of such a talented couple'.

It only takes a few words for it to be clear how far Liam is prepared to go for a payday.

'It was wonderful,' he says. 'I felt so privileged. I'd love to think at least some of their talent rubbed off on me.'

There's a laugh from the audience – someone must be holding cards off to the side, telling them what to do, because it was more desperate than funny.

'That's insane,' Martha rages. 'He was at boarding school most the year and then summer camp in the holidays. As soon as he was old enough to leave, he was out the door. I only had to wait a couple of years and then I followed him.'

She takes the remote control from the table and mutes it.

'I can't watch this any more,' she says.

'Sorry.'

'It's not you.'

Martha rubs her temples and the enthusiasm of earlier, the promise of a sister night, has gone. We're not the people we were six or seven years ago. She downs another glass of wine and opens a second bottle, then scooches herself into the corner of the sofa, wriggling to get comfortable.

'That's why I bought cushions,' I say.

She smiles thinly. 'When are you going to get your own place?' she asks wearily.

'Am I a bad tenant?'

A shake of the head. 'Not that, Char. You're better than this. Before everything happened, you were getting good grades at school. You were smart.' A cough. 'You *are* smart. You got the brains and the looks in this family. You're twenty-three years old, you have money. You can do anything you want.'

I shake my head. 'I don't want their money.'

'So forget it – but you're still better than this.'

We look at each other and I'm not sure what to say. I know she's right. It's what I told Liam years ago.

'It was a decade ago,' Martha says softly. 'That's long enough. It's time to move on.' She leaves it hanging for a moment and then plucks her phone from the table, adding that she's going to call Mason.

As she disappears into the kitchen, Martha closes the door, leaving me alone with the TV. Liam is talking again and the presenter is still flashing her cleavage in his general direction. It's all a bit flirty and hard to tell if it's fake. It probably is, or else she has serious self-esteem issues.

I turn the sound up.

'…They were great parents,' Liam says. 'The best.'

I pause it. Rewind. Repeat.

'…They were great parents. The best.'

Pause. Rewind. Play. Over and over. I'm not sure how many times I listen to him speaking. He's smiling as he says it.

'…They were great parents. The best.'

I'm so engrossed that I don't realise Martha is back in the room. She's standing in the doorway, phone in hand. It feels like I've cheated on her.

'…They were great parents. The best.'

She turns from the television to me as I pause it once more.

'That boy will do anything for money,' she says.

TWENTY

SETH. NOW

I'm not sure when it happened, but television news has got to the point where it's taking the mick. I remember the old days with Dad when the six, nine or ten o'clock news came on and it was all serious. It felt like it meant something. Now it's all cheapo videos ripped off the internet of cats falling in holes or toddlers singing along to some pop song.

There's speculation, too. Loads of it. Everything from hinting that the killer of Charley's parents could be back, to mentioning the Willis Curse.

A news broadcast talking about a curse.

It's ridiculous.

All I can hope is that Charley's seen some of the attention, that she knows people care for her. That *I* care for her.

I don't know what to think. Has she left me? Has she left the life we wanted for ourselves? Or is it something far more serious than that? She's been taken? Everything's conflicting. I don't know whether to be angry or upset. In the end, all I feel is empty.

The journalists from the front of the house have, for the most part, disappeared off to wherever they came from. For now, whatever Fiona told them is enough – but I'm not stupid enough to think that'll be it. The longer Charley remains missing, the more this will be a story. More questions for the police, more questions for me. No new answers.

Fiona has gone, but Emily has been minding the house. No sign of Charley, of course.

'What did the brother want?' Emily asks. We're in the kitchen and she's cooking spaghetti. I didn't ask her to, but she insisted she wasn't going to leave until I ate something.

I dig out the Post-it note from my pocket. It's become slightly screwed up, but I flatten it on the kitchen counter. 'He gave me the name and number of some publicist who used to know Charley's mum and dad. He reckons she can get the media to go away.'

Emily glances towards it as she stirs a pot of tomato sauce. It looks like she's making enough food to last a week. 'Pamela…' Em rolls the name around her tongue. 'What does she get out of it?'

'How do you mean?'

'People don't usually work for free.'

'Good point…'

'Didn't you ask?'

It sounds so simple when Emily says it like that.

'He made it sound like it was a family favour thing,' I reply. 'As if they all knew each other from the old days and Pamela wanted to help…'

Emily doesn't bother to hide the scepticism. Sometimes she's really good at being the *older* sister.

I get to escape her gaze because my phone starts to ring. It's Raj, but he doesn't have much to say. *Is Charley back?* No. *How are you?* Fine. *If you fancy a pint…?* Not today. *Okay, well if you need anything…?* He leaves it there and says goodbye.

In the meantime, Emily has found half a dozen plastic tubs and dumped a mound of spaghetti into each. She's busy spooning meaty tomato sauce on top when I get back into the kitchen.

'No excuses,' she says.

'For what?'

'Not eating. These can go in the fridge and there's some left over that you're going to eat before I go home.'

'I'm not hungry.'

'I don't care.'

'I ate at the service station with Liam. We had Burger King.'

She tilts her head. 'Do I actually have to call you a liar, or are you going to do what you're told?'

There's no point in arguing with my sister when she's in this mood. If she ever settles down with someone, she's going to spend the first year bullying them into the type of person she can stomach being around.

Okay, that's not true. It's only me she's particularly harsh on and, yes, touchy-feely or not, I do know that's because she cares.

I take the plate through to the dining table in the living room and then start to eat.

'See,' I tell her.

'I'm not leaving until you've eaten it all.'

'Can you stay and do the dishes?'

'Don't push your luck.'

I do eat it all, but it's hard to say it was particularly enjoyable. It's not Emily's cooking, more that I don't think I'd enjoy anything right now. Food's only function is to help me get through a day. To be awake and alert for when Charley calls, or arrives on the doorstep.

When I'm done, I carry the plate into the kitchen and leave it in the sink. I turn into perhaps the most unexpected thing.

A hug.

Emily rests her head on my chest and puts her arms around my back.

'You're supposed to hug me back,' she says.

I do… sort of. I find myself patting her gently on the back as if she's a puppy wanting reassurance.

'You're useless,' she says, smiling kindly when she pulls away.

'It feels weird,' I reply, not only meaning the hug.

'Are you going to be all right?'

'Yes.'

What else can I say?

Emily steps away and then nods at the Post-it note that's still on the side. 'Are you going to call her?'

'Probably.'

'Be careful,' she says.

'Of what?'

'I don't know, little brother. But I *do* know that people like that don't take on jobs unless they think they're getting something in return.'

TWENTY-ONE

Pamela the publicist might be many things, but she's definitely not a person who hangs around. Within an hour of me talking to her on the phone, she's driven to my house, parked, marched up the driveway as if it's her place and then breezed inside.

I can imagine she was quite something in her youth because she's got a no-nonsense air about her now, even though she's got to be sixty years old. She has big platinum blonde curly hair, expensive clothes, high shiny heels despite being inside, plus bright red lips and nails with matching thick-rimmed glasses. When she talks, the words flow into one another as if she can't get her thoughts out quickly enough. I feel exhausted simply being in her presence.

Apparently she doesn't do soft furniture, because she's taken one of the hard-backed chairs at the dining table, onto which she's unpacked an A4 diary planner.

'I think the best thing for now would be a public statement,' she says, not bothering with the preamble. 'If Charlotte *is* watching, perhaps that would persuade her to come forward. If the worst has happened, it can't do any harm.'

She speaks matter-of-factly, no concern about what 'the worst' could be.

'The police assigned me a family liaison officer,' I reply. 'Should I tell them?'

'You can – they've got their own media team, but the thing to remember is that the police will always look out for their own.'

'What do you mean by that?'

'I've seen individuals who've been completely unprepared. They've been put in front of cameras, nervous and stumbling over their words. That creates an impression in the minds of the public.'

'What impression?'

Pamela looks up from her book. 'That you're guilty, darling.'

'I haven't done anything wrong.'

'But that's the problem. It's doesn't necessarily *matter* whether you've done anything. If the police stick you on camera and you're sweating like a baboon and babbling incoherently, people are going to make up their minds.'

She smiles as if this is the simplest thing in the world. I'm not sure what I expected, but it wasn't this.

'I just want Charley to come home,' I say and then add: 'She prefers Charley.'

'That's what we all want, hon. I've known her since she was an infant. I was there when Annie and Paul brought her home from the hospital, God rest their souls.' She crosses herself. 'You might have seen some of the old photo spreads…?'

I haven't. Seeking them out to goggle at pictures of my wife as a newborn would be weird.

'Such a tragedy everything that's happened in that family. Lovely people, too…'

'She's not dead.'

Pamela peers over her glasses at me. 'Of course not, darling. I'm not saying that. I'm thinking of you.'

In a weirdly warped way, I believe she actually *is* thinking of me. I remember some of the press conferences or interviews I've seen over the years. Unconvincing family members shuffling around and making themselves look like closet serial killers. Perhaps it *is* a police ploy to hang people out to dry. Make them look guilty and let the nation decide. You only get one chance with the public – look at Christopher Jefferies. That poor sod hadn't done anything wrong, but the public and media decided he looked a bit eccentric so probably had murdered Joanna Yeates in Bristol.

'Charley never wanted the attention,' I say.

'Oh, I don't blame her – not after what happened. Poor girl.'

'She liked living away from everything where nobody cared who her parents were. If I do an interview, it's going to bring everything up again.'

Pamela fixes me with that stare which makes me feel like I'm a schoolkid about to be told off for not understanding something simple.

'It's already out there, Seth. Did you not see the stories today? What do you think people will be saying tomorrow? Or the next day? It's not a case of bringing it all back to the surface – it's already there. There are two ways to do this. One involves letting things spiral potentially out of control. Before you know it, people will be looking into your past, talking to school friends, finding anyone who's ever had a bad word to say about you.'

'What's the other way?'

'That's where you get to tell your side of things in a controlled environment. No dodgy police press conference where some pea-brain with a pencil asks if you murdered your wife.'

'Murder? She's not dead. I've not murdered anyone!'

I didn't mean to, but I'm actually shouting. Pamela's directness has brought up those dark feelings deep down. That tiny voice telling me that she *is* dead. That somehow it *will* be blamed on me, or, worse still, that I'm somehow responsible indirectly. Perhaps I said something? *Did* something? At the time, I thought it was innocent, but Charley took it the wrong way?

'I'm not saying you did, honey. I'm not saying she's dead – I'm telling you what other people will be saying. What they *are* saying.'

Pamela is right, of course. It was only a few hours ago someone was online implying I was shagging my sister. Nobody takes time to check anything nowadays – and once it's on the internet, it's already too late.

'I'm not sure you realise how big this could be…'

Pamela is talking to me as if she's my mother. I'd naturally take against this, wanting to go against advice if only to make a point.

A stupid point.

The problem is that she's right – again. I have no idea what the police are doing. Fiona herself admitted I wouldn't usually be assigned a liaison officer – but then she appeared. Who's to say she wasn't sent to keep an eye on me? Perhaps I was followed to the service station? Maybe they're listening to my phone calls? Checking my emails? Following Emily? It might not be a missing persons case at all, they could already be thinking murder.

'What do you get out of this?' I ask. 'I don't have money. Neither does Charley.'

'Consider it a family favour.'

'But you don't know my family. You and me have only just met.'

Pamela smiles and there's a moment where our eyes lock. She's being genuine and I'm not sure this happens too often.

'Do you know, I actually cried when I found out what happened to Annie and Paul.' She crosses herself once more and then points to her eyes. Caked-on make-up has largely covered her wrinkles, but it's there that I realise her age for sure. Sixty is probably underplaying it. '*Actual* tears,' she adds. 'I've had so much Botox I doubt my tear ducts work nowadays, but do you know how many times I've cried since I started doing this job?'

'I don't know.'

'Twice. Once for Princess Diana; once for Annie and Paul Willis.'

Another time, another place and I'd be laughing. Pamela is deadly serious, though. I believe everything she's told me. She doesn't seem the joking type.

'Look,' she says. 'You have every right to be suspicious – but after what happened to Annie and Paul and then poor Martha, this was always going to be big. You might not know it, but your life has changed. It might not be baseball cap and sunglasses in public, but there's no point in pretending everything can carry on as normal. If you put your story out there, that's it done. If you don't, the papers, the radio stations, the news channels; they'll go searching. They've got pages and time to fill – and everybody has skeletons. You might think you've gone through life making no enemies, but there'll be someone in your past who remembers you. Someone who didn't get as good a mark as you at school; some kid on the football squad who couldn't get in the team because of you; someone at uni who wanted to go out with a girl, but you got there first. There's always someone. You've got the choice to either let the public hear from that nutter, or hear from you.'

After she's put it like that, it doesn't seem like there's much of a choice. I can't think of anyone off the top of my head, but she's right. Sometimes I wonder if there's more nutters than normal people.

'What do I do?'

She claps her hands and then writes something in her giant book. 'Ten o'clock tomorrow morning,' she says.

'Isn't that a bit soon?'

She checks her watch. It's a little over thirteen hours away. 'Not really. I could get people here within the hour if I wanted.'

Pamela removes one phone from an inside pocket and a second from her bag. She checks both, mutters something I don't catch, and then puts both on the table.

'You know Diane Young, don't you?'

'Who?'

She gives me that scolding look again. 'Diane Young. This is right up her street. She's got a nightly news show. Well-respected, intelligent, loves her gin… and she owes me one.' Pamela is already reaching for the phone. 'She used to know Charley's parents, too. I think she was an entertainment reporter back in the day. Anyway, she'll be very sensitive to you and your needs, she won't ask anything you're uncomfortable with.' Pamela flicks through the pages in her book, then picks up both phones and starts to stand. 'Unless I'm very much mistaken, and I'm *never* very much mistaken, I think Diane was one of the reporting team who covered everything that happened with the sister.'

'Martha?'

A nod. 'She's familiar with the family history and the... um... well, you know...'

'Know what?'

Pamela lowers her voice, as if saying it too loudly will make it true. 'The curse.'

TWENTY-TWO

4 YEARS AGO

Charley Willis, 24 years old

Mason looks like he hasn't slept in a week. His skin is so pale, it's practically grey. The only colour in his face is the black of the crow's feet around his eyes. The poor guy is drifting around as if he's floating, dead-eyeing everyone as he shakes their hands and thanks them for coming.

Nobody can think this is a good idea.

Everybody's giving it the usual bow of the head. The condolences. One after the other. Over and over and over.

I'm sitting on the floor in the corner of the hall, knees to my chest, watching the human wall of black mooch around the scratched wooden floor.

The kids who've been dragged along have no idea how to behave. They'd rather be playing, but their parents have instead kitted them out like they're extras in an emo band and then given them nothing to do. A few have made a brave break for it, heading to the buffet and piling up their plates.

A small ginger lad I don't know spots me watching and offers a bashful flat smile. He's ignored the savoury and gone straight for the cake. His plate has Battenberg, mini Swiss rolls, three chocolate biscuits and a couple of cream puffs loaded on top of each other.

I return his acknowledgement with one of my own and then he spins and carries his plate off to the far corner, where some of the kids have created their own little eating circle on the floor.

There's a large part of me that wants to join them. Kids don't flannel around with their choice of words. None of this 'sorry for your loss' BS. It's all upfront. *What happened? Why? Oh.*

Done.

That's so much easier. Then it's back to PlayStation or kicking a ball around.

That was Martha's way, too.

When Mason has finally finished thanking everybody, he turns in a circle. At first he stares past me, then he realises I'm the one in the corner wearing black like everybody else.

He floats across, scuffing his feet aimlessly. 'Thank you for coming,' he says. It's only us in the corner. I don't have to reply because he instantly adds: 'Sorry. As if you'd be anywhere else. I'm thanking people out of habit.'

His chest rises dramatically as he takes a deep breath. His bottom lip bobs but he just about holds it together.

'How have you been?' he asks.

'Awful.'

'Me too.'

He lowers himself onto the seat next to me, offers me his hand and I take it. He's cold.

'Martha really loved you, Little C,' he says.

Loved.

Past tense.

'She would've done anything for you.'

'I know.'

We sit like this for a few minutes, his hand in mine; me on the floor, him on the chair. He's sobbing softly but I've done my crying.

'I don't believe what they're saying about her,' I say. 'There's no way she'd leave you behind, no way she'd leave Dillon and Daisy.'

Mason sighs, his heading dipping to his knees.

Dillon and Daisy are on the other side of the room with Mason's mother. Daisy is sleeping in a car seat, oblivious to the fact she's at her own mother's wake. She'll never remember this. Probably not Dillon, either. He's only three and yet they've found him a dinky little suit. He's so bloody gorgeous – and yet I can barely look at him because the suit represents the occasion.

The back room of the pub is very Martha, I suppose. Low ceilings, cheap booze, cakes at the buffet. All a bit grimy, just the way she likes it.

Liked it.

Mason slips his hand out of mine and rubs his eyes. There's colour in his face now – scrubbed red skin around his eyes and nose.

'Did she say anything to you about why she was at your parents' house?' he asks. He's questioned me before, but if repeating himself is the only way he can rationalise what happened, then I'd have to be quite the cow to deny him that.

'Nothing,' I reply.

'Did she say if she was unhappy?'

'The opposite – she was *really* happy. She was looking forward to you all going to Cornwall. She'd sent me a link with photos of the cottage.'

'It's just you hear these thing about postnatal depression and all that.'

'If she had a problem then she never mentioned it – and she never showed it. She was tired, but that's not the same.'

'But why would she be at your parents' house at all?'

Mason looks up finally, throws both hands into the air. He's been asking this question over and over. It will be what keeps him awake every night.

I know.

That's what *I'm* thinking when I'm staring at the ceiling at three in the morning.

'I don't know,' I tell him. 'It's been in limbo for eleven years. Uncle David keeps filing slightly different legal disputes. I'd pretty much forgotten about it. I don't know why she'd go there now.'

His body is arching up and down as he breathes in and out. All I can do is rub his back, hoping he knows that he's got to keep it together for another hour or so, if only for the kids.

'Have you *seen* what they're saying?' he breathes.

I don't point out that I was the one who said I didn't believe it. No point. 'I've seen it,' I reply.

'How can someone say that? Why would they think *she* burned the house down?'

That's the problem when it comes to speculation. It's always from those who know a person only through the picture that's painted. Martha is, and always will be, the wild child, even though she was never like that. Not really.

But the wild child broke into our parents' old house and set it on fire. She either got caught inside, or that was how she chose to commit suicide.

Choose one.

Except there's no way that's what happened.

The people who know her… who *knew* her – Mason and me – know she wouldn't do that. She *wasn't* the wild child. She was a wife, mother and sister and, my God, did she love those kids.

None of that matters because it doesn't fit what people want to believe. The Willis Curse; The Cursed Family; The Mysterious Willis Family. Take your pick.

There are photographers at the gate of the pub hoping for the money shot. They didn't get their photo of me crying eleven years ago and they're sure as hell not getting it now.

Liam's nowhere to be seen. I'm not sure why I thought he might show up. I'm the only Willis here. The last one standing.

I'm staring at the floor because I know everyone is looking at me. Mason's friends and family. Martha's *friends*. The ones I've never met – which is all of them. I can feel them watching. It's not Mason, it's me. My damned family. My damned curse.

Mason stands, turns to the corner to try to compose himself.

'Please stay in touch,' he sobs. 'Dillon loves you. Daisy will, too. You're the only link back to their mother.' He coughs. 'It's only you left.'

TWENTY-THREE

SETH. NOW

Five in the morning.

Again.

I've slept on the sofa once more, still in yesterday's clothes. There are empty Stella bottles on the floor and I know the filthy spaghetti plate is still in the kitchen sink. It's probably beginning to crust. Emily would be furious. Mum, too, if she knew who I was.

The red digits on the satellite box beam across the room and the sun is already on its way up, shining through the open curtains into the living room.

Why am I awake?

It's not as if the sofa is particularly comfortable, certainly not as much as the bed… but that's *our* bed. Charley and I bought it when she was moving in. An IKEA special. If a relationship can handle a trip to a giant Swedish warehouse, it can handle anything.

I sit up straighter when I hear something tapping. It's only gentle, like the scraping of the water pipes.

Maybe it's Charley, gently tapping on the floor, urging me to follow her upstairs. *Come on up, it's much comfier in bed than on the sofa.*

There it is again… tap-tap-tap.

I jolt up as I realise there's somebody at the front door. I'd not closed the curtains and there's a police car at the end of the drive. Fiona is at the door. I race around from the living room through the kitchen to the front door and pull it open.

'It's not what you think,' she says straight away. 'I didn't want to ring the bell in case you were completely out of it. We can do this later if you want.'

'Do what?'

'We were wondering if you can come and identify a wedding dress…?'

TWENTY-FOUR

I've never been in a police car before.

I remember having a Matchbox toy one when I was a kid. It was part of some sort of set, along with a fire engine and an ambulance. I'd sit on the kitchen floor while my mum cooked, zipping them back and forth.

'*I'll break my neck on one of those cars*,' she'd say. '*Is that what you want?*'

I'd offer to go into the living room or outside, but she'd smile and tell me to move into the corner instead.

I wonder how many parents have ever broken their necks when it comes to things they claim they might break their neck on. Probably none.

Being inside a police car is not that different to being in a regular car. Someone I don't know is driving and I'm in the back seat with Fiona, the liaison officer. The passenger seat is empty and there's that seed of doubt planted by Pamela that makes me wonder why. Is Fiona here in case I try to jump out? Aren't there child locks anyway? Do they think I've done something wrong?

It's only as we move away that I realise there are no journalists or photographers outside the house any longer. Either that, or I missed them. Perhaps there's a photographer up a tree and he snapped a picture of me getting into a police car. That will look good, won't it? Exactly the type of thing Pamela told me to be careful about. Anyone who's not a police officer in a patrol car looks guilty of something by default.

Too late now, I suppose.

'Where did you find a wedding dress?' I ask.

'We got a phone call late last night,' Fiona says. 'A farmer from a few miles outside of town found it on the edge of his property. It was tangled into a tree.'

'Do you get many reports of stray wedding dresses?'

'None.'

That sounds ominous.

'It could be some sort of fancy-dress thing,' Fiona adds, although it doesn't take much for me to know she's trying to put a brave face on things.

'Sometimes there are stag or hen parties on their way to the city in a minibus,' she adds. 'We don't want to make any assumptions about what it is, about who it might belong to, without first asking you.'

'But you think it's Charley's?'

Fiona doesn't reply, but that's enough of an answer in itself. They've not sent her out to find me at five in the morning with no reason. They've got a photo of Charley in her dress, so they'll have a pretty good idea of what it looks like.

I rest my head against the door and close my eyes. It's not that I feel unwell as such, more that everything is sluggish. When Fiona says something, it takes me a few moments to process. It's as if I can feel those electrical impulses trudging around my nerve endings, taking their time about it.

Slooooooow.

And then I realise the implication. It's obvious. I'm not sure why I didn't pick up on it before. If it *is* Charley's dress that's been found, that means she was undressed at some point. It's not like she took a change of clothes with her. All of her things are back at the house.

I open my eyes and blink back into the car.

'You already know it's her dress, don't you?' I say.

Fiona says nothing.

THE WILLIS CURSE

by SAMANTHA BAILEY

(Archived four years ago)

Liam Willis fidgets constantly as he tries to find the words. We're in a booth, think faux leather and coffee stains, him on the side that offers a view of the door. His gaze snaps off towards the front of the café as the bell tinkles, but it's nobody he knows.

'You don't have to answer,' I assure him, but he shakes his head.

'It's not that,' he stammers. 'It's just I don't know what to tell you.'

Perhaps his nervousness is because he's aware that, like it or not, he's a part of this so-called jinx. If it can affect his parents and sister, is he next in line?

'I don't know,' he repeats. 'I mean... a curse? You think it's nonsense. It's like all those horror movies. You think it's all made up and then it keeps happening.'

In his own way, Liam has spelled out the exact dilemma this reporter had when asked to talk to the eldest Willis child.

A curse? That's ridiculous – except that it *does* keep happening.

Eleven years ago, it was Paul and Annie Willis. They were the beloved television personalities slayed in their own home while their youngest daughter, Charlotte, cowered in an upstairs wardrobe. The killer has never been found.

It's only now that the open verdict has been reached on the death of middle child, Martha, that we can truly ask, 'Is there a Willis Curse?' Perhaps more specifically, is the Willis *house* cursed?

Three deaths on the same spot, all unexplained.

I ask Liam if he feels threatened, expecting an instant rebuttal. That's not what happens. He looks up to the ceiling, lost in thought.

'I'm not sure I'd say threatened,' he replies.

'What would you say?'

'Worried.'

Liam was born when his parents were at the height of their fame. Paul was a household name when that meant something. A charismatic and friendly family figure, he could shift from giving away cars on a Friday-night game show to showing off the latest technology on a magazine show by Monday.

If he was the king of evening TV, then wife Annie was the queen of breakfast. Along with her health-conscious recipes, her yoga and exercise routines inspired hundreds of thousands of women to lose weight.

Liam went to a boarding school, but he assures me he never felt abandoned.

'They always found time for me,' he says. 'I'd be home on weekends and we'd take holidays together. We'd talk on the phone all the time. They wanted the best for me.'

Two years after Liam was born, his sister came along. Little is known of Martha Willis in the early days, though Liam says she was a happy youngster. It was much later that she became the so-called 'wild child', well-known for her drinking, drug-taking and bed-hopping antics around Camden.

As the Willis machine rolled on, the couple became more and more popular until reaching the apex of their careers when they jointly hosted the *Royal Variety Performance*.

A year after that and, according to media rumours at the time, their marriage was in trouble. Liam calls that suggestion 'total rubbish', with the only definitive fact being that Annie Willis gave birth to a third child nine months after those rumours surfaced.

Charlotte Willis was the catapult that sent Paul and Annie back into the limelight. With bouncing blonde curls and twinkling green eyes, she was a glossy magazine darling from the day she was born. Annie Willis wrote two books about parenting and co-presented a show with her husband that followed similar themes for almost six years. Paul Willis, meanwhile, found himself as the face of *Wheel Of Fortune*.

It's said that everyone knows where they were when they heard of the death of John F. Kennedy or John Lennon – but a few generations on and many identify with where they were when they heard of the Willis Massacre.

In the aftermath, Charlotte controversially went off to live with wild child Martha, while Liam tried to crack America.

'It's harder than it sounds,' Liam says with a rueful smile.

'It sounds pretty difficult.'

'I got through to a few final auditions for pilot shows – but never more than that. I don't think they were looking for Brits at the time and I never quite mastered accents.' He pauses and then adds: 'Good times, though.'

I don't press on what those 'good times' might have entailed, but the smirk says plenty.

'What is it that worries you?' I ask, taking him back to his own choice of words.

'In what way?' he replies.

'Is it the so-called curse that worries you, or is it that your parents' killer was never caught?'

Because that's the terrifying truth. A killer *is* still out there and, according to the inquest, there is now a third death that's unexplained.

Martha burned to death in a fire at her parents' house a few months ago. Her husband and friends insist she was happy, that there was no reason for her to take her own life. The police and fire investigators have been unable to shed any further light on things.

Perhaps the curse is not a curse at all. Perhaps, like most demons, it is human. The police say there is no connection – but they have taken eleven years to not find a killer.

'She might have set the fire herself,' Liam says, somewhat out of the blue.

'Your sister?'

'Yes.'

It's an astonishing allegation.

'Does that sound like the type of thing she would do?'

'We didn't talk much. She was angry.'

'About what?'

Liam shrugs, unable to offer anything more specific. Martha is not around to defend herself, but Liam's thoughts do not match the coroner's. In his report, Martha was noted as a 'loving wife and mother' as well as a 'devoted sister'.

The sister is, of course, Charlotte Willis. Liam has remained, to some degree, in the public limelight. Martha struggled to shake off the 'wild child' tag – but little is known of the final Willis youth. For someone whose childhood was consumed in the spotlight, it is perhaps no surprise that her adolescence has been spent shunning it.

As for the possibility of that Willis Curse, Liam does eventually decide that's it something in which he does not believe.

'It can't be real, can it?' he says later in our conversation.

'Why do you say that?'

He pumps up his chest, flashes a toothy smile as if he's auditioning to host one of his father's famous game shows. 'Because I ain't going nowhere,' he says.

TWENTY-FIVE

SETH. NOW

Pamela the publicist arrives at quarter past seven, laden with two soft suit bags. I can only imagine what time she got up because she's got a full face of make-up and her hair is as high as the night before. She tells me there's more in her car, hands me the keys and then disappears into the house. I'm already lugging the suitcase from the back seat of her BMW when I realise I could have told her to get it herself.

She has a way of giving orders that means there's not even a question of refusing to do something. This is probably how Mussolini started. One minute he was telling someone to get the bags from his car, the next he was founding fascism.

The reporters and photographers have seemingly gone. I lock her car, then the front door and carry everything into the living room. Pamela is clinging onto a pair of suits and presses one against my chest, muttering, 'no, that'll never do' to herself.

'I have my own suits,' I tell her, but she's not listening, she's pressing the second one against me instead. It's dark grey with light grey stripes.

'Do you have any Savile Row?' she asks.

'Who?'

'This one,' she says, passing me the second suit. 'That's a four-thousand-pound suit, but it doesn't look it on camera.'

'How much?!'

'I'm owed a few favours – I guessed your size last night. You can borrow it for today.'

I take the suit and hand her the suitcase. Inside is an overwhelming selection of shirts, ties, cufflinks, socks and even underwear. She brought underwear!

There's an iron in there because 'I wasn't sure you'd have one'.

She might be many things, but Pamela is not afraid of work. Before I know it, she's erected some pop-up expandable ironing board and is busy pressing a shirt. The iron zips back and forth with ruthless efficiency and it's only when I mention the wedding dress that she stops to look up.

'They found Charley's dress?'

'In a hedge a few miles away.'

This is the first time I've seen her something close to flustered – and even then it's only a blink that gives her away.

'I had to identify it,' I add.

'How do they think it got there?

'No idea. There was a bit of a rip at the bottom, but that might have happened at the hotel. She accidentally stood on it earlier in the day. There was no blood, the zip still works, it wasn't torn. She must have taken it off.'

I'm still trying to get my head around it myself as the pace of the iron across the shirt increases.

'That's very evocative,' she says. 'Very powerful.'

I've tolerated Pamela so far, but this is what takes me to the edge. I can't take the bubbling condescension any longer: 'This is my wife you're talking about.' I don't realise I'm shouting until it's too late. 'She took *off* her wedding dress at some point. It was left in a hedge.'

Pamela puts the iron down, smiles sadly and rubs my arm. 'I know, honey. I know. I meant that it might jog someone's memory. We're hoping someone comes forward to say they remember something. We want Charley to be found. That's all I was saying.'

She removes her hand and somehow has me feeling like I'm the monster here.

I say sorry and even though she replies that it's fine, I apologise a second time.

It's like I'm not in control of myself. I can't blink away the image of Charley's wedding dress. The police had wrapped it in clear plastic, ready to be tested for whatever. It was unmistakably hers: sleeveless; smooth and shimmery across the top with a dotted trail of small decorative imitation pearls along the back. The first time I saw it was when she walked along the aisle – but that was enough that I'll never forget it.

Pamela has moved on. She passes me the shirt to go with the suit. It's plain white, the type of which I have half a dozen upstairs. Then she hands me a navy tie, cufflinks, socks and underwear. 'Brand-new,' she assures me. 'Diane's getting here for eight ready to go for ten, so best get a shift on.'

It's no surprise that the clothes fit perfectly, nor that Diane Young turns up at *exactly* eight o'clock. She's in her own chauffeur-driven car, but there's a satellite truck behind and half a dozen blokes lumping equipment.

Pamela is in her element, throwing around air kisses as if she's married to the invisible man.

Everyone spends two hours running around setting up lights and cameras in the living room while I'm in the kitchen with Pamela and Diane, who goes over the list of questions.

The two women are seemingly from a similar mould but with a decade between them. Diane is immaculate: brown bob of non-moving hair, bright red nails, scarily white teeth. She oozes authority. It's a good job they apparently get on because I dread to think how an argument between them might go. Like planets colliding.

I find myself marvelling at how much stage-managing goes into making something look authentic. My living room is still mine and yet it's been dialled up to eleven. Someone's got hold of the wedding photo Emily had given the police. They've printed it out, framed it and placed it between two pot plants I've never seen before. That's all in the background of the shot, with the foreground two huge leather-backed chairs that I've also never seen. It's smart yet not too over the top. 'Man of the people,' Pamela says.

Everything's happened in such a whirlwind this morning that I can't quite take it all in. I'm pretty sure I'm not comfortable with any of this – the wedding photo especially – but it's too late now. It's three minutes to ten and the cameras are ready to roll. We're not live, but Diane says they need editing time for her evening show. They're also going to drip snippets onto the news broadcasts.

We sit in silence for the three minutes until the producer or whoever he is says everything is ready. Diane thunders into action, reeling off the age-old list of tragedies through which Charley has lived and then reiterating that she's been missing since the wedding on Saturday. I'm mentioned in there somewhere, but it barely registers.

'I can't imagine how hard this is for you,' Diane coos.

I mumble something about wanting Charley back, missing her. Hoping she's watching. We rehearsed this in the kitchen, but the lights are making it feel like a midsummer's day in the desert and I'm struggling to concentrate.

'Can you tell the viewers how you met?' Diane asks.

'It was at her shop,' I say. 'She runs a sandwich place with her friend. It's called Martha's—'

'A tribute to her sister, of course,' Diane adds.

'I'd gone in for breakfast and there was this woman behind the counter wearing a bright green apron with a frog on the front. I remember looking up to the menu and then I saw her smiling at me. I was the only customer there and we got chatting.'

'Did you recognise her as Charlotte Willis?'

I grope at the words for a moment. 'Charlotte' has thrown me off. She's never been that to me.

'That's not the type of thing I'd have noticed. She was just the woman behind a counter who wanted a chat.'

Diane flashes her ferociously white teeth. They're dazzling under the bright lights. 'When did you find out who she was?'

'We went walking on the following Sunday – it was Charley's idea. We were on this towpath next to the canal and she said she had something to tell me, that I'd find out soon enough. I didn't know what to think, but she said she was very googlable. She said I'd probably heard of her parents, and as soon as she mentioned their names, I remembered. She didn't have to say any more after that. We laughed about whether googlable was a real word.'

Diane nods, adjusts her glasses slightly. 'Was it intimidating?'

'What?'

'The weight of Charley's history. The family dynasty. I can see how that might weigh on a person.'

I take a second, not sure how to phrase it. 'I figured there was nothing either of us could do about it, even if we wanted to. Your past is your past. We liked spending time together, so that was all that mattered.'

Pamela told me to sit as still as possible. Hand movements are fine but full-on fidgeting makes a person look shifty. The more I think about not moving, the more it feels like I need to. My body is doing its best to betray me by creating itches that I'm trying hard to ignore.

'I understand you met around two years ago,' Diane says. 'Some might say it is a little quick to meet, move in and marry within that period. What would you say to that?'

Before I sat down, Pamela told me not to shrug. '*Use your hands,*' she said, so I do, offering both hands palms up.

'Everything felt right. She asked me.'

Diane leans in, mock surprised. She already knows this. 'Charley asked *you*?'

'About a year ago. It wasn't all one knee and tears, that's not what we're like. We were talking about her moving in and she said perhaps we should get married, too. Simple as that.'

It's time to get serious now, which is indicated by Diane taking off her glasses. I'm not sure if she needs them at all. Perhaps the lenses are plain glass and the whole thing is for show? She doesn't fold back in the arms, dangling them off to the side instead as she leans in to look me directly in the eyes. Regardless of any advice Pamela gave, it's impossible not to wilt under Diane's gaze.

'Moving on to Charley's family,' she says, 'has she ever spoke to you about that horrible day when she was thirteen?'

'I've never asked and she's never said.'

'Are you not curious?'

'Not really. I'm in love with the person she is today. Whatever happened then is gone. If she wanted to talk about it, she would.'

A nod. 'I'm sorry to ask this, but with all the talk after what happened to Martha Willis and now your wife's disappearance, do *you* believe in the so-called Willis Curse?'

I almost ask her to repeat herself. Of all the questions we ran through in the kitchen, this wasn't on the list. I blink at her, turn slightly to glance towards Pamela, who is sitting close to the camera. Or she was. She isn't there now. I'm searching for the words.

'I don't believe in curses,' I reply, although I stumble slightly over the words.

Diane reaches for and touches me on the wrist. 'That's probably a poor choice of words. I don't think we're talking about a curse in a horror movie sense. Do you believe that bad luck can perhaps follow a family? That misfortune can run through generations?'

She removes her hand and sits back, locking me into her stare.

'I think that, for the most part, we're the sum of our own decisions.'

'Does that mean that, for whatever reason, your wife might have made a decision to leave?'

I blink again. We've completely veered from the script.

'I can't believe that,' I manage.

'So you think she's been taken through force…?'

I open my mouth, stumped momentarily until the words come: 'I don't know what to think. I just want her to come home.'

TWENTY-SIX

It's twenty to six in the morning.

Technically, that means I've had a lie-in, although I have no idea what time I actually got to sleep. I'm on the sofa and the television is flashing away as the news channel regurgitates the same stories on a loop.

The bonus questions of Diane's interview were apparently agreed with Pamela because they wanted an authentic reaction. The pair of them were delighted with everything and the interview aired last night. I watched myself over and over, all the while listening to my phone ping with messages of support. Until I watched myself, I had no idea my voice was like that. It doesn't sound that deep to me, but as soon as the TV me opened his mouth, it was like the bass had been turned up. That would be fine if I had anything like the frame to pull it off, instead I sound like I've had some sort of body transplant.

None of the texts were from Charley but the missed call count is up to a whopping (193). It's Wednesday morning, so that's approximately eighty-three hours since she disappeared. That is two-point-three-two-five calls every hour or, to put it another way, one call every twenty-five minutes and forty-eight seconds.

I've had a lot of time on my hands.

I find myself trying to decide whether one call every twenty-five minutes and forty-eight seconds is still a bit stalkery. Then I get lost in trying to calculate how much the average would be brought down if I called right now. Or, if I were to wait for, say, an hour and then call, how much would that drag the average out?

I think I'm going slightly mad.

I got three texts from my sister.

8:04 p.m.: Did u steal that suit?
8:51 p.m.: Have u eaten today?
11:32 p.m.: Seriously have u eaten today? Don't make me come over!!!

I text her back, managing to get two lies into one short message as I tell her I was asleep when her final message arrived and that I did eat.

If toast counts, then the second part of the message isn't technically untrue.

My phone pings right away with her reply.

5:52 a.m.: You lie.

I've not touched the food that Emily cooked. I had some toast last night while TV me was busy scaring young children with the deepness of his voice. I put a couple of slices into the toaster and sit watching them. I've never noticed it before but the toaster makes a really low clicking sound. Like a pair of crickets chatting to each other.

I really am going mad.

When the toast pops, I take a photo and send it to Emily with a caption that reads: 'No need to come over – I don't need anything turning off and on again'.

She fires straight back: 'Dickhead.'

As much as she's been rock-like since Saturday, I really don't want to see her today. I'm not sure I want to see anyone except Charley. I'm hoping that after the interview last night and the subsequent clips on the news shows that somebody's memory will be jogged. Either that or Charley herself has seen it and will get in contact.

My mind is full of conflicting thoughts. I told Diane I couldn't believe she chose to leave – and that's the truth. But there's a part of me that hopes she did because the alternative would be so much worse. If she left through choice, that's something we could be able to work out. Perhaps it was some sort of emotional flashback and she needed time by herself? Maybe she was caught up in the sentiment of the day and it all became too much for her? She might have run off along the hotel's service lane and found a car and… I don't know. But anything like that is better than thinking somebody snatched her.

It's precisely six o'clock when my phone starts to ring. Pamela the publicist.

'How are you this morning?' she asks.

I mumble something about getting a good night's sleep but can tell she isn't listening to the answer. She has other things to discuss.

'Have you seen the story in the *Mirror* this morning?' she asks.

'What story?'

'I tried to stop it, but they'd already done some deal and didn't want to lose the money. Rest assured I'll be taking it up with the powers that be.'

'What story?' I repeat.

There's a slight pause. 'You're probably better looking it up yourself.'

They say you should never search for your own name on the internet, but when I hang up, I commit the cardinal sin. A lot of the stories have me as an aside. They're about Charley and the fact she's missing. Either that or another rehash of the endless Willis Curse stories, where I'm a throwaway name. All of that is fine.

It's almost worrying how close Emily was to the truth. The plus point is that no one's calling me a dog rapist. What they *are* calling me is a dog killer.

'Is Willis hubby a dog killer?' to be precise.

Even the headline manages to be inaccurate, considering I'm not a Willis. I suppose, strictly speaking, I *am* a dog killer – but the same could be said of any vet. If a pet is put to sleep for humane reasons, that's technically one animal killed by a human. It's a normal part of the job, though. To put a creature out of its pain and suffering is surely the kind thing to do?

They've found some bloke whose bulldog died after having a seizure at the clinic a little over a year ago. It wasn't long after I'd started working there. One of those truly unavoidable things. The dog was epileptic and had a history of seizures. The owner had brought him in for precisely that reason. When the animal had another fit, this time while on the operating table, it suffered a brain haemorrhage. Truly awful. It's shocking, but, at its core, one of those things that couldn't be avoided.

According to the owner, that makes me a dog killer.

There's more too. Another paper has been speaking to the farmer who found Charley's wedding dress in his field. The police hadn't released the information – and I'd not spoken about it on-air to Diane for precisely that reason. Now it's out there anyway.

The farmer says he knows Charley because her shop buys dairy products from him. 'She always seemed so friendly,' he says. His name is Jan Astley and he runs Astley Farm. I don't know him, but his signs are all along one of the country roads leading towards the motorway. There's a small farm shop tagged onto the side of a house that sells cheese, butter and meats. Charley and I have visited a couple of times before. From those two instances he manages to say: '…they always seemed like such a happy couple'.

It's extraordinary. He's said something which, in essence, is friendly and flattering and yet I still read the sentence over and over, slowly becoming angrier. It's probably the word 'always' that does it. *Always*. He saw us twice when we bought things from his shop and yet that means we '*always* seemed like such a happy couple'.

The longer this goes on, the more I can understand why Charley has done everything she could to keep away from such attention. Who would want this life?

I spend much of the rest of the morning reading everything that's been written about Charley in the past few days. It ranges from the relatively tame – straight stories with phone numbers for information – to the delusional. There are conspiracy blogs that say her parents were part of the illuminati. Charley is apparently a lizard and her 'so-called' disappearance is simply a case of her reverting to her true form and then having to hide. If the articles aren't bad enough, there are the comments underneath, with at least one person 'confirming' the theory. 'TruthTeller1214' says they once saw her reverting to her lizard form in the disabled toilets of a Waitrose.

All the while, the text messages buzz through: Raj, Emily and Alice asking if I'm okay. I don't reply. Not yet, anyway.

It is a little before midday when the doorbell goes. I get up from the floor and look through the window. Pamela was right about one thing – the journalists have disappeared since Diane got her story – and the only car parked on the road outside my house is a battered people carrier. Its owner is at the door: Mason.

I've not seen him since the wedding and can't remember a time when we've ever been alone. He's Charley's brother-in-law, so we only meet if he's brought Dillon and Daisy over, or if we're visiting them. Mason and I are really good at the whole nodding-at-each-other thing. We'll mumble the odd 'all right'; 'how are you?', that sort of thing, but that's it. We're world-class at the nodding, though.

It's probably indicative to how many actual friends I have around here that I was considering asking him to be my best man.

When I open the door, he smiles weakly. 'I thought I'd see how you were doing,' he says.

'Oh, right…'

It's a little awkward, but I invite him in and then, because we're British, I offer him tea. He's milk, no sugar.

The kettle is busy bubbling away as we sit tongue-tied in the kitchen.

'Where are the kids?' I ask.

'At Mum's. They've been helping out during the holidays.'

'Right...'

'I saw you on TV,' he says.

'It wasn't really my choice to do it.'

'Hopefully she'll see it and come home...'

We sit silently for a minute or so and though it could be awkward, it genuinely does feel like a moment of support. It's odd how two men sitting in close proximity not talking can actually be a heartening glimmer of help.

'I met Liam a couple of days ago,' I say.

'Charley's brother?' Mason seems genuinely surprised.

'Right. He called and asked for a chat. I thought he might know something about where Charley had gone, but he put me in touch with a woman who set up the TV interview.'

The kettle clicks off, but neither of us move.

'Martha never had any time for him,' Mason says. He stops and twitches slightly. 'Did he ask you for money?'

'No... Should he...?'

'Martha used to say he was always going on about money. He'd pop up in magazines and on TV shows every now and then with snippets about their parents. Martha and Charley didn't want anything to do with it.'

'I never knew. Charley never really talked about him.'

Mason nods. 'He didn't come to Martha's funeral, but he came to the house a few days later. He was all friendly and apologetic, saying he was too upset to be at the funeral. Then he ended up asking for money.'

I'm not sure how to reply at first, so get up and fill a pair of mugs with hot water instead. 'Why did he think you'd give him money?' I ask.

'Liam, Martha and Charley got around a million each after their parents died. They were supposed to divide the house between them, too – but that got caught up in a dispute over the ownership. Did you know that?'

I dribble in the milk and pass Mason his tea. 'Yes. Charley gave away most of her money. She kept enough to set up her shop and that was it.'

'Martha bought our house outright with hers and put the rest into these high-interest bonds that will mature when Dillon and Daisy each turn eighteen. I couldn't access that money even if I wanted to. She wanted to make sure it's a legacy – but Liam didn't know that. After she died, he wondered if she'd left any for him in her will. She hadn't, of course – they barely even spoke. She left it all to Dillon and Daisy.'

I sit back on the stool with my own mug. 'Why did he think Martha would leave him money?'

'I have no idea. I've not seen him since then. I'm surprised he didn't ask you.'

'He sounded like he wanted to help. Said we should go for a pint in the future.'

Mason holds a hand up. 'All I know is that Martha wanted nothing to do with him.'

'Charley as well…'

We both take a moment. We've said more to each other here than in the previous two years we've known one another.

'Did Martha ever say why they fell out?' I ask.

Mason shakes his head. 'Did Charley?'

'No.'

He sucks on his lips, glancing towards the window and then back. 'I suppose I always got the sense that with whatever happened to their parents…' He tails off, unsure how to phrase it and then looks directly at me. 'I always thought Martha was hiding something.'

He delivers the line like a sledgehammer and I can sense what's behind it. He's thought this for years but never said it out loud. He didn't bring it up with Martha and it's not the kind of thing he'd talk about to Charley. All this time, all those years, it's lingered at the back of his mind. Now, finally, he's actually said it.

I don't know how to reply.

'I know that's a horrible thing to say about your wife,' he adds. 'I wanted to ask her about it, but I could never put the words together. And then it was too late…'

He turns away and puts the mug down, staring off through the window towards the back garden.

'Have you ever been to the house?' he adds.

'The Willis house?'

A nod.

'Never,' I reply.

'I go once or twice a year. After what happened to Martha, I guess I feel close to her there.' Another pause and then he looks back to me again. 'Do you want to go?'

It's something that's never occurred to me. You read about the shrines that people create. Where fans might go on a pilgrimage to see Graceland, where Elvis died; or to stand on the street where John Lennon was shot. If Charley had wanted to go, I'd have been with her, supporting her, but she never mentioned it.

I stay silent too long.

'It was only an idea.'

Mason smiles sadly and I can see a flicker of what he's gone through since what happened to his wife four years ago.

I put my mug down on the side and push myself up from the stool. 'Let's go.'

TWENTY-SEVEN

3 YEARS AGO

Charley Willis, 25 years old

Everyone knows who I am.

It's enrolment day, not even the official beginning of term, and yet the sideways glances haven't stopped. People must genuinely think I can't see them when they lean in close to the person next to them and mutter a couple of words. Some of them point slyly behind their other hand.

You know who that is, don't you?

It's mainly women who have signed up to the catering management college course but there are a few men and the age range is everything from eighteen or nineteen all the way up to fifty-odd. I thought I'd be one of the oldest, but there are a few of us in our mid-twenties. I knew there was a chance I'd be recognised, but it's been twelve years since everything happened at the house. It had all gone away, but then, after last year with Martha… I guess it's all back again.

We continue to traipse around on the campus tour, but I've stopped paying attention. Instead, whenever someone gives me that sideways *look who it is* glance, I return it with interest. I might not be in my sister's league, but I did learn a thing or two from her and can more than pull off a ferocious death stare.

Without exception, everybody peers away quickly when they realise they've been rumbled.

The tour guide is constantly cheery and says something about new refitted kitchens before striding off along a corridor. The group filters in behind him as I drift to the very back. We head, blinking, into the sun and then cross a courtyard. I mooch slower and slower, allowing a gap to develop as we approach the next building.

Perhaps I should go home? There are probably online courses where I don't have to actually meet people. It sounds really appealing and yet the whole point of this is that I'll be able to open my own shop at the end of it. That's going to mean dealing with people every day. People to buy from and sell to. Some of them might recognise me, too – and what do I say then?

'Hi.'

I jump slightly as I realise a woman has slowed as well. She's around my age, all smiles and flustered enthusiasm with a curly blonde bob.

'Er, hi…'

'I'm Alice,' she says.

I wonder if I should come up with a fake name – but remember I've already enrolled with my actual name. Plus they gave me a sticker. It had 'Hi, my name is' printed at the top and then some bloke wrote 'CHARLEY' in capital letters underneath. It took him three attempts – and three stickers – to get the spelling correct. I have no idea why I wasn't allowed to write my own name.

Alice points to the sticker on my chest. 'Charley,' she says.

'Right.'

'I figured I'd say hi,' she says.

'Hi.'

I'm hoping she'll leave me alone, but she's matching my pace and has that slightly delusional, overly enthusiastic look about her, as if she might start dribbling at any moment.

'Do you fancy a coffee?' she asks. 'After this is done, I mean.'

'I don't really drink coffee.'

'We could go for a pint if you prefer? There's this pub on the other side of the roundabout on the way in. The food's not bad there…'

'I don't really, er…' I cut myself off before I add the word, 'eat', because that's pushing it a little. I need better excuses for ignoring people.

Alice slows even further and, for some reason, I find myself doing the same. We stop in the middle of the paved area as the rest of our class amble ahead. 'Do you want the truth?' she says. 'People have been talking about you. One of the old women recognised you and she told everyone who you were. I think it's the highlight of her week. If she had any idea how to use her phone, she'd be asking for a selfie. Me? I don't care. Whatever. I like your boots.'

I look down to my feet and, in fairness, I am wearing my favourite boots. They cost eleven quid from a market stall but are probably the most comfortable things I've ever had on my feet. It's hard to fight back the smile.

I start to walk after the others and Alice is still at my side. 'What are they saying about me?' I ask.

'Y'know, the usual. Willis Curse and all that.'

'Original then?'

'What do you expect? For most of this lot, the most excitement they get is accelerating over a humpback bridge.'

I laugh and it's becoming increasingly hard to maintain my stony exterior.

'So why are you here?' Alice adds. 'I didn't get the grades to go to uni and then got sick of doing agency work. My dad lent me a bit of money and here I am.'

It's a big moment, because the question she's asked, whether she meant it or not, is so personal. If I open myself up, then that's it. It could be on the internet within an hour.

'I promised my sister I'd stop arseing around,' I say, figuring I have to trust someone sooner or later.

'Oh…'

It's obvious Alice knows who that is. Everyone saw the stories – that's why people recognise me, after all.

'Do you think we should catch up with the others?' she adds.

'Not really.' I motion towards the campus café on the far side of the forecourt. 'We can go for a coffee if you want.'

Alice smirks and I know then that I like her. 'I thought you didn't drink coffee?'

TWENTY-EIGHT

SETH. NOW

I've seen photos of what the Willis house used to be. It wasn't quite a mansion, but it was a grand detached property with towering pillars at the front. It was classy but in a dated way, a monument to the seventies. I don't know if Charley's parents had it built for them, or if they bought it as it was, but everyone knows it now as the Willis house.

I suppose that's how I'd always pictured it if ever I thought about it, but it's nothing like that at all. It's a big hole in the ground, part building site, part tip. The pit is probably five metres deep or more. Three times my height. There are intermittent pools of murky water dotted along the bottom, with thick concrete pillars lined with twisty metal placed even deeper into the foundations. A crane sits in the centre, entombed and abandoned in the mud, and there's a crusty cement mixer on its side in the corner. Long planks of wood have been dumped at various spots and there's a spade sticking out from the ground next to the crane.

As for the house itself… there is no house. The whole area is one large patch of dirt.

Mason and I stand on the edge, peering down towards the site below.

'What happened?' I ask.

'The house was supposed to be sold with everything split three ways between Liam, Martha and Charley,' Mason says. 'Their uncle said he had a claim to it, though, and it ended up being batted back and forth by solicitors for a decade or so. It went on and on. After what happened to Martha…' He tails off for a moment, breathes deeply and then forces himself on. 'After that, it was sold as land for development. The house itself was apparently quite run-down – which is understandable as it was empty for eleven years. Once all the solicitors were paid, there was basically no money left.'

'Charley got a cheque for a couple of thousand pounds. I don't think she ever cashed it.'

'Same here. Didn't feel right.'

Despite the state of the site, it is being used. A crow swoops down to one of the pools of water and drinks from it.

'They were going to build luxury flats,' Mason says. 'I have no idea why they'd do that out in the middle of nowhere. I saw the plans once but didn't pay much attention. The letter was addressed to Martha, but she was gone by then. The developer ran out of money and I don't know what's happening now. It's been like this for about six months.'

It really is a mess.

A second crow joins the first and then they get into a squawking match until the original one swoops away.

If it wasn't for the gates at the front of the crumbling driveway, nobody would know this hole was here.

'Charley gets a letter now and again,' I say. 'I think it's from the solicitor who sold this place, but she doesn't bother with it. I always thought she wanted to forget this place entirely.'

'Can't blame her…'

It was all before I met her but that is about as true a statement as can be. From hiding upstairs as her parents were murdered below, through to her sister dying in the fire that scorched this place to the ground, it's no surprise Charley wanted to pretend this house never existed.

'Do you think you'll ever know what happened with Martha?'

I've said the words before thinking them through.

Mason turns to look at me and I swear I've never seen a person so close to tears without actually crying. His bottom lip is trembling and his eyes are so wide that I can see more white than any other colour. Before I can take anything back, he's speaking.

'I don't know why she was here,' he says. 'It was a normal day. Daisy was only a year old, so it was a full-time job looking after her and then Dillon was three, so he was busy charging around, pulling things over and generally trying to hurt himself. We used to take one child each. Everything was fine and she said she had to go out and get a few things done. We both used to do that. If we needed bread or something, we'd go get it just to have an hour away from everything. It was one of those things you don't really say out loud but we both knew what was going on. I used to mooch around Asda for forty-five minutes, or sit in the car park by myself. You'd get a bit of peace and then it'd be back to trying to stop Dillon eating dirt.'

He chuckles to himself, gives that same *bloody kids, huh? Be grateful it's not you*-look from the wedding reception.

'Anyway, she said she had to nip out for a bit and it was fine. It was the code we never talked about out loud. I figured she wanted a break. Then she didn't come home. The next thing anyone knows, this place was on fire. They found her inside after it had been put out. Her car was on the driveway.' He points off towards the spot where his people carrier is now stopped.

'But the house was abandoned at the time?' I ask.

'Right. I have no idea why she'd be here. The only thing was her phone records. Someone called her not long before she left the house, but it was one of those disposable mobiles. Could've been anyone.'

'I never knew that.'

He shrugs. 'It was mentioned at the inquest. It's one of those things where it might have been nothing. Probably was. Wrong number, or whatever. They only spoke for sixteen seconds, so it's not like Martha had a proper conversation with whoever it was. Then people started saying *she* burnt this place down. That it was suicide because of what happened to her parents. Then it was all about a family curse, or a curse on this house. By the time the inquest said open verdict, nobody really cared.'

Mason coughs, squeezes his nose and bows his head.

'There's no way she committed suicide,' he adds. 'Something happened here four years ago and something happened here fifteen years ago.'

It's pathetic, but I don't know what to say or do. I end up patting him on the shoulder as if he's a sickly child. I don't know enough to constructively add anything, but all I can think of is what Liam told me at the service station.

'*It's the Willis women. They think differently to you and me. They do weird things.*'

Whatever others think of him, it's hard to deny he's got a point…and, if that's the case, what does it mean for Charley?

TWENTY-NINE

2 YEARS AGO

Charley Willis, 26 years old

Alice drums her palms on the counter next to the till to create a drum roll. She counts me down: 'Five-four-three-two-one! Go!'

I flip the sign from Closed to Open and then unlock the door, swinging it inwards with a jingle and wedging it ajar.

Martha's is officially open for business!

'Is there anyone there?' Alice asks.

I move onto the front step and peer both ways along the street. There's a kid sitting on the nearby wall picking his nose, but that's it. Cars are creeping past on the way to the main junction that will take them out of town, but nobody is looking anywhere other than the road. I step back into the shop and shrug.

'No.'

'Oh…' Alice's shoulders slump slightly. I know precisely how she feels.

'It's only seven o'clock,' I say cheerily.

'I thought someone might come in for breakfast on the way to work…'

'They still might.'

It was an early morning of coming in to bake cakes, make sandwiches and boil down some soup. Things are still cooking in the kitchen. It's not like we expected a queue for our first morning, but one person would have been nice. We've had signs up for weeks, plus there was a notice in the paper at the weekend.

'I'll get those cupcakes out of the oven,' Alice says. She forces a smile but isn't too good at hiding how disheartened she is.

Everything is gleaming in the café, from the whooshing espresso machine to the display cabinet that's filled with potential lunches for people. The floor is so clean, people could eat off it – not that we were taught that on the catering course. We have a dozen tables scattered around the small space anyway.

Mum and Dad's money, I think as I gaze around the shop, before blinking the thought away.

I take my frog apron from the hook and tie it around myself and then head back to the front step, hoping a friendly face might be able to persuade a person or two inside. Cars continue to creep past, all potential customers on their way to work. Surely somebody needs to buy lunch… or pop in for breakfast…?

Nobody even bothers to turn to look.

Seven becomes quarter past, then half past. Alice pokes her head out from the kitchen intermittently, looking steadily more disappointed each time.

Quarter to eight, then eight. An entire hour and not one customer. People do go by. There's a woman with a pram, kids on the way to school, a couple of men running to catch the bus. Nobody gives the shop a second glance.

Eight fifteen, half eight. Nobody. Alice spends a bit of time in the doorway and then returns to the kitchen, saying unconvincingly that business will pick up later. 'Word of mouth,' she says. I'm not sure she believes it herself.

Our first customer arrives at three minutes past nine. It's a man wearing loose jeans and a long-sleeved T-shirt. Nothing too special, and he trips over the step on his way in. He tries to right himself and then bumbles into one of the chairs before managing to catch himself on a table. By the time he's done all that, he's twisted a full one-eighty and is facing the door again. For a moment, I wonder if he's going to leave. I've not even seen his face, but that might be for the best to save his own embarrassment, given he's managed to nearly fall over twice in barely a second.

Then he turns and blinks up at the menu on the wall above me. He scratches his head and then looks to me, a crooked smile on his face.

'Whoops,' he says.

There's no particular reason for it to be funny and it's probably the stress of the past two hours, but I find myself laughing.

'What's the soup of the day?' he asks.

'I don't think I can serve you that,' I reply.

His eyes crinkle. 'Why?'

'You'd probably spill it on yourself. I don't want to get sued.'

He grins wide and laughs to himself. 'Good point,' he says. 'How about a cake instead?' He nods at the display cabinet and goes all googly-eyed, like a mother with a newborn.

'What's your name?' I ask.

He peers up, looks at me properly for the first time. 'Seth,' he says. 'What's yours?'

THIRTY

SETH. NOW

It's a little after four by the time Mason drops me outside the house. We spent a long time at the Willis house, not really saying much. The Willis women undoubtedly leave questions in their wake. Who actually killed Annie and Paul? The person was never found. Why was Martha at the house, how did it catch fire and why was she inside?

And Charley.

Why did she disappear after our marriage ceremony and where is she?

It's not a lot to hang onto the slimmest silver lining of them all, but I do feel closer to Mason after the day. We've each married into whatever's going on with this family; we each have the same questions.

'We should do this again,' he says as he pulls on the handbrake. I suppose he means spending time together, not visiting the house.

'Whenever you want,' I reply. 'Text or call. You can bring the kids if you can't get a sitter, or I'll come to you…?'

He nods appreciatively and offers his hand. We shake and then I get out of the car. It's odd, nothing has really changed, and yet I feel better. A problem shared and all that. He pulls away and then I realise I'm exposed on the street. The neighbourhood watch tyrants ready to spring outside and ask what's going on. Before anyone can notice, I hurry along the path and let myself into the house.

I realise the missed call count hasn't increased through the entire afternoon I've been with Mason. That twenty-five-minute average will definitely be on the way down. Less and less stalkery as the day wears on.

Into the kitchen and the living room… except something isn't right.

In the centre of the draining board is a single upturned glass, with spotty drizzles of water peppering the sink.

It can't be mine; Mason and I were drinking tea.

'Hello?' I shiver as my voice echoes around the house. No answer.

I have my own keys and Charley's were among her things that Alice returned. Nobody else has a key for our house. I rush into the living room, but there are no broken windows. None in the kitchen either.

The back door has a key in it.

Not mine.

Not Charley's.

I stare at it for a few seconds until the truth that should have been obvious dawns. I'm so tired that everything's sluggish. The key turns and the door unlocks as I head out to the back garden. I reach up to the overhang above the door, running my hand along an indent between the gutter and the tiles. I hid a key there years ago after locking myself out. It's not that high off the ground and I don't have to stretch – but the key has gone.

Only two people knew about that key: me and Charley.

Back inside. My spine is tingling.

'Charley?'

No answer.

Our bedroom is directly opposite the top of the stairs. I head up to where the door is closed. I'm pretty sure I left it open.

It has to be, doesn't it?

The door creaks inward and I realise I'm holding my breath. The bed was still freshly made, largely because I've not slept in it since the wedding. Now the covers are scragged to the side, creased from the shape lying underneath. There's a mop of messy golden hair on the pillow, a body curled into the sheets.

My heart is thundering.

'Charley…?'

THIRTY-ONE

6 WEEKS AGO

Charley Willis, 28 years old

It's hard to take in how beautiful Liam's girls are. I remember that kick of elation I had when teasing him about his looks back in my old flat after he returned from LA. That sneering, snidey me that feels so long ago. I don't think I'd say that to him now and, besides, he's created two of the most stunning children I've ever seen.

Skye and Jasmine are back in their cots side by side and I swear they can understand each other, even though they're only three months old. Jasmine will babble a series of burps and bubbles and Skye will respond. It's incredible to see them.

'I don't know what to say… they're so gorgeous.'

And they are. They really are. All parents think their children are beautiful, despite the truth in front of them. It's the harsh fact of life that nobody ever says they're looking at an ugly baby because, for the most part, people aren't total maniacs. Every child is gorgeous in the eye of the beholder.

Helen looks exhausted, but she's smiling weakly. I wish I knew her better. It's not like I have much family.

'They'll happily mumble away to each other,' she says.

A glance to Seth and he knows what I'm thinking. Neither of us have said it out loud yet, as if talking about what we want might somehow curse it.

No, not curse. Not that word. Something else.

Either way, we have the wedding first.

I turn to Liam, but I'm not sure what to make of him. He's standing in the doorway of his living room, hands in pockets. He's been watching this whole time, barely saying anything to either Seth or me. I wondered if they might bond over football or something. Blokey stuff. They've not really talked.

When Liam called, I didn't know his number. I almost didn't answer, assuming it was a salesperson. He asked if we wanted to meet his twins and all my instincts said no. The prospect of visiting the children weighed heavier.

We've changed, I suppose. Definitely me and probably him. You say and do things when you're younger because everything in life seems so bloody important. Everyone who says no is out to get you. Anyone who thinks differently to you is out to make your life worse. Then you grow up and realise life is what it is. None of those things matter in the end. You can sit and stew, find conspiracies where there are none, or you can get the hell on with it.

Like it or not, you can't choose your family. Liam's my family. Helen, too. And those beautiful girls.

I nod at him. 'You all right?'

'Just watching,' he replies. Liam glances to his wife, then back to me. 'Do you want to help me in the kitchen?'

'Sure.'

I give a small nod to Seth to let him know I'm fine and then follow Liam through the house. It's gorgeous. I naturally assume Helen chose most of it because it's really classy – all varnished wood and polished surfaces. Perhaps that's the bitchy side of me creeping through.

The kitchen is tough marble worktops, huge built-in oven, gleaming hose taps and a large American-style fridge. All very functional and smart.

'This is lovely,' I say. 'All of it. The house, Helen, the girls. You've done so well.'

Liam is resting against one of the countertops, smiling thinly, not really committing.

'Are you all right?' I ask.

'They're going to repossess it,' he says, holding a hand up to indicate the house. 'All of it. We're nine months behind. Helen doesn't know.'

I stare at him but his features don't move. He's looking at me blankly. Not his sister, just... nothing.

All I can think of is the two beautiful children in the other room. 'Oh, God...'

'I invested in this company,' he says. 'We'd buy a load of luxury cars and then hire them out for the day. People would get to drive a Ferrari or whatever. It was guaranteed money.'

I find myself rubbing my eyes, unable to believe we're here again.

'It's all Uncle David's fault,' he adds. 'If he hadn't been such an arse about the house, we could've sold that years ago and split the money. That's what Mum and Dad wanted.'

'You got a million quid fifteen years ago.'

He shrugs. 'That's nothing, is it? Loads of people are millionaires nowadays. You can barely get by.'

'Liam! People get by on a lot less than that all the time. Do you even know what minimum wage is?'

I know he doesn't. He scowls at me as if I've slapped him in the face. It's pure hatred.

'How much have you got left?' he asks.

'I'm not giving you money.'

'You got a million, too.'

'So what? I'm going to have my own family to think of.'

He's nodding along, teeth bared, jabbing a hand towards the living room. The cosy family picture is long gone. 'It's not me you're punishing,' he snarls, 'it's those girls in there.'

It takes me a moment to process what he's said, let alone the spite and venom with which he spoke.

'Oh, you *really* are a piece of work,' I reply. There's a part of me that's always been able to channel Martha. 'That's why you got in touch, wasn't it? Nothing to do with meeting Helen or the girls. Not about making up. It's all about money. It always is.'

'C'mon, Charlotte—'

'That's not my name!'

'Whatever. Can't you help me out? We're brother and sister.'

'Even if I wanted to help you out, I don't have any of Mum and Dad's money left. I kept some to put together the shop and that's it. I gave the rest away.'

Liam boggles at me. 'You *what?*'

'I put some in an account for Dillon and Daisy and I gave the rest to Uncle David's kids, like he always wanted. I didn't care when I was thirteen and I don't care now. I always felt bad for them. If he hadn't acted like such a dickhead with the solicitors, Martha would've helped him out years ago. The only reason she didn't is because they were as stubborn as each other.'

Liam can barely get the words out: 'You gave *all* your money to Uncle David after everything he put us through?'

'Not *all* of it. I told you – I spent some on the shop. I gave quite a bit to charity. I never wanted it. I tried to tell people.'

Liam is so stunned that he staggers to the side, using the hose-like tap to support himself. 'You didn't *want* the money?'

'No.'

'I don't understand.'

We stare at each other and it's hard to believe we share any genes at all. I don't understand him and he sure as hell doesn't understand me.

'This is about Martha, isn't it?' he says out of nowhere.

It's my turn to be shocked. 'What?'

'You always loved her more than me, didn't you? It was always you two against me.'

'She was there for me, Liam. She took me in after everything that happened. She went through all the paperwork to become my legal guardian. We had all these social worker visits because they were convinced she was some wild child. She had to wee in pots to prove she wasn't a crackhead.'

'What about me?'

'You went to Hollywood for four years. We got one postcard. When you got back, you came over, asked for money, and then disappeared again. You only ever get in contact when you want something. When I was a kid, Martha was the one who would visit Mum and Dad's and would sit and play with me. I barely saw you. I didn't know you. She was my sister, you were someone who turned up every now and then with your hand out.'

Liam is boiling. I remember how angry Uncle David used to get, but Liam is worse. His face is red, teeth grinding together, fists balled.

'I really need your help,' he says, although it doesn't sound like much of a plea.

'I don't have any money, Liam. I run a sandwich shop. How much do you think we make?'

'Your fella then.'

'He's a vet. It's not that much money for patching up dogs and cats. He doesn't own the practice – he works there. He's still in debt from his training.'

Liam is nodding again, pacing back and forth, seething. I take a step towards the door and the safety of the living room, but I'm terrified for Liam's poor kids, not to mention Helen. I don't particularly want to leave them while he's like this, but, beyond that, what are they going to do when the house is repossessed?

Liam stops pacing, looks me dead in the eye, and then he says the words he can't possibly say: 'I know about Mum and Dad.'

PART TWO: GENESIS

THIRTY-TWO

SETH. NOW

Charley rolls over in the bed and opens her eyes.

It's her.

It's really her.

There's a moment in which I wonder if I'm dreaming it. If my mind is playing tricks from the lack of sleep and food.

But it's not.

She's back.

Charley wriggles against the tightness of the covers, trying to move into a sitting position. Her hair is a dirty, tangled nest; her left eye dark and blackened, cheek swollen.

It's still her, though.

I sit on the bed and Charley lunges for me, wrapping her arms around my back and *squeezing*. Neither of us say anything, but her chest starts to bob as she sobs into my shoulder. All I can do is hug her back. I want to grab her, hold her, not let her go, but she's such a mess that I don't want to hurt her any further.

We stay like that for a long time. She hugs me and I hug her. Neither of us say anything.

Eventually, she levers herself away and dabs her eyes with the bedclothes. She wipes away something from my cheek and it's only then I realise that I've been crying too. She winces as she touches her left eye.

'Are you okay?' I whisper.

'I'm done crying now,' she replies. Her voice is husky and low, one eye raw and red, the other scarred black and purple.

I don't know where to start. Where was she? Why? How is she back? What happened to her eye? Everything blurs into one.

'Do you want a cup of tea?' I ask instead.

She nods, rubs my arm – and I notice she's still wearing her wedding ring. 'I really do.'

Charley is wearing her pyjamas, fleecy and warm. She slips on a pair of slippers and rounds the bed. I let her lead the way downstairs, not wanting to take my eyes from her in case the mirage disappears in front of me. She reaches back and takes my hand and she's real.

She ends up making the tea herself. I watch as she fills the kettle and turns it on, then grabs a pair of teabags. Two sugars into my mug, none in hers, bottle of milk on the side ready to rumble. Wait.

She's real.

We sit on the same stools where Mason and I sat earlier.

'We're going to have to call the police,' I say. 'They're still looking for you.'

She nods and I'm unsure if that means she already knows. Surely she does?

'Not right now,' she croaks, resting a hand on my knee.

Her nose is slightly squashed, possibly from whatever has blackened her eye. She rests her head on my shoulder and I wish I was brave enough to ask the questions. If I was only now meeting her, I'm sure I would – but there's something about her I can't describe. It's not *how* she looks; it isn't the physical injuries. It's something behind her eyes. A glassy emptiness. I know that if I ask now she won't answer. She needs time.

The kettle flicks off and she lifts herself up. Hot water in each mug, splash of milk in both and we're done.

'I've been out with Mason today,' I say.

Her eyebrow flickers. 'Oh.'

'We went to your parents' house. He says he goes there sometimes when he's thinking of Martha. I didn't know it was a building site. I thought there'd be a house.'

Charley stares through me and I can't figure out if she knew the house was gone. She must have done.

'I always hoped you'd spend more time with Mason,' she says.

'We agreed we would. He's busy with the kids, so doesn't get a lot of free time. We'll try to work things out, though.'

'That's nice.'

She sips her tea, loops her fingers through the mug and she's still real.

'Emily's been great,' I add. 'She filled up the fridge and cooked a load of spaghetti. She's been texting every couple of hours to make sure I'm eating properly.'

It's not quite a smile, but Charley nods along. 'How did the pictures come out?'

'From the wedding?'

A nod.

'I've only seen a few. They looked great. I think she did a good job.'

'Something for her portfolio…'

There's a break. I've been driving the conversation but have no clue where to go from here. My wife has been missing for four days and we're talking about my sister's photography portfolio.

'How's your mum?'

I blink back into the kitchen. 'Sorry?'

'Your mum,' Charley says. 'How is she?'

'Oh… I don't know. I've not seen her since Sunday. Emily says she's been confused; she keeps thinking it was her wedding to my dad. She gets upset when he's not around.'

Charley rubs my elbow. 'Oh, Seth…'

'She said she saw you.'

The hand disappears.

'Who did?'

'Mum. She says she saw you in the corridor when she was on the way to the toilet. She reckoned you were by the French windows and that you told her to tell me you loved me.'

Charley turns away, staring through the window, much like Mason did a few hours ago.

'Right…'

That's all she says. Not a confirmation, not a denial. There's a part of me that is furious, that wants to jump up and demand a reason. We got married – and then she disappeared. She at least owes me an explanation.

But then I see her black eye, the swollen cheekbone; the empty, broken stare… and I'm not angry at all.

'Alice was worried about you,' I say. 'She came over with your things. She reopened the shop this morning. She says trade was up, but I don't know if that's a good thing. Probably rubberneckers wanting to get a look at the place.'

Another sad bob of the head.

'I met Liam, too.'

Up until now, everything I've said has been met with a stoic nothingness, but at the mention of her brother's name Charley spins to face me. Tea sloshes over her mug onto the floor. 'My brother?'

'Right. He called me.'

She stares, seemingly unable to take it in. Her eyebrows are twitching. 'He called you? On the phone?'

'On Monday morning. It was in the paper what had happened and he asked to meet in a service station. Em waited here in case you came back and I went to meet him.'

'You met?'

'Outside a Burger King.'

'What did he say?'

'He put me in touch with this publicist. She set up this public appeal interview thing. I don't know if you saw it, but it was on TV last night.'

Charley gives no indication at all that she knows what I'm talking about. Her mouth is open, her stare distant.

'Did I do something wrong?' I ask.

It takes her a moment, as if we're on some sort of time zone delay, but her attention flickers back to me.

'I think we should call the police now,' she says.

THE REBIRTH OF BRITAIN'S GOLDEN COUPLE

by SAMANTHA BAILEY

(Archived 28 years ago)

Annie Willis hasn't stopped grinning since she welcomed me into her house. Millions know her as a 'lifestyle guru', the woman who brought yoga to breakfast television. Plenty more know her as the author of numerous bestselling books, but, for now, for the first time in nine years, she has another role to play: mother to a newborn.

'You forget how exhausting it is,' she tells me with a weary smile, bobbing a cocooned ball of swaddling on her shoulder. I can see a few wisps of blonde hair, but that's all.

'It's like you go through everything one time – or twice if you're me – and then it all falls out of your mind,' Annie adds. 'You remember the good stuff – the weekend trips, teaching your kids how to read, that sort of thing. You block out all the lack of sleep and the hours you spend worrying.'

The Willis house is exactly as one might expect. *Less Is More* sold half a million copies as Annie gave Britons advice on how to declutter their lives – and that is something she lives up to herself. The hallway has perfect lines of varnished wood, a pair of elegant lamps and a vintage telephone sitting on an antique dresser. That's it. No need for fancy touches or over-the-top showing off. After all, less is more.

Annie leads me through into what she calls the 'reading room'. The rug is plush and fluffy – 'a gift from a friend in India' – and the walls are lined with steepling ornate bookshelves that are filled bottom to top.

'Books are my downfall,' Annie confesses. 'I know I live by less is more – but that's not the case with books. You have to have one indulgence.'

Annie's own books are there, of course, but there is no pride of place. The cookery books she authored are filed in alphabetical order along with everyone else's. No preference given here – and she has quite a collection. I don't count, but there is comfortably a couple of hundred.

'I've always loved cooking,' Annie says, noticing my interest. 'I started collecting years ago, long before I was on television. Some of those are my mum's hand-me-downs.'

The cookbooks are barely the start. There's a lot of non-fiction: more lifestyle guides, craft books, fitness manuals and biographies dominate the shelves. I pick out a biography at random – that of a household star I won't name. The inscription is on the inside cover: 'To Annie and Paul, forever love'. The author has drawn a heart and then signed his name inside.

But I've become distracted.

The subject of why I'm here is babbling happily away to herself as Annie lays her gently in a crib. The cot is typical Annie Willis: made of wood with smooth lines. Functional yet classy.

I get my first proper look at the child and she's breathtaking. Only a few months old, yet already with a shock of bright golden hair.

'She started smiling at three weeks,' Annie says.

It sounds early, but looking at this beautiful baby beaming up at me, I can believe it.

'Say hello, Charlotte,' Annie coos.

As little Charlotte opens her mouth, there's a moment where I think she might do just that. A small burp erupts and then Charlotte chortles to herself once more.

Annie, 41, has been a fixture on British television for a little over a decade, finding fame initially with a short five-minute slot after the weather on ITV. Husband Paul, 45, got his break seven years before that when he finished second on popular talent show, *New Tricks* with a ventriloquism act. Within two years, he was hosting the programme.

By the time Paul was picking up his runner-up award, he and Annie had already been married for two years, having been in a relationship for a further two. They met as redcoats at Butlin's one summer and, as Annie points out, have barely spent a night apart since.

I ask if it was love at first sight and there's a moment in which it feels like Annie has been transported back to those heady holiday camp days. She stares off towards the corner of the room. 'I'm not sure if I believe in that,' she says. 'There was a spark, for sure. I think we were attracted more to each other's desire to succeed. Paul was working so hard at his ventriloquism and I was part of a magician's act with someone else. For some entertainers, it's all about putting on a show and then going back to a room with a bottle of wine, or whatever. We were never like that. We'd both work and work to get better.'

'So it was more of an intellectual meeting?' I venture.

'Exactly. That and the will to thrive.'

And thrive they did.

For some, children would be a barrier to success, but Annie has never been one to listen to the word 'no'.

'When I got the television job, I didn't realise I was pregnant,' she says. 'I was doing all the yoga stretches, not knowing I was carrying. There was a time where I thought I was putting on weight. When I told the producers I was having a baby, there was horror on their faces. I thought they'd fire me – it was different times then – but everything came together. Instead of the yoga I'd initially pitched, we ended up running what were essentially prenatal Pilates classes for everyone, all live on breakfast television!'

It's that ability to react to changes in circumstances that have arguably been the key to Annie's success. Within weeks of giving birth to son Liam, she was back on screen with advice on such taboo subjects as breastfeeding and post-childbirth weight loss. Not long after that, she was showcasing recipes for young children and teething toddlers. Two years after Liam, Annie gave birth to Martha and then moved onto giving advice about how to juggle a pair of children.

As Annie's career went from strength to strength, so too did Paul's. He moved from presenting entertainment programmes to game shows and serious documentaries, proving himself to be one of the country's most versatile entertainers.

At their peak, it is estimated their weekly reach was more than half the population.

Annie smiles sheepishly when I put this to her. 'It's weird when you say that,' she says. 'I'd do my slot in the morning and then come home and be a mum. Paul might have a filming block, but he'd almost always be home in the evening to kiss the kids goodnight. We were so busy being parents that we didn't register the other stuff.'

'Didn't you get noticed?' I ask.

'Oh, all the time. I'd be at the supermarket and there'd be women following me around. They'd be looking at what I put in my trolley and then put the same thing in theirs! The manager noticed and used to help me out – he said I was the best advert he ever had, but it didn't feel like that. I'd be trying to stop Liam from grabbing things off the shelves and Martha would be waving at everyone, all the while people are telling me their problems and asking for advice.'

The fondness with which Annie speaks makes it clear these are memories she holds dear. 'Was that as good as it got?' I ask.

The question seems to take her by surprise, but Annie stops to think. She's standing at the side of Charlotte's crib, rocking it gently back and forth.

'That's a good question,' she says. It takes her a few moments to gather her thoughts. 'I suppose it is in many ways,' she replies. 'It's hard to quantify, isn't it? All those things we've done. We did these radio roadshows one summer and tens of thousands of people would come out. I guess it's those smaller interactions that meant so much, though. I'd get letters from people, writing to ask what they should do about their circumstances. I'd try to reply to everyone and then, sometimes, you'd get another letter to update you about everything. It's nice to know you made a difference.'

Charlotte is asleep now. Annie gazes lovingly at her daughter and then takes a seat in the nearby lounger. She invites me into the one next to her and then puts her feet up. 'First time today,' she says.

For a person who's worked so hard for so long, the strains and stresses do not show. Annie Willis is an unquestionable beauty, famed for her natural look. She's lost little of that through the years and has regularly been christened a 'dad's favourite' by certain tabloids.

She laughs off that suggestion. 'They don't see me at three in the morning when Charlotte's crying.'

It was three years ago that Paul and Annie Willis hosted the *Royal Variety Performance* together. From that pinnacle, it was hard to see where else either of them could go. Unfortunately, the only way was down. A year later and newspaper rumours were swirling that the golden marriage was in trouble.

'It was never what they made out,' Annie insists. 'They took it way too far. I think it was a researcher on one of Paul's programmes who sold a story. They were fired for that, but it was already too late because people believe what they read.'

I wonder if she's going to add anything else. When she doesn't, I point out, politely, that she hasn't actually answered the question. Was the marriage in trouble?

'No,' she replies, unequivocal this time. 'Look, every marriage has its ups and downs. If you think it's going to be perfect all the way through, then you're kidding yourself. We had a couple of arguments about personal things, but it was never anything more serious than that. Having a few cross words doesn't mean you're going to divorce.'

Despite that, times were harder for the couple. Breakfast television had moved on from yoga to high-intensity aerobics and with Liam and Martha growing up, there was less material to interest the viewing public. Annie was quietly dropped from breakfast television, much to her chagrin.

'They betrayed me,' she says. 'They promised I had a job and then offered it to someone else. I don't have much else to say about that but facts speak for themselves.'

For their part, the production company say there was no duplicity, insisting it was a 'natural parting of the ways'.

After that disappointment, Paul then discovered that he, too, had been dropped from his popular car magazine programme. Within a period of approximately eighteen months, they had gone from being at the top of the television tree, to each being unemployed.

'That's a bit of an exaggeration,' Annie says and, for the first time, there's a bristle to her tone. 'There was technically a time where neither of us were *on* TV, but that doesn't mean we weren't working. I was writing a book and in talks with a couple of companies over various projects, while Paul was launching his own production company. Things take time. There was never any panic.'

For some, being 40 and 'between jobs' in the entertainment world would mean the end of a career – but Annie Willis has never been 'some'. The announcement of her pregnancy around a year ago was met with widespread delight among the public. Critics said it was a shameless attempt to get back into the public eye, but they were drowned out by a groundswell of well-wishes.

One thing is certain, the birth of Charlotte Willis has given Annie a new lease of life in more ways than one.

'There are lots of women out there having babies into their forties,' she says. 'That's the way of the world now. People want to have a career and still have children afterwards. It's not the case that women can't have both nowadays. They want to hear stories like mine.'

'What next?' I ask.

'Paul and I are going to present our own show,' she says. 'I suppose there will be elements of what I used to do, but we're moving on to reflect the times. Some men stay at home and some women go out to work. Some families have a couple where both work. There's no shame in men spending time in the kitchen or changing the baby; just as there's no shame in women getting involved in the family finances, for instance. That's the reality we're going to reflect.'

In many ways, Annie and Paul Willis are the textbook guide on sustainability. They refused to give up when some said they should. Each obstacle was overcome by reinventing themselves for a new generation.

The last word, of course, goes to little Charlotte. She gurgles a request and Annie dashes across the room to check on her daughter.

'I think she's got wind,' Annie says with a smile. 'At least burping a baby will give us something to talk about when the first episode goes out.'

The Willis Way begins on Wednesday at 8pm on ITV.

THIRTY-THREE

SETH. NOW

The posters in the police station are beyond laughable. There's a photo of some kid lying in the gutter, giving a glossy-eyed stare to the camera. Underneath is a note about under-age drinking. I can't believe anyone has ever been put off having a sneaky pint because of something like this.

Yes, officer, I was going to stab a guy in the head, but, because of your poster, I decided not to.

All of them are essentially a variation on 'don't commit crime', some with an 'or else' implication at the end; others with a more '*please* don't commit crime'-vibe.

They're not quite as bad as the ones from outside churches. They'll have something like a giant pig on the front with, 'Jesus is like a pork loin' underneath, followed by a confusingly contrived explanation of why it's not been written by a maniac. Even that's marginally better than the ones that have a massive picture of the sky and a headline along the lines of 'God's Blue-Sky Thinking'.

I swear more people need to be sectioned.

The clock on the wall above the posters continues to move very slowly. It's like a time portal where everything has braked to a crawl. Minutes are lasting ninety seconds and someone's crammed a couple of hundred minutes into an hour.

Nine p.m. My lie-in this morning means I've been up for fifteen and a quarter hours, although I think I was still awake after midnight, so it's been a lengthy day either way.

Fiona, the family liaison officer, appears from nowhere, hovering in front of me and pointing a thumb towards a vending machine that's been humming and farting incessantly. 'Do you want something to eat?' she asks.

'You sound like my sister.'

'Someone cleaned out all the KitKats, but it's got pretty much everything else.'

I shake my head and she sits down next to me. 'I'm sorry you're still waiting,' she says.

I nod along the corridor in the vague direction Charley headed with a pair of officers a few hours ago. 'What's happening in there?'

'Standard stuff. They're asking where she's been, what she's been up to, that sort of thing. Establishing whether a crime took place…'

It's a very polite insinuation. She could've said, '*Whether your wife decided to walk out on you for no reason.*' I guess that's what all the training's for.

'Is the fact she's been a long time a bad sign?'

Fiona purses her lips and doesn't respond immediately. I already know the answer. Of course it bloody is. If her explanation was, 'I was sick of my husband, so hid in the back of a Nissan Micra for four days', she'd have been done by now.

'It's all standard,' Fiona repeats. 'I'm sure everything will be finished soon.'

We sit awkwardly for a moment.

'Charley never said anything to me,' I say. 'She didn't say where she'd been, or what happened. I'd gone out for a drive with her brother-in-law and, when I got home, she was in bed. She let herself in with the spare key.'

I'm guessing this is precisely what Charley has said because it doesn't seem much of a surprise to Fiona. She nods to one of the least mental posters. SUPPORT IS AVAILABLE, it reads. There's a stock photo of some woman whose face is obscured as she buries her head in her hands.

'Help is there if you want it,' she says. 'I can get you a brochure if you like.'

I'm not one of those people who thinks asking for help makes you weak. On the other hand, I can't believe the solution is sitting in a comfy chair and paying some bloke a few hundred quid to listen to your problems. In other words, I don't live in New York.

It's complicated.

For now, I don't know what I'm dealing with. If Charley walked away from me, is that something we can work through by ourselves? If she was attacked, is that something with which she can cope, or will she need to talk to someone other than me?

Could I handle that?

Would there be such uncontrollable fury at whoever was responsible that I couldn't contain myself? I took vows to, among other things, 'protect' her – and hours later I failed. What does that make me as a husband? The only way I could've messed up worse is by shagging someone directly after the ceremony. That would've put a real damper in the 'honour' part of the vows, let alone the 'be faithful to'.

Fiona probably knows all this herself. She crosses to the poster and rearranges the leaflet box underneath, plucking one out and passing it to me.

'It's only something to consider,' she says.

'Thank you.'

I glance across the words and then fold it into my pocket. We sit silently for a few more moments and then a pair of doors click open along the corridor. There are four officers with Charley in the centre. None of them are smiling. It's like a funeral march as they approach. When she reaches me, Charley pulls my arm, wrapping it around her and pressing herself into my chest.

'Is that it?' I ask.

'For now,' an officer replies. 'You can certainly go home. Do you want—?'

'No,' Charley replies quickly, twisting and pulling away. She bats away a yawn and thanks the officers. Fiona says she will be in contact the next day and that she's there if we need her – and then we're off out into the car park.

As we head through the double doors, Charley holds out her hand and I take it. She's cold, trembling.

'Are you all right?' I ask.

'Yes.'

'Do you need to go to hospital?'

The bruise around her eye has evolved into a kaleidoscope of colour, less black, more purple and green. It's spread outwards from her socket as well.

'I just want to go home.'

We get into the car. I'm driving but can barely concentrate on the road. I accidentally put it in third rather than first and then bunny-hop into a stall.

Charley says nothing for the entire journey. She leans her head on the rest, clasping the seat belt to herself. The radio is silent and the only sound is the engine.

It's dark by the time we're home and I park on the driveway. There are no journalists hanging around, but I wonder if the neighbours are watching. It won't be long before news gets out that Charley is home and then everything will start up again. The public will want answers. They're not allowed to be concerned about someone without later getting the full explanation of precisely what they were worrying about.

Charley doesn't move when I switch the engine off. The head-lights dim to nothing and we're in the shadow of the hanging, swaying branches from next-door's tree.

'What was the officer going to ask you about?' I say.

'Whether or not I wanted someone to sit outside the house overnight.'

'For security?'

'I guess.'

'Do we need that?'

'No.'

Neither of us talk for a moment and then I force out the words: 'Do you want to talk?'

I so want her to say yes. I wonder if she can sense the begging tone in my voice. It's a while before she responds. I can make out the shape of her face in the gloom but no specific features. I see her lips curve into an O.

'Tomorrow,' she says. 'I promise.' She turns sideways and takes my hand. She's still cold. 'I love you.'

It's the first time either of us have said this since she got back. I wondered if she'd ever say it again. There's a tremble to her voice. Nervousness, perhaps? Apprehension?

But what can you do? Someone says, 'I love you' and, assuming you're not a total arsehole and they're not a lunatic stalker, you say it back. It's the law.

'I love you, too,' I reply.

Charley squeezes my hand. I mean it. The problem is that I am no longer sure about who it is I've married.

THIRTY-FOUR

20 YEARS AGO

Charley Willis, 8 years old

I hear the doors before I hear his voice. Father bangs his way through the house and then his footsteps clatter across the hard floor of the hallway.

'Charlotte? Where are you?'

He's shouting at the top of his voice. '*Look what you've done now,*' is what Mama will be saying if she's anywhere near him. I wonder if I can get away with hiding in the wardrobe. I'm supposed to put all my dirty clothes in the hamper, but there's a little space behind it where I can fit myself. Sometimes, when Mama and Father are shouting as loudly as they can, I squeeze myself inside and cover my ears.

'Charlotte! Get down here now.'

It will only be worse if I try to hide from him, so I creep onto the landing and look over the railing towards him at the bottom. He glares at me, spitting with anger.

'What did I tell you?' he shouts. 'Get down here.'

I want to take my time to try to figure out what I might have done, but the longer it takes to get down the stairs, the angrier he's going to be.

I run down them two at a time, holding onto the rail to make sure I don't fall. When I get to the bottom step, I stop a little out of his reach. Martha left home a few weeks ago. Mama said she wasn't old enough – she's only seventeen – but my sister said she didn't care. Later, she told me she *did* care but that she couldn't take it any longer. Mama called her a selfish bitch, plus more bad words, and she's not been home since.

I stay out of Father's reach as he reels back to show me the back of his hand. I flinch because I know I should. '*He'll never hit you,*' Martha once whispered. '*He'd never risk leaving a mark. Remember that. It's important.*'

Perhaps she's right? He's never hit me, but there are so many times when I think he will.

He sneers as I cower onto the steps.

'What the hell is this?' he shouts.

I'm covering my face with my arm but look underneath my elbow to see a thick stack of papers. I slowly unfurl my arms to see what he's holding.

'I don't know, sir.' I'm careful to remain respectful.

He flips the pages around to show some felt-tip swirls on the back.

'Don't give me that,' he continues. 'Don't you *dare* give me that. What have you got to say for yourself?'

I stammer my reply: 'I thought… I thought it was plain paper. I was trying to draw an elephant.'

He holds up the page high in the air. 'An *elephant*? Have you ever *seen* an elephant? It looks nothing like this. Nothing! Is there something wrong with you?'

'No, sir.'

My father flips the pages around again. There is a page of typed writing on the front. 'Even if we put to one side your appalling lack of artistic ability, how am I supposed to rehearse for this role when you've scribbled all over the back of the script?'

'I'm sorry, sir. I didn't know. I thought it was blank.'

'Why didn't you look?'

'I thought I had.'

He throws the whole stack into the air, letting them fall to the ground. The pages swish and swirl around his feet and mine, some blank side up, some print side up; others showing off my drawings.

'You're going to pick all this up,' he says. 'Then you're going to put everything in order. I don't care how high you can count. You better learn fast. When you've done that – and you *will* do that – you're going to go into the kitchen and stand in the corner facing the wall. Do you understand me?'

'Yes, sir.'

He stares at me, arms behind his back. 'Well? What are you waiting for?'

I spring into action, sweeping up as many pages as I can and twisting them all so they're at least facing the right way. All the while, Father stands and watches. He doesn't say anything specific but tuts and snorts at various intervals.

Father might think I don't know how to count, but I really want to show him I can, to make up for spoiling his papers. It's lucky that a lot of the right numbers are together. Thirteen to nineteen don't need sorting and everything from thirty-two to fifty-one have somehow remained in order. I get a little confused around the 110s, but the task is nowhere near as hard as I thought it would be.

When I hand the script back, Father snorts: 'You took your time.'

I know to be polite and respectful, but I also know there are times when it is better to say nothing. This time, I say nothing.

'Well?' my father adds. 'What are you doing standing in the hall? Why aren't you in the corner?'

I do what he says, heading into the kitchen and the corner close to the back door. I suppose this is my spot. I've spent a lot of time here recently. Sometimes there are spiders that crawl up and down the wall and I like to whisper to them, wondering if they understand. It's not the corner that's the problem, it's the standing up. Sometimes my knees wobble and because I'm not allowed to use the wall to hold myself up, it's really hard to stay standing.

Mama comes into the kitchen after a while – I don't know how long because I can't see the clock when I'm facing the wall. If I were to be caught looking, I'd have to stay for longer.

'Not again,' she says.

'Sorry, Mama.'

'Why can't you behave? You're going to end up like your sister. Is that what you want?'

'No, Mama.'

I can hear her chopping food behind me. Every now and then the fridge will open and close, or the oven will buzz. I know all the noises of the kitchen. My favourite is when the microwave pings. Sometimes, when it's just me in my room, I'll try to copy it. 'Ping!'

Usually I'm allowed to move after a while. Sometimes it's before my knees wobble, sometimes after. It hurts more this time, though. Perhaps I've been here a lot longer, but I can feel my legs starting to twitch. I hope she won't notice, but…

'Stand up straight,' Mama scolds.

'Sorry, Mama.'

I manage to do as I'm told but not for long. I don't know why people's bodies don't do what they're told. I don't want my legs to wobble, so why do they? It's quite naughty of them, really. Perhaps that's why *I'm* so naughty?

'Straight!'

I try to do what Mama says, I really do, but my legs won't do what I want. It feels like I need to sit and, even though I don't want to, a small whimper escapes from my mouth.

'Stop snivelling!'

'Sorry. It's just… I really need the toilet, Mama.'

'You were told to stand in the corner.'

'I'll come right back, Mama. Honest I will.'

'You'll do as you're told.'

It's so hard, but I have to touch the wall. I'm going to fall over otherwise.

'What are you doing?' Mama asks.

'Please. I can't stand any more. Please.'

'Are you defying your parents?'

'No, Mama. No. I want to stand.'

'Then do it.'

I take my hand from the wall and somehow, I don't know how, I do manage to stand. I close my eyes and think about other things. About going back to school, or being allowed to watch television on Saturday mornings and how much fun that is.

'This is for your own good. There's no way I'm having you turn out like your sister.'

'I know, Mama. I know.'

It's like this is magic me. There was a me who couldn't stand any longer and now there's a me who can. Like I've got new legs.

I'm not sure why it happens, perhaps because I was thinking of other things. I wasn't thinking about why I was being punished, so I probably deserve it, but my leg is suddenly warm and wet. I don't even know what it is at first. I think perhaps I've spilled a drink, I'm always doing that. But then I realise I'm doing a wee on myself. I'm doing a wee with my clothes on. The warm and the wet spreads lower down my leg and then it's on the floor. There's a puddle that's spreading around my feet.

I don't know why it happens, but I'm crying. It's not like I mean to and I try to bite my tongue, like Martha does, to hold it all in. I can't do it like she can, though, and then I'm crying.

'You're not standing up straight,' Mama says. I wonder if she knows I've gone number one on the floor, but she must do. 'Straight!'

Time passes. I don't risk looking at the clock, but there's a point where it feels like I can't cry any longer. Mama always says that crying is a waste of time. I'm not going to get my own way, so why do it? So I stop. It's like an order I give myself. Stop crying now, and I do.

I can smell food, but Mama doesn't offer me anything. She turns off the kitchen lights and then I can hear her voice in the dining room with Father. Everything's dark, but perhaps I could turn and squint at the clock. Except… what if someone sees?

More time passes. I'm actually quite good at standing up straight. Mama would be proud. If my stupid knees hadn't wobbled in the first place, if I didn't touch the wall, I'd have been allowed to move by now. It's all my stupid legs' fault.

The light comes on and there are footsteps. Father's, I think. His sound different to Mama's.

'You think the world revolves around you, don't you, young lady.'

It is my father. I thought it was. He doesn't sound angry any longer. It's his disappointed voice.

'No, sir,' I reply.

'Let me tell you something: it doesn't. You will learn respect. Do you understand me?'

'Yes, sir.'

He doesn't reply and I wonder if he's waiting for me to say something.

'Father?' I say.

'Yes.'

'I'm sorry.'

'Your apology is not accepted, Charlotte.'

'Please can I go to bed, sir?'

He doesn't say anything at first and I bite my tongue, trying to make my legs stay straight. *Please*. I don't say it out loud. *Please don't wobble*. I think the words so loudly that I wonder if other people might hear them anyway.

'No,' he says firmly. 'You will stand in the corner until I say otherwise – and do not think that just because it's dark you can lie on the floor. If I find you in any position other than standing where you are now, there will be absolute hell to pay. Do you understand me?'

I try not to cry. 'I do, sir.'

He turns the light off and then it's quiet. More time passes.

Sometimes I hear the odd sound from upstairs. A voice or a laugh. I don't know. My tricks aren't working any longer. I can't make my legs obey and so I have to be naughty. I lean on the wall and sit on the step. I try to keep my feet out of the puddle, but it's all over my shoes and starting to smell.

It's hard to keep my eyes open, but I have to. A couple of times, I think I hear a squeak from the steps so I jump back into position. I wonder if Father knows. Or Mama? Sometimes Father says he has eyes in the back of his head, or that he knows what I'm thinking. Perhaps he does?

After all, I try not to be naughty, but it's no good. I guess it's just who I am.

THIRTY-FIVE

SETH. NOW

Charley and I sleep on opposite sides of the bed, facing away from each other. I guess it's the opposite of spooning. Forking? I don't know what it should be called.

I lie awake and listen to her breathing, waiting for her intakes of air to deepen and lengthen.

It doesn't happen.

Or it probably does, but I'm asleep first.

It's the first time I've slept in a bed since Friday – five nights – and the next thing I know, I'm jumping awake. I don't remember the dream, it was there and it's gone, but the clock tells me it's seven o'clock.

'Shush…'

Charley is there. She holds my hand, squeezes it. 'I'm here,' she coos.

And she is.

She brushes the hair from my face and kisses me on the forehead. Her fingers slide along the curve of my cheek as I blink up towards her. I remember seeing her in the shop for the very first time. The way she smiled when she said I couldn't have soup. I think I knew then we'd end up getting married.

'How long have you been awake?' I ask.

'A while.'

'What have you been doing?'

'Watching you sleep. You were so peaceful…'

'I've not really been sleeping.'

She cups my chin with her hand and kisses me on the lips. Our first proper kiss since she got back. Since after the registrar said we were officially man and wife.

'I was abducted,' she says.

After the hours, the worry, the questions… after everything, it's as simple as that. Three words. Charley speaks so matter-of-factly that it's as if she's describing a normal day at work. *Ran out of soy milk, customer left an umbrella, saw a man with the most ridiculous wig I've ever seen.*

'Abducted?'

I'm like a parrot with a sore throat, but what else can I say?

'I was in the corridor near those doors at the back. Someone tapped me on the shoulder and when I turned, there was a man in one of those scream masks. I thought it was some sort of joke. There was that other wedding party and I didn't know if it was some theme…'

She reaches for a glass of water on the side that she must have fetched while I was sleeping. She sips and then offers it to me. I shake my head and she returns it where it came from.

'He had a knife,' she says. 'He told me to go outside. I still thought it was some sort of joke. I thought it was Raj or someone. Then he handed me this hood thing. He told me to put it on and then he pushed me into what I think was probably a van. I don't know.'

Although I'm under the covers, I'm shivering. Or I think I am. Charley is stroking my hair.

'We drove for miles,' she says. 'I was in the back, but he'd tied the hood. I could breathe but was getting bumped and banged around every time we went over a pothole or whatever.'

'When were you in the corridor?'

She blinks at me. 'Sorry?'

'When the guy in the mask was there. Mum said she saw you.'

Charley squints and her fingers have stopped massaging my scalp. 'I don't think I saw her.'

We look at each other and I realise I have no idea what she's thinking. I wonder if she believes I've just questioned her story when all I was doing was worrying about my mother.

'He kept me on a farm somewhere,' Charley says. 'Or a garden, like one of those really big ones that some people have out here. I'm not sure. I told the police I didn't know. I was in this shed-type thing and it smelled bad every now and then. Like when you're driving along and the wind changes.'

'You were in a shed?'

She nods. 'He brought me food every morning and evening, but he made me wear the hood every time.'

'So you never saw him?'

'Never. He left me some clothes, basic stuff – jeans and a top, nothing fancy – but he took the wedding dress.'

'They found it. I had to identify it.'

'I know. The police told me. I'm sorry.'

She removes her hand and I want to tell her she has nothing to be sorry for. I want to, I really do – but she's already moved on.

'He asked me questions about my mum and dad.'

'What questions?'

'I don't really remember. He'd make me wear the hood and then he'd sit and talk to me, He'd want me to tell him normal things that people already know. What their names were, whether I had brothers and sisters, what it was like growing up… that sort of thing.'

'Why?'

It's such a stupid question that I immediately apologise.

'He never said,' Charley whispers anyway. 'The police asked if I'd ever had a stalker. I'd never thought about it until they asked.'

'Had you?'

There's a second or two in which I think she's going to say yes, that there's a whole chunk of her life about which we've never spoken.

She shakes her head. 'No. They said sometimes people can develop an obsession with others, even though they've never met.'

'Is that what they think happened?'

'I don't know.' Charley sits up straighter. 'Can we go downstairs and get some breakfast?'

I'm in such a daze that I'd do pretty much do anything she asked. It's one thing after another. Man in a mask, knife, van, farm, shed, stalker, breakfast. What on earth? This isn't the type of thing that happens to people like us. We keep to ourselves. We work locally, watch TV in the evenings like anyone else. Somehow we've ended up in another world.

Charley dresses with her back to me and I find myself watching, looking for scars or scrapes. Her shoulders and back are smooth and clear. When she catches me watching, she says nothing. She continues getting dressed and then squeezes my hand on the way to the stairs.

When I get to the kitchen, she already has bread in the toaster and the kettle is fizzing away. We make aimless ridiculous small talk about butter and Marmite, about needing to buy instant coffee. I don't care about any of it because the voice at the back of my mind is screaming for the rest of the answers.

Charley is so calm that I wonder whether she's in shock. I don't know enough about it, but it's the thing everyone says, as if that explains it all. She makes toast for me and then herself, plus two cups of coffee. Then we sit and eat together, as if this is all perfectly normal.

She rinses the plates and leaves them to dry as we head into the living room. Charley takes the sofa and I'm on the lounger. There's silence for a long while, me not daring to ask. Where to begin? What to ask?

'Do you want to know the rest?' she asks and it's like the silliest question ever.

My answer is there and gone and I don't even know what it was. The sentiment was 'hell, yeah'.

'I thought I was going mad,' she says. 'I was in there by myself all day. I'd make up games like counting the grooves in each piece of wood. Sometimes I didn't know if I was awake or asleep. There wasn't a bed, I only had the floor. The only time anything changed was when he knocked. He'd tell me to put on the hood and then he'd wait. I think he could see me. One time I didn't put it on and he wouldn't come in until I had. That's when he'd bring food and ask the questions.'

'Did you recognise the voice?'

Charley shakes her head. 'No… just a man's. The police asked a lot of questions about accents, but I don't know. I think I stopped listening properly.'

'Did he… touch you?'

It might be a quirk of timing, of me asking at the wrong moment, but there's a fraction of a second where it looks like Charley is trying to hide behind her mug.

'No.'

There's a small silence between us and I wonder if I have any right to ask. It's not like she's my property. Is this the sort of rampant misogyny some people are accused of when they ask what they believe to be an innocent question? Have I crossed some feminist line?

What would I have said if she'd replied that he had touched her? Would it change anything? It's not me who was taken and yet I feel numb.

'Did he let you go?'

'I tried the door one time and it was open. I'd pressed against it loads of times but it hadn't moved. It was like a reflex to try. I pushed it and then it opened.'

'Just like that?'

'I guess. He must have forgotten to lock it.'

'Where were you?'

'I don't know. It was dark. The moon was out. I wasn't going to poke around to get a proper look – I just ran. Next thing I know, I'm in the woods. There are all these snaps and creaks coming from the shadows. I'm trying to tell myself it's from squirrels, nothing serious, and yet I keep thinking of the scream mask, so I keep running and running.' She points to her eye. 'It's where I got this. I tripped over a log or something and landed face first. I don't even know what did it, probably a rock or something, but I got up and kept going. I was running for ages. I was so tired. Then I was on a road. I didn't know which way to go, so I picked right and carried on running.' She presses her lips together, not quite a smile. 'I guess all those gym classes paid off.'

'How did you get here?'

'The sun came up. I was still running, but then I thought maybe whoever it was would drive past and see me. I cut through a hedge onto this field and kept moving. The next thing I know, I realised where I was because there was a road sign for the town. I keep going, thinking someone might stop at any minute. And then, I don't know… I guess I'm here. I knock and there's no one in, so I go round the back and use the hidden key.'

She takes a really deep breath and squeezes her eyes closed.

'You know the rest because—' Charley stops herself mid-sentence and peers out towards the street. Her head dips. 'They're here,' she says.

I think police, men in masks, but it's none of that. The reporters are back.

THIRTY-SIX

I don't have a chance to move before my phone starts to ring. Pamela the publicist. Charley is frozen in her seat as I take the call. There are no particular niceties this time.

'Can I speak to Charley?' she asks.

'How do you know she's here?'

'Everybody knows.'

I mute the call and turn to my wife. 'It's the publicist your brother recommended. She wants to talk to you. I can tell her to get lost if you want…?'

Charley reaches out and takes my phone. I only hear one half of the conversation, but it doesn't last long anyway. 'Tomorrow,' Charley says. There's a pause and then: 'No, I'm not doing it today. If people harass me, I'm not doing it at all. Tomorrow.' One more break. 'No – only then. I'll do whatever you want tomorrow and that's it. I'm not doing anything today and I'm not doing anything after tomorrow. One day. I don't care about the rest. Do whatever you need.'

She listens as Pamela says something else and then hangs up before passing me back my phone.

'I've got to get my own phone,' she says.

'What happened to yours?'

She shakes her head. 'I don't know. I guess he took it. I thought I had it on me.'

I thumb my way through to the correct screen and then hold it up for Charley to see.

'Two hundred and four missed calls?' She's smiling. 'Is that how much you love me?' she asks. 'How long was I away? I would have expected at least three hundred.'

She laughs at her own joke but I don't know when I'll laugh again. I'm finding it hard to breathe properly, as if I can never quite take in enough oxygen at once.

'What were you saying about tomorrow?' I ask.

Charley clambers up, crosses to the window and pulls the curtains. She switches the lights on before sitting again. 'Pamela said she's got offers streaming in.'

'Is that what you want?'

It takes her a while to reply. Charley fidgets and fusses, sips her coffee. Looks anywhere except at me. 'It's the only way they'll go away,' she says. 'I've been here before and said no to things. If I'd said yes, perhaps they'd have gone away for good.'

I'm not so sure about any of that. It's true they left *me* alone after the interview – but I'm not Charley. I'm not the story. My parents weren't national treasures.

'Are they offering money?' I ask.

'That's what Pamela says.'

'And that's what you want?'

There's a moment where we look to each other and I'm not sure I know who she is. It's never been about money. Not once.

'They're going to keep coming back until I say something anyway, so I may as well get something out of it. I can put it away for Dillon and Daisy.'

'Do you think we should ask that Fiona what she thinks?'

'Who?'

'The family liaison officer. She—'

'No.' Charley shakes her head vigorously. 'I'm done with the police. I'll do the interviews tomorrow and then I'm done with the media, too. I want to forget everything.'

'What about a trial?'

Charley's eyes narrow. She's so hard to read. 'What trial?'

'If they find out whoever took you. What then? You'll have to deal with the police and media then.'

'That's different.'

I want to argue but, really, I don't think I have it in me. I guess it's not my decision anyway. I wasn't the one who was taken. This isn't about me.

The pair of us turn as there's a sound of something scrabbling at the back of the house. It sounds like a cat scratching at a locked cat flap.

We don't have a cat.

'If that's one of those damned reporters…'

I fly up off the sofa and for the first time since I woke up, I am furious. I race into the kitchen, unlocking the back door and wrenching it open, ready to do who knows what.

The person at the door leaps away as I pull it inwards.

She yelps. 'Oh!'

It's not a reporter at all, it's Alice.

She blinks at me, surprised. 'Is it true?' she asks.

Charley slots in at my side and then edges past me, stepping onto the back patio, where the two women embrace.

'You're back…?' Alice whispers the words as if she's not too sure.

'I'm back.'

They release each other and Charley leads Alice into the house. I poke my head out to make sure there are no interlopers in the garden and then lock everything back up. I close the kitchen blind for good measure.

In the living room, the two women are on the sofa together. 'I saw the crowd out front, so parked round the corner,' Alice says. 'I had to climb over a hedge to get into your garden. I'm so glad you're safe. Is everything all right…?'

I know exactly what Alice is asking and it's not specifically whether her friend is well. There's the implicit undercurrent that I had of wanting to know everything that happened.

Charley shakes her head, bows slightly. 'I can't talk about it again. I've been over it twice already. I'm sorry…'

Alice reaches out and squeezes Charley's hand. 'Oh, honey, the fact you're back is the main thing.' She delves into her bag and pulls out a mobile phone. 'I thought you might need this,' she says. 'It's my old one. I got one of those pay-and-go SIM cards from the newsagent. You might have to register online; I don't know.'

Charley takes the device and turns it over, examining the screen. It's a bit scratched from pockets and bags but would probably get a few quid on eBay.

I check my own phone and there are texts from Emily, Raj and a couple of other people, asking if Charley really is back. I tap out a few quick responses and then turn it off. Today is not a day for interruptions.

'What do you want to do today?' I ask.

Charley doesn't look as if the thought of doing something has entered her mind.

'We can visit Mason if you want?' I suggest.

She glances towards the window and the unwanted attention beyond. 'I just want everything to go back to normal,' she says.

There's a moment in which Alice and I share a look of mutual understanding. For Charley, for her friends, for me, there is no normal after this.

THIRTY-SEVEN

17 YEARS AGO

Charley Willis, 11 years old

'What the hell have you done to your arms?'

Martha grins at Mama as she turns sideways to show off the tattoos. There are spikes and swirls twisting around her wrist and climbing up towards her elbow. 'Don't you like them?' she asks. 'It's not finished yet. I think I'm going to have it all the way up to my shoulder.'

I know she's doing this to make Mama angry. It works.

Mama turns around from the cooker. 'You look like a slut,' she says.

I don't know what a slut is, but it makes Martha smile. 'Thank you. That's exactly the look I was going for.'

I'm sitting in the corner by the back door, peeping around the fridge. I wonder if they know I'm in the kitchen with them. Mama definitely did, but she probably forgot I was here.

Just as I think I might have been forgotten, Martha spins and looks at me. She's cut her hair since I last saw her. It's short and black. Far darker than when she lived here. Her tattoos are so bright and colourful that, even though I know I should hate them – Mama does – there's a part of me that wants to touch her skin to find out if the shapes can be felt.

'Hey, Charley,' she says.

Mama peers around Martha towards me and gives me the look she does when she would rather I wasn't around.

'It's *Charlotte*,' Mama says.

'Whatcha up to?' Martha asks.

'Watching Mama,' I say.

Martha looks between us, but I'm not sure why. I want to ask about the tattoos, perhaps even see if Martha will let me touch her arm, but I don't think Mama would like that.

Mama looks even more annoyed and I'm not sure if it's with me. I think it might be Martha. She takes hold of my sister's arm and spins her around. 'Will you stop trying to drag your sister into your sordid little world.'

'Take your hands off me.'

They stare at each other for a couple of seconds and I wonder if one might end up hitting the other. Mama says Martha is a bad influence.

Mama lets go of my sister's wrist and then turns back to the cooker.

'If you want your money, you're going to lose that attitude, young lady.'

'I'm twenty years old, you senile hag. Don't call me "young lady".'

Mama spins again. She's holding a wooden spoon. She ignores Martha, looking at me instead. 'Do you see what I keep telling you, Charlotte. This is what you'll turn into if you don't listen to your father and me.'

Martha shakes her head and turns to me as well. 'That's a lie. *I'm* what you'll turn into if you listen to these two egomaniacs.'

'*Martha!*'

They glare at one another again, then Mama grinds her teeth together and speaks while barely moving her lips. It's scary when she does this.

'You listen to me, *young lady*. Pamela went out of her way to set this up and you're going to do as you're told. You are *going* to smile. You're *going* to be polite. If the reporter asks you something, you will give a thoughtful and considerate answer that I would approve of.' She points to Martha's arm. 'And you're going to cover that up, too. Some of your old clothes are upstairs. Go and find something with long sleeves.'

'What if I don't?'

'Then don't. Go away – but don't ever expect any more help from your father and me. Don't think we don't know about what you get up to in that hovel of yours. The drinking, the boys. If you're going to act like a drunken whore, the least you could do is not get pictured doing it.'

They stare at each other again. They're pretty much the same height, so they're eye to eye. It's so horrible that it makes me shiver. I don't want them to argue.

Martha eventually turns and leaves the kitchen. I hear her stomping up the stairs in a way that would get me in trouble.

Mama lets out a loud breath and looks to me. 'Is that what you want to turn into?' she says.

'No,' I reply, knowing that is what she'll want to hear.

'Sooner or later, that girl is going to bring shame on this family and she doesn't even care.'

'She's naughty, Mama.'

Mama is wagging the spoon in my direction, but she finally smiles. It's not a big one but it is for me. 'She is.'

I like it when Mama smiles for me.

After that, Mama turns back to the cooker. She takes a tray of roast potatoes from the oven and lays it on the side. They're bubbling away, the smell filling the kitchen. Roast potatoes are my favourite. Mama sounds like she's in a good mood because she's humming to herself.

It doesn't last long because Martha storms back through the kitchen door. She's wearing a cardigan over her vest-top.

'Happy?' she asks, sounding angry.

Mama points to Martha's chest. 'You can do something about that, too.'

'They're breasts, Mum. What do you want me to do about them?'

'Cover them up. The magazine wants photographs of us acting as a family and I'd really like it if my eldest daughter didn't look like she should be hanging around on a street corner.'

'I'm thinking about getting my nipples pierced. Do you think I should tell your reporter that?'

'Don't you—'

I'm not sure what happens then because there's a really strong pain in my stomach. It's like someone is poking a knife into me really hard. I don't mean to, but I let out a little cry.

'What's wrong?' Martha asks.

'My stomach hurts.' I'm bending over so that I'm almost folded in half. It helps make the knives go away.

Martha comes and sits next to me on the floor. 'Has this been happening a lot?'

'Every day.'

Mama bangs the spoon on the side of the oven and then wags it in my direction. 'For God's sake, Charlotte. You're such a drama queen. Why do you always have to make everything about you? Time and time again, you do the same thing. There was that time when we had Ted and Veronica over and you wet the bed. Then your father was getting that award and you thought it would be a good idea to be sick in the car.'

She smashes the spoon onto the cooker once more.

I don't even remember wetting the bed. Mama talks about it all the time, so it must have happened. I've said sorry, but she keeps bringing it up.

Martha's fingers are cold as she touches my middle gently, asking where it hurts. She turns back to Mama.

'This could be a kidney stone,' she says.

'It's not a kidney stone,' Mama replies.

'How do you know?'

'Because Charlotte does this all the time. Something is going on in the family and she'll try to make it about her.'

Martha holds my hand and bites her tongue. There's a small stud through it and I wonder if Mama knows.

'Perhaps you should take her to a doctor,' Martha says.

'Oh, go away, Martha. Go and sit upstairs until the reporter gets here. You don't live here, so you don't know what your sister's like. The only thing you know about the medical profession is where to get the morning-after pill.'

Martha squeezes my hand and stands. I can feel her trembling. 'You are such a bitch,' she says. And then she walks out of the room.

Mama continues stirring whatever she's stirring. I can see her shaking with rage. I really want to hide, but the knives are still stabbing into my stomach. Mama waits until Martha has gone.

'You know the blue dress in your wardrobe…?' she says.

I'm not even sure Mama is talking to me because she's doesn't turn around.

'Charlotte? I'm talking to you.'

It's hard to speak, but I grit my teeth and try to sound normal. 'Sorry, Mama. Yes, Mama. I know the dress.'

'I want you to put that on. Wear those flat black ballet shoes you have. Comb your hair and then you can come back downstairs and lay the table. Okay?'

'Yes, Mama.'

I do what I'm told, but my stomach is still hurting. It's hard to stand at first. I try to use Martha's trick of biting my tongue and also my wall trick of closing my eyes and thinking of something else. It's really hard and there's a time where I have to bend over and touch my toes to make the pain go away. I do manage it, though. I have a glass of water from the bathroom and everything feels better.

It's not long after I finish laying the table that the doorbell sounds and Mama tells Martha, Father and me to be ready.

Even though I've put my dress on, the writer is wearing jeans – which Mama has told me in the past is disrespectful. She is carrying a big bag and has a notepad and pen with her. She says her name is Samantha and is really smiley. She knows my name and calls me pretty, which is nice of her. I try to smile back but it hurts because of my stomach.

Samantha and Mama talk about photographs and they agree that pictures should be taken before we have tea. Samantha says she has a friend outside and it's a man with a really big camera. He has keys attached to his belt and they jangle every time he walks.

It's really hard not to make any noises because my stomach is hurting so much, but I think I manage it. The photographer takes lots of photos of us all together. He starts with us at the table, ready to eat, then he takes us into the reading room and makes us all sit around as if we're reading a different book each. Mama gives me an Enid Blyton story and tells Samantha how it used to be hers when she was my age.

We take more photos in the garden and more again in the living room. Each time, the photographer says things like, 'Can you move your arm out a little bit, Charlotte?' I do what he says, but Mama has a look in her eyes that tells me she isn't happy.

The photographer eventually says he has enough pictures and then Mama goes into the kitchen to serve our food. Samantha gets to sit at the head of the table, which is usually Father's spot. This is the first time Martha has eaten with us in a long time. She visits on Saturdays or Sundays sometimes, but Mama says it's only ever because she wants something. Martha once told me it's because she wants to make sure I'm all right, but I don't know who to believe.

Mama has made a full roast dinner, which is my absolute favourite. She tells Samantha it is the type of thing she has put in her new cookbook, which is called *British Classics*. Mama talks about her book a lot. She's written another one with Father – but I can't remember what that one's called. I won't tell her that, though.

Martha is acting really strangely. I've never heard her say 'please' so many times before, let alone 'thank you'. Samantha asks her what life is like now and Martha says things are good and that she's trying to figure out what she wants to be. Mama smiles and says she supports her daughter, but the funny thing is that I've heard them arguing about this before. Mama will say Martha is a freeloader – whatever that means – and Martha replies that she can do what she wants.

Father doesn't say a lot. He's wearing a suit and talks about the book he's written with Mama. Samantha then turns to me and asks if I'm aware of how famous my parents are. I repeat the lines Mama told me to say, that 'they will always be Mum and Dad to me'. I have to remember to say 'Mum and Dad' instead of 'Mama and Father' and nearly forget.

Samantha says it's really sweet and asks what I want to be when I grow up. Mama had given me a list of questions she thought Samantha might ask and then made me remember each of the answers I was allowed to give. We've spent the past week going over them again and again. She wouldn't let me go to bed last night because I kept getting words wrong.

'I want to be just like my mum,' I say. Mama smiles at me. *For* me. She's happy. Samantha writes something on her pad and says that's very nice.

I'm hoping she's going to ask some more questions because I spent such a long time learning what to say. It makes me a bit sad that she starts talking to Mama instead.

Everything is going really well, but I am only halfway through finishing my plate when my stomach starts to hurt so badly that I think I need to scream. It feels like someone is pinching my side, digging their fingers into my front and back so hard.

'May I be excused, please?' I ask.

Mama is halfway through a sentence, but she turns to look at me instead of Samantha. There is a moment where her eyebrows dip in the middle and I think she might shout. It's only there for a second and then she smiles at me.

'Of course you can, Charlotte.'

I slide out from the chair, being really careful not to make it squeak. Father hates that. As soon as I'm in the hall, I run for the toilet. I don't know why it's happening now, but I know I'm going to be sick. Mama says it's dirty, but I can't stop myself. I kneel over the toilet and then my stomach starts to squeeze. It's in my chest, then my throat and then I feel the lumpy, sludgy goo covering my lips before splashing into the toilet. It happens three times before I'm able to sit back on my knees.

It's hard to breathe and the smell is horrible. I've also got a bit of sick on the top of my dress and Mama is going to be so angry with me.

Before I can think of what to do, there's a knock on the door and then Mama hisses my name. I manage to reach across and unlock it before she pushes it open.

She looks at me and then turns to the toilet bowl.

'I can't believe you're doing this now, Charlotte,' she says.

'I'm sorry, Mama. I tried not to.'

She lowers her voice to a hiss: 'Don't you know how important this interview is?'

'I'm really sorry.'

'Time and time and time again, you try to make things about you, don't you?'

'It was my stomach, Mama.'

'I don't care what it was. You're going to go upstairs and don't even think about coming down. I'm going to have to say you were feeling tired, or something.'

She takes a small step backwards and looks along the hallway and then turns back to me.

She leans in really close so that we're eye to eye. I don't think her lips move but she speaks anyway. 'You really are a horrible child, aren't you? I wish you'd never been born.'

THIRTY-EIGHT

SETH. NOW

Pamela the publicist is treating Charley as if they are long-lost friends. We get the full rigmarole of 'I remember when you were *this* high', 'Oh, you poor dear' and 'Do you know, I first met your mother when she was still at Butlin's', and so on.

Charley told me yesterday that she doesn't ever remember meeting Pamela before.

Diane Young arrives a little after nine in the morning and then it's a whirlwind of action. There's a specialist make-up artist who leaves Charley looking utterly unlike herself. Her look, if you can say she has one, is natural and generally untouched.

Not now.

She looks like she might at Hallowe'en and the only part of her face they haven't painted is her eye. If anything, it's darker than it was yesterday and I wonder if they've blackened it further.

'New look,' she says to me quietly when we're alone in the kitchen.

'I don't like it,' I reply.

'Me either.'

It's only a fleeting moment before somebody comes in to drag her off for a chat with Diane.

I'm a spare part and though I don't really mind, there's still a part of me that feels fairly put out. I do live here, after all.

With little else to do, I find a spot on the stairs. Engineer types run back and forth along the hallway, carrying cables and equipment, while I read some of the news stories.

Alice stayed for a while yesterday and talked to Charley about shop stuff. Charley seemed to think she'd be back at work by Monday at the latest, but Alice said she'd get one of her friends to help her out for at least a week. After that, Charley and I spent the day together. There didn't seem much point in leaving the house to potentially be followed, so we closed the curtains and watched television.

I don't think either of us was particularly paying attention.

I wonder when regular, everyday things will begin to feel normal again. It seems a long way off.

We've not heard any updates from the police, but the news websites are reporting that the police are looking for a man with a local accent. That seems to be the only new thing they have. There is some insinuating that the person who abducted Charley could be the person who killed her parents. Because the police haven't made any sort of link, the official reports can't say as much, but that doesn't stop people in the comments sections. Some columnist has written a comment piece wondering, 'Why can't the Willis family be happy?'

Pamela finds me in the end. She's at the bottom of the stairs as calm as ever. 'They're starting if you want to come and watch,' she says.

'Is that a good idea?'

'Charley's asking for you.'

I'm not sure why that takes me by surprise but it does.

I follow Pamela back through the house into the living room, which has been redressed in much the same way it had been when Diane was interviewing me. The smart seats are back and so is our framed wedding photo. Charley gives me a small smile as I sit on the sofa at the far end of the room. With the lights, camera and equipment, plus Diane, Pamela, Charley, me and two cameramen, the room feels very full and very warm.

Diane starts with yet another recap of Charley's history and my own interview. Then she leans in and softens her voice. 'Would you like to tell everyone what happened to you?'

Charley does, repeating the story she told me yesterday. Not looking like herself is one thing – but she doesn't sound like herself either. It feels like she's going through the motions. Some of the things she says are word-for-word what she told me. Not similar, not using a couple of the same words, but identical.

Diane doesn't know this, of course. She's at her absolute heart-wrenching best, leaving the most perfect of pauses to punctuate what Charley is saying.

Pamela is enraptured by it all and hasn't touched her phone since the interview began. It's the longest I've seen her last without tapping out an email.

After the television interview, Charley will have a sit-down with someone from a magazine, then a pair of newspaper journalists. One after the other, just like she wanted.

The problem is that no one's questioning the obvious stuff. Or perhaps the police are, but they're not ready for another cross-examination yet. I've heard the story twice and had plenty of time to think about everything she said since the first time.

A man planned well enough ahead to bring a knife to our wedding, meaning he knew when and where we were going to get married. But how? We only invited a small number of people and didn't post anything publicly precisely because Charley didn't want the media to pick up on it.

That same person knew about the hotel and the service exit. He was careful enough to wear a mask at first and then make her wear a hood to hide his identity… and yet he left a shed door unlocked.

He gave Charley clothes to change into, took her wedding dress… and then left it in a bush where it would be found. I've been trying to think of a reason why. Perhaps it was to push the blame onto someone else? Or make the police look for her in an area away from where she actually was.

I'm sure there *is* an explanation, but I've not thought of something that feels right.

Then there's the big question.

Why?

There was no ransom demand, no robbery. He didn't touch her. Didn't hit her.

Didn't *kill* her.

So why?

Diane doesn't ask any of those questions. I don't blame her – it's not why she's here and it's not the story she's trying to tell. This is all 'my hell' and the family curse. It's the same thing that's been peddled for fifteen years.

I've not really been listening, but then the big question comes from Diane. She removes her glasses for maximum earnestness. 'I'm sorry to ask you this, Charley, but do you think the person who abducted you could possibly be the same person who broke into your house all those years ago?'

Charley bites her tongue and then gulps. It takes her a couple of seconds to answer. When she does, her voice is solemn, her gaze distant.

'I really don't know.'

THIRTY-NINE

Charley spends most of the day repeating her story to the journalists Pamela has picked out. It's one after the other, once over tea while the TV crew were packing away; then in the garden as the sun shines high.

We eat together in the evening – Emily's spaghetti – and avoid talking about anything to do with what happened. Charley starts a conversation about perhaps going on holiday in a couple of weeks, bringing forward the honeymoon. She spends some time online looking for destinations, but we don't make any decisions.

I can't remember what was on television, but we definitely watched something. We didn't talk about whatever it was. I ask Charley if she wants to watch Diane's programme, but she doesn't. 'I'm done with that,' she replies.

We sleep in the same bed, but it is forks again. Her on one side, me on the other. I don't know what to say to her.

The following morning marks a week since we married. A week since Charley disappeared. I'm awake first and leave her sleeping, heading downstairs to put the kettle on. The fancy furniture of the day before has gone, as has the framed wedding photo. I don't know who took it. It might even be in a cupboard somewhere.

Charley comes down at a few minutes after nine, still in her pyjamas. She offers a sleepy 'morning' and then we hug in the kitchen, making small talk about whether we slept well. The death of conversation.

We're interrupted by the doorbell, which is something of a relief. I'm hoping it's Alice or Emily, someone to help the conversation along, but it's the family liaison officer, Fiona.

She doesn't hang around.

'We've arrested someone,' she says.

Charley is resting against the sink and stares back all the way along the hallway, open-mouthed. 'You've arrested someone?'

'I can't give any further details at the moment, but I'm hoping we can take you to see something.'

'Where?'

'We want to take you to a site.'

'For what?'

'I think it's best if we simply go there…'

Charley is stunned to the point that she seems unable to speak.

Fiona comes into the house, along the hall into the kitchen. 'Are you all right?' she asks.

Charley stumbles her reply, saying that it's a bit of a shock, before clearing her throat. She's using the sink to hold herself up. 'When do you need me?' she asks.

'As soon as possible.'

It takes her another couple of seconds, but Charley finally clicks into gear, saying she'll get changed and heading upstairs.

Fiona and I are alone in the kitchen and we listen until the footsteps on the stairs have stopped.

'Looks like you had a busy day yesterday,' Fiona says.

'She wanted to get it all out of the way. She says that's it now, no more interviews.'

A nod. 'Our media team weren't too happy.'

'I'm not the person to tell.'

I wait to see if Fiona is going to say anything else. When she doesn't, I ask if they've really got their man.

'I don't want to say too much,' Fiona replies.

'But you must have a reason to arrest someone…?'

'We do.'

That's all she'll say on the matter.

'Can I come, too?' I ask.

'I don't see why not – but it's up to your wife.'

Charley reappears not long after, having changed into shorts, a fitted T-shirt and walking boots. She doesn't mind me going with her and so we both end up in the back of a police 4x4 heading out of town. Fiona is in the passenger seat and it's then I notice the driver is DS Stanley. The detective slows as we move away from the housing estates and shops into the vast carpets of green.

'I'd like you to pay attention to the surrounding area,' Fiona says. 'If there's anything you recognise – a gate, a tree, a ditch – anything, you should say so.'

Charley fixes herself to look out the window as we trawl along the back roads like a pensioner on a Sunday afternoon. I recognise odd junctions and signs, but it is proper backcountry territory as we head along rocky tracks and trails, bumping our way up gravelly hills and then lurching from side to side on the way back down.

There are a couple of occasions where I know we're repeating ourselves, taking the same paths, the same roads.

Charley is silent and so is Fiona. DS Stanley seemingly knows where she is going, taking the various twists and turns without instruction. She hasn't spoken yet.

We drive for more than an hour, but it's hard to figure out how far we've actually gone. It might be thirty or forty miles in total – but I don't think we've gone more than perhaps ten miles from the house.

That was the other thing with Charley's story. If she effectively walked and ran home over the course of a night, then she couldn't have been that far away, especially if she spent some of her time running in circles around a wooded area.

There are plenty of woods circling the town, some small, others vast and largely untouched. From Charley's description of her escape, I'd imagine the police would easily be able to put together a map of possible places she was kept. It would have to be within ten, perhaps fifteen miles of our house; close to woods that would be dark at night without a built-up area nearby.

We are seemingly exploring all of it.

It's a long while before Fiona twists and fights her seat belt to turn towards the back seat. 'Anything?' she asks.

Charley shakes her head. 'I don't think so.'

'Do you recognise any of the junctions?'

'Only the one I told you about at the station. Nothing today.' She pauses and then adds: 'It was dark.'

We eventually loop back towards the town, picking up speed on the A-roads until we take another turn onto a single lane road that is banked high on both sides by towering, overgrown hedges. Sergeant Stanley hasn't bothered to slow this time, accelerating until we reach a rather ominous sign.

Astley Farm Shop.

We bump over a cattle grid, through a pair of thick concrete pillars and then we're on the farm. Charley's dress was found in a hedge somewhere close to here.

The farm shop is a small building off to the side of a barn. There's an A-frame sandwich board at the front advertising pheasant and venison for sale. There are wisps of straw and hay across the ground and then a paved driveway leading to a sprawling house and garden. Beyond that are acres of fields, with trees on the horizon. The unmistakable smell of animal waste hangs in the air.

When the vehicle stops, Fiona clicks off her seat belt and climbs out. Charley is in a state of bewilderment, remaining still in her seat, staring through the window to the farm beyond. Fiona opens the back door and then the prickles begin at the back of my neck.

'Are you all right?' Fiona asks.

Charley unclicked her seat belt. 'I, um…'

'It's okay to be apprehensive.'

Fiona helps her down and they round the vehicle until they're the same side as me and DS Stanley – who finally speaks, acknowledging me with a frosty 'morning'. The hairs on my neck are standing on end.

It was only a few days ago that Jan Astley was in the papers talking about how he'd found the wedding dress, saying that we 'always seemed like such a happy couple'. It felt odd when I read that, almost a personal invasion even though it was a positive remark. I don't know him.

I turn in a circle to take in the farm and the doubts that were beginning to fester suddenly evaporate. *This* is what makes sense. The farm is massive and there will definitely be some sort of shed somewhere. He'll have access to vehicles like vans and 4x4s. There are fields and woods over the back. It would be easy for someone to run for help and end up going in one big circle while it was dark.

As for Jan Astley… he knows Charley because he sells his goods to her. Perhaps he's one of those obsessive types? He found the dress so he could be some sort of white knight, or as some sort of double bluff?

Then there is his interview with the paper – with that creepy line about us. I remember reading somewhere that people who commit these sorts of crimes can often not resist inserting themselves into investigations.

It all makes sense.

Charley grabs my hand and squeezes so hard that I let out a little yelp. She's taking long, deep breaths as she turns, like I did, to take in the surroundings.

Neither of the officers say anything at first, but they're both watching her.

'Do you want to come this way?'

It's the first time DS Stanley has spoken to Charley. She's still got a hatchet face and the grey-eyed non-committal stare. She gives nothing away.

She leads us along a rickety stone track, around the side of a barn and then we trace the wooden fencing that surrounds a giant field of dirt.

It doesn't take long to see where we're headed.

At the far end of the field, a good five minutes' walk, is an outhouse that's too big to be a shed but too small to be a barn. I figure it might be some sort of storage building, with brick walls and corrugated metal for the roof. There's a heavy metal door hanging open and a line of police tape circling the entire structure.

When we get to the tape, we stop and nobody makes a move to pass to the other side. The building is ten metres or so away, close enough to see what it is but not enough to notice anything specific from the inside. The outside is unremarkable. It's breeze blocks, not bricks, unpainted except for a large '9' written in red spray paint on the side.

'Does any of this seem familiar?' the detective asks.

Charley lets go of my hand and stands, staring. It feels as if everyone is watching her because a small nod will mean so much.

'No,' she whispers.

She shakes her head.

'No. It's not here.'

The two officers are staring at her and there's a moment in which everything stops. They were definitely expecting a different answer.

'Are you absolutely positive?' DS Stanley asks – even she seems surprised.

'It's not here,' Charley says, before turning to me and taking my hand. 'I want to go home now.'

WHERE THERE'S A WILLIS, THERE'S A WAY

by SAMANTHA BAILEY

(Archived 17 years ago)

Annie Willis glows as she offers a hand towards her daughter. It's a little over a decade since I last visited this house and met Charlotte Willis for the first time. She was only a few weeks old then, unaware of the fame into which she'd been born.

'It's all about family for me,' Annie says.

Charlotte crosses to her mother and smiles, accepting the cuddle and then wriggling out of it in the way embarrassed children do.

'That's the thanks I get!' Annie smiles.

Charlotte turns away from me, utterly angelic with her ringed curls and dinner plate emerald eyes. Her mother asks if she's finished laying the table and then Charlotte heads into the dining room.

Annie is giving me something of a cooking demonstration before I sit down with her family for a roast with all the trimmings.

'What do you think is Britain's most traditional meal?'

Annie's question has taken me by surprise, largely because it's usually me doing the asking. I tell her that I've always been partial to fish and chips and she laughs as she continues stirring a large tray of gravy.

'It's hard to argue with that,' she replies. 'But, for me, fish and chips is all about the seaside. It's Brighton pier, Bournemouth or Weston-Super-Mare. There's a recipe in my book for fish shop batter – but it only scrapes into my top ten. I wanted to write about meals that were associated with the home, with family. Meals that everyone can eat together.'

I've only been in the house for a few minutes but it radiates the kind of homely cooking that takes me back to my parents' house when I was growing up. I suppose many would say this is precisely the key to Annie Willis's longevity as a so-called 'lifestyle guru' – it's that ability to make everything feel like it's fit for a family. She's the nation's mother.

'I've got chicken tikka masala in the book's top five,' she adds. 'I know that came out as number one in a public poll for favourite dish the other year – but, for me, nothing beats a good roast.'

As she opens the oven door and sends a gust of roast potatoes and red meat spiralling into the air, it's hard to disagree. Rather embarrassingly, I find my mouth salivating at the feast to come.

It's not long before I become one of the privileged few to find out what it's like to eat a meal cooked by one of the country's favourite chefs. I'm not a food critic and there's little point in trying to describe the succulence of the meat, the crispness of the roast potatoes, the way the Yorkshire puddings have raised to perfect domes, the soft, sweet vegetables, or the rich gravy.

All I will say is this: Sorry, Mum. This is the best roast dinner I've ever had.

It's not only the food by itself, of course. Annie Willis has spent more than twenty years on Britain's screens in some form or another. Husband Paul can add seven more years to that. Generations of Britons have grown up watching their programmes or reading Annie's books. Annie is now 52, while Paul is 56. They're institutions, king and queen in their own right.

And, with that, they are excellent company.

The three of us are joined at the table by daughter Charlotte, now 11; and, rather unexpectedly, eldest daughter Martha, who recently turned 20. Annie assures me that their other child, Liam – who is 22 – would have been present but for work commitments.

It's reassuring to know that a couple who've pitched themselves as parenting role-models still have such a strong relationship with their children.

'I'm here all the time,' Martha tells me over dinner. 'In many ways, I wish I'd never moved out. People don't tell you how expensive everything is. Cheese, for instance! I couldn't believe how much cheese costs.'

Apart from expressing her surprise at the cost of dairy products, Martha is otherwise quiet and polite. There's not much hint of the so-called 'wild child' here. She speaks when spoken to and is particularly courteous towards her sister. She says she's figuring out what she wants to do with her life and it's hard not to feel an inkling of understanding. After all, her mother's shadow is a large one out of which to emerge.

Charlotte herself is an absolute delight. Softly spoken with exquisite manners, she's like a character from a period drama. I ask what she thinks of having such famous parents and she replies that they will always be Mum and Dad to her.

Paul Willis grins that famous grin when I ask if he's thinking about retirement. He tells me a story of a former colleague who gave up a career in show business to retire to the sun.

'He was back within three months,' Paul says. 'The game is in your blood. It retires you before you retire from it.'

From there, he is a goldmine of stories, reeling off tales of friends in the entertainment business, the likes of which I would love to print but unfortunately cannot.

Charlotte asks for permission to leave the table and then disappears upstairs to play. 'She's at that age,' explains Annie.

After we have finished eating, Martha is asked to clear the table and she dutifully obliges in a way I suspect would have parents all over the land tearing their hair out. 'Are your children always this helpful around the house?' I ask.

'Charlotte is,' Annie replies. 'Martha does her share when she's over. It's the way they were raised.' She takes her husband's hand. 'I suppose it's something about our generation. It's how we were brought up, too – to show respect for your parents. We've passed that onto our children.'

I ask about advice for parents whose children perhaps aren't as cooperative, but Annie exchanges an amused glance with her husband.

'I'd love to tell you more,' she says, 'but it's in the book… the other book.'

I suppose this is the first moment of awkwardness since I arrived. The first real shill. It's why I'm here, of course, and yet I won't pretend it's not an abrupt end to that thread of conversation.

The Willises have two books coming out in time for Christmas. There is the previously referred to *British Classics* cookbook from Annie; and then a joint project: *Perfect Pearl: 30 Years At The Top*, which celebrates their thirtieth wedding anniversary and chronicles their climb to the top of British entertainment.

This is Annie's twelfth cookbook but, while the first nine topped the charts, it is a different story with her most recent releases. New faces have appeared on Britain's screens, with fresh-faced and – yes – *younger* chefs coming up with their own recipes. I ask if this jars.

There is an unquestionable bristling as Annie replies – but at least she's honest. 'I suppose it's the way of the world, but what my husband and I have always managed to do is adapt with the times. People wrote us off ten years ago. Then five years before that – and so on.'

'Is that why you've written the books?' I press. 'To prove yourselves?'

It is Paul who answers, but the merriment of his storytelling has been replaced by something more serious. 'What do we have to prove?' he asks. 'I was presenting shows before some of these newcomers were born. I've forgotten more than they'll ever know.'

Annie takes that moment to tap her husband on the hand and there's an unspoken admonishment.

'I suppose it would be easy to be bitter,' Annie says. 'Of course it would – but we'd rather do our own thing. I still get letters every week from people saying they wish we were back on the television.'

It's coming up to three years since *The Willis Way* came to an end. It was a show in which Annie and Paul gave advice, ranging from parenting tips through to general family budgeting. Critics never took to the format, saying it was dated, but that didn't stop viewers tuning in – especially in those early years. One of the further accusations was that it was exploitative. Daughter Charlotte appeared on the show more than twenty times before her first birthday. By the time she was six, she'd done much of her growing up on screen. Detractors argued she was too young to give consent to that level of intrusion. That led to an appearance on *Newsnight*, where Paul infamously called the presenter a 'stupid son of a bitch'. For some, it was the final straw; for others it was a father defending the honour of his daughter.

Either way, eighteen months later and the programme was cancelled.

Since then, appearances in the public eye have seemingly dwindled for the couple, though Annie denies that is the case.

'We have lots of work,' she says, 'it's just not of the type we were doing before. We open fetes, I do cooking demonstrations at events all around the country, I was at a dozen book festivals last year – and so on. People think that if your faces aren't on television every day, then you're done for. We're dispelling that notion, but, ultimately, people will write what they want.'

I put it to her that her words seem like a direct challenge to me, considering I've been invited here specifically to write an article.

'Sorry,' she replies. 'That's not what I meant at all. You're here, you're able to see our family for what it is. I was talking about the people who write things and haven't even met us.'

That's a fair point. Earlier this year, Annie was photographed leaving a supermarket wearing no make-up and workout gear that showed what some called a slightly slack stomach. It all seemed so at odds with the toned yoga guru that breakfast viewers were so used to seeing. The headline – 'Wide-Load Willis' was unquestionably mean-spirited and raises broader issues about how people in the public eye are treated, women especially. Questions were even asked in Parliament.

'Of course it hurt,' Annie says, although I have the sense she is carefully watching her words. In all honesty, I don't blame her. 'It sends out the message that you can't leave the house unless you've spent hours getting ready. It goes beyond me.'

I ask if it has harmed her prospects of finding another job on television.

'Perhaps,' she concedes, 'but I suppose that's why we've written the books. It doesn't have to be about being on screen every day. There are still people out there who'd like to hear from us.'

Martha takes that moment to drift into the living room, telling everyone that she's washed up. She says she's going to go upstairs to check on her sister and there's unquestioning tenderness between the siblings.

I ask what's on the horizon and the couple exchange another of their silent glances. It really does feel as if they can read one another's minds.

'We keep moving onwards,' Paul says.

'What does that mean?' I reply.

'Who knows – but someone told me twenty-seven years ago that I'd never make it as an entertainer. He said I wasn't natural enough, didn't have good enough hair. Can you believe that? Hair!' He shrugs. 'We've proven people wrong once, so now we'll do it again.'

British Classics by Annie Willis and _Perfect Pearl: 30 Years At The Top_ by Paul and Annie Willis will both be released in October.

FORTY

SETH. NOW

The police drop us back at the house and say they will be in contact if they need anything. I can't stop myself from looking online, where rumours are rampant that Jan Astley has been arrested. I have no idea what that means, whether it was a hunch or some sort of tip; whether Charley denying she knows the site means he'll be released. It feels like quite the mess.

Perhaps the police wanted it to seem like they were doing something?

After we get back to the house, Charley is quieter than ever. She says she has a headache and returns to bed. When I check on her half an hour later, she's either sleeping or she's really good at faking it.

I don't know why I'm even having those thoughts. Of course she's sleeping. Why wouldn't she be?

Emily calls and we talk about Mum for a while. She's stuck in one of her cycles of thinking she has jobs to do. She wants to clean the house she doesn't live in, cook meals for children who are no longer children and go to shops that went out of business more than a decade ago. I've not seen her in six days, a fact of which Emily reminds me by spelling out precisely how the past few days have gone. When we put Mum in the nursing home, we agreed we'd share the job of visiting her day-to-day. It's not been very joint in the past week.

One more person I've disappointed, I suppose. Or two – Emily *and* Mum.

I spend a while in the living room doing little but sitting. I dread to think what the news is reporting, having peeked at what was online. I don't know how to talk to my wife, or whether I'm making things worse. Fiona said there was someone I could talk to and I find myself hunting through pockets looking for the leaflet.

Wherever it is, I can't find it.

Raj, my best man at the now tainted wedding, is the person who finally comes through with a short but simple text: 'Can we meet?'

That sounds heavenly. A quiet pint somewhere with whatever sport's on in the background. He can tell me about a week in the life of his brothers and sisters. There's always something crazy going on.

I wake Charley briefly, whispering to ask whether she minds me nipping out with Raj. Her eyes barely open as she mumbles that it's fine.

Fifteen minutes later and I'm outside Raj's house in the car.

This is the first time since she returned that I've been away from Charley. It feels both strange and a relief at the same time. I spent so many hours wanting her to come back and, now she has, I have no idea how I feel about it. I thought she was one person and, now, I'm not so sure.

That makes me a particular type of scumbag, doesn't it?

Raj bustles out from his house and climbs into the passenger seat.

'Where do you want to go?' I ask.

'Somewhere quiet. Do you remember that pub out by the river we went to last summer? The one with the big garden that floods every winter. Let's head out there.'

I expect him to launch into an endless babble of information. He talks a lot at the best of times and we've not seen each other in a week. But he's the exact opposite, sitting quietly with his head against the rest, watching the road.

'You all right?' I ask.

'Yeah. You?'

'As you'd expect.'

I risk a glance sideways, but he doesn't say anything. I would've expected him to mention Charley in some way, if only to ask if she's okay.

'How's Rafi?' I ask.

'All right.'

That's it. No elaboration. No tales of the girl he's been rejected by this week. After that, I give up, wondering if it's me. That's the most likely explanation, isn't it? Charley's not really talking to me and now Raj. It's only the madman who thinks everyone else is mad.

I follow the country roads out past the Astley farm and there's a moment where I think about turning in. I can see a flicker of police tape off in the distance, but the gates are closed and there is no sign of anyone being home.

Raj says nothing and I continue driving.

The pub is roughly halfway between our town and another. It's an old brick building with a thatched roof that sits by itself. In the winter, there's a raging fire and cosy home-cooked meals. In the summer, everyone spreads out across the beer garden and lounges in the sunshine.

When we arrive, the garden is bustling with people. There is a bouncy castle in the furthest corner close to the river, with children racing around as their parents enjoy an evening out of the house. It's Saturday evening, probably the busiest time of the week – and the mass of people provides some degree of anonymity. As I find a spot on one of the picnic tables in the opposite corner to the bouncy castle, Raj heads inside. He returns ten minutes later with two pints and a lemonade.

'I'm driving,' I remind him, nodding to the two pints.

'These are mine,' he says. I think he might be joking, but he isn't. He necks the first in one go while still standing; then he wipes his chin and slides in opposite me.

'You look like you needed that,' I say.

'Yeah...'

He takes a mouthful of his second pint and swallows.

'Are you sure you're all right?' I ask.

'First time I've drunk since the wedding,' he says.

'I'm not entirely surprised.'

Raj doesn't say much at first. He has another mouthful and then wipes his face with his sleeve. 'I swore last Sunday morning I was never going to drink again,' he says with a sigh. 'Why'd you let me have so much?'

I snort with laughter at him. 'I figured it was up to you. If things had been different, I might have been as drunk as you at the end of the night.'

He shudders at the moment but has another drink anyway.

'I don't remember much after the ceremony,' he says. 'Rafi says I was popping in and out for air.'

'He told me that, too.'

Raj shudders at the half-memory. 'Never again, man.'

I nod at his pint and he rolls his eyes.

'Yeah, I know...' He has another mouthful and then adds: 'I should've got three.'

'You on an all-nighter, or something?'

A shake of the head. 'I remember being in a bush.'

'When?'

'At the wedding – that little courtyard bit out by the back doors. When I was out there, I must've fallen into a bush or something. I keep getting flashes of all these twigs and leaves in my face. I asked Rafi about it and he said that's where he found me when he came out to check on me. He said I was sleeping.'

He stops and has another – larger – mouthful. He's had a pint and a half of lager and I've had one sip of lemonade.

'I told you I got a new phone for the wedding, didn't I?' Raj adds.

'Right.'

'I thought I could take some photos but my old one had a rubbish camera. Only problem was I didn't have a clue how to use the new one.'

He takes out his phone – new and unscratched – and puts it on the wooden slat of the table between us.

'I still don't really know what I'm doing,' he adds.

Raj has another mouthful of his pint and stares up at me. From nowhere, there are tears in the corners of his eyes. I ask what's wrong – and it's hard to believe this is all about understanding how to use a phone.

He glances away again as a young lad roars past. He's had his face painted as a lion and is being chased by his father. They loop around our table and then race back towards the bouncy castle.

'There are hundreds of photos on the phone,' Raj says. 'I didn't look until this morning. There are *literally* hundreds of photos of bushes and tress.'

'From where you fell into the bush?'

'Yeah.'

I laugh, thinking this is a joke, but he does nothing but stare into nothingness.

'What's wrong?' I ask.

'I think I was trying to take a selfie.' He adds, 'I was so bloody drunk, I don't even know. I vaguely remember trying to switch it from the back camera to the front… or the other way around. Whichever way it is to take a picture of yourself. I was in the bush and that's all I really remember.'

'That's all right… we've done way worse than that when we were lashed. Remember that bloke Frank at the football Christmas party last year? Imagine explaining that to your missus…'

Raj doesn't laugh. He shakes his head. 'I'm really sorry, mate. I swear I didn't know. I *swear*. I only found them this morning. It took me ages to grow a set of balls and text you. I wimped out twice.'

'Wimped out of what?'

Raj swipes a couple of things on his phone and then passes it across. 'There are more,' he says.

There's a photo on the screen, slightly out of focus but clear enough. Leaves dot the edges of the picture but the framing is otherwise perfect.

Charley is standing outside the back doors of the hotel in her wedding dress.

'Keep going,' Raj says.

I swipe to the next photo, which is a total contrast to the first. Charley is still there, but she's at a 45-degree angle. There's a man at her side wearing a cap. He's in the next photo, too. And the one after that.

'I know it's only the back of his head, but do you know who he is?' Raj asks.

The photos are a mix of clear and fuzzy; angled and well framed. Some are upside down, others completely obscured by leaves and twigs. I have no idea what Raj thought he was doing when he took them.

The final picture is the most damning. Charley and the man walking away from the wedding, heading through the gap in the plants towards the car park. This is the exact spot where I spent hours of Saturday night and the early hours of Sunday hunting. When I press the screen for information, there is a time attached to each photo.

'Do you know him?' Raj repeats.

I don't reply. The mask, the knife… it was all a lie. Charley simply walked away.

Raj sighs and downs the rest of his pint. 'It's worse than that, mate.'

I scroll back through the photos, taking them all in and then starting all over. 'How could it be worse?'

'Raf had been messing with my phone. He'd set everything to auto-upload to the cloud. You know what I'm talking about? Where you can back all your photos up.'

'So there are copies?'

A shake of the head. 'It's not that. It's a public photo-sharing site. You know what it's like. People take pictures of things and then dump them online for their friends to see. You can either do it manually, or there's a setting so it happens by itself. Raf says it can be public or private – but all of mine are public.'

Raj sighs. 'Cats. Bloody cats – you get hundreds of pictures of someone's mangy cat.' He picks up his glass but it's already empty. 'These photos have been online all week but nobody bothered to look. All they had to do was search for my name but no one noticed.'

There's more. I can see it in his face.

'What are you saying?' I ask.

'I got an email at lunchtime. All the info is there. Timestamps, my name. You can see Charley's face!'

'Who was the email from?'

He shakes his head. 'I'm sorry, mate. I wish I'd known. I'm so sorry – but it's out there now. The bloke was a reporter.'

FORTY-ONE

15 YEARS AGO

Charley Willis, 13 years old

At first I can't figure out why I'm awake. There is no light seeping through the top of the curtains, which means it must still be dark outside. Mama says people only wake up at 'ungodly hours' if they've been lazy during the day. There was a time a couple of years ago where I kept waking up at five in the morning, but if I ever mentioned it, she would find me more jobs to do the next day. In the end, I decided to lie in bed quietly instead. Sometimes I'd remember to bring books up from the reading room and I'd put the light on. They were good mornings.

I started sleeping better eventually, but I'm not really sure why. Perhaps Mama *was* right and I was working harder during the day?

But now I'm awake again, even though it's not the morning. Mama won't let me have a clock in the room because she says timeliness should breed itself. I don't even know what that means. I do have a watch, though. Martha gave it to me. It's on my side table and I scrabble for it in the dark, bumping and banging on the wooden surface. I wait for a few seconds, listening in case the noise has woken either Mama or Father. I make lots of racket, they say. When I press the light button on the side of my watch, I can see it's 3:24.

It's *really* early. I'm not sure if I've ever been awake at this time before. Mama would say I must have been very lazy yesterday.

I roll back onto the bed, but it's then I realise my thighs are warm and sticky. In fact, the backs of my knees are as well. It's like when I'm getting dressed after being in the bath but I've not quite dried myself properly. I push the covers away and I suppose my eyes have become used to the dark because I can to see what I'm lying in. There's a thick dark smear all across my sheet. It has drenched the lower half of my pyjamas.

There's a horrifying moment where I think I've wet myself. I've not done this in such a long time and I can't think of any way I'm going to be able to hide it all. Mama will be so angry.

I reach across to my nightstand once more and flick on the light. It flashes bright and white, leaving me blinking and seeing stars. It takes a while for the twinkling pinks and greens to dissolve until I can see what has really soaked the covers.

It's blood.

My blood.

At first I can only stare at everything. The sheets are cream and bobbly, or they were. The blood has covered a wide circular pool. We talked about this at school, but it was all very embarrassing. I remember some of the other girls giggling. I didn't listen to it all, I'm not sure anyone did. I wanted to ask Mama about it but then forgot.

What do I do?

I push back the rest of the covers, but the top sheet is speckled with blood as well. When I take off my pyjama bottoms, I feel the tackiness of my skin, which has changed colour to a greasy red.

It's coating my hands and, as I swing my legs out of bed, I realise blood has dripped from the bottom of my knees onto the floor.

Oh, no.

I hug my knees to my chest and sit on the bed staring at the horror scene I've created.

'Mama…'

My voice is a whimper at first, but then I'm crying out for her.

'Mama!'

I'm not sure how long it takes, but I start to hear footsteps on the landing. They get louder and then my door swings open and a hand switches the main light on. I'm blinking again, seeing stars from the sudden switch. Mama is in the doorway wearing a long pink nightdress that hangs to her ankles. Her hair is frizzy and wild, her eyes mostly closed.

Everything is going to be all right.

It takes her a few seconds to open her eyes properly, almost as if she's sleepwalked here. I used to sleepwalk when I was younger. Showing off, Mama said. Looking for attention, even though I don't remember it.

Mama says a bad word.

'Look at the state of you,' she adds. 'Just look at what you've done.'

She steps into the room, looking at me and the mess I've made. When she gets close to the bed, she jumps back.

'It's on the carpet, that's going to take ages to get out.'

She rubs her eyes hard and scratches the side of her face.

'You're absolutely filthy,' she says.

'I'm sorry, Mama.'

'Those are perfectly good sheets you've ruined. That's money down the drain. You know how hard your father and I work – but do you have any consideration for others…?'

It sounds like she's asked me a question, but I'm not sure she has. All I can do is apologise again. She is shaking her head, not listening.

'Disgusting,' she says before turning to me. 'This is *disgusting*, you know that? Don't you know about towels and tampons? Didn't you think? Do you need to be told everything?'

'I'll clean it up, Mama. Honest. Can you get me some new sheets, though? I'll clean everything in the morning.'

Mama turns back to the mess at the bottom of the bed. I've made myself small enough that I'm sitting on the clean part of the bed, except that my thighs and knee are tacky and horrible.

She yawns but doesn't cover her mouth with her hand, even though I get told off if I do the same. She switches off the lamp on my nightstand, leaving only the main light on.

'You made this mess,' she says. 'And now you can lie in it.'

She steps away towards the door, her back to me.

'Please, Mama. Please. I'll clean it in the morning. Please.'

She doesn't turn. 'You can lie in your own filth and think about what you've done. Think about the money you've wasted. Do you know how much nice sheets cost? Bedding? Nightclothes? You can lie there and think about how selfish you are.'

Mama switches the light off and stands in the door frame, her shape creating a shadow against the gloom beyond. I can see only her back.

'And don't you dare move until morning.'

Then she closes the door.

FORTY-TWO

SETH. NOW

It's half past nine when I get back to the house. The downstairs is silent, as if Charley is still missing. There is an upturned glass on the draining board – the only sign that she's moved from our bed since I left.

The laptop is still on the floor close to the window in the living room, the charger not plugged in. The battery is down to twenty per cent when I flip the lid and wait for the Wi-Fi to kick in. When it does, I type in the web address that Raj gave me.

He's right. All the photos are there. The leaves and twigs, the weird angles. Charley in her dress, the back of the man's head. No knife. I suppose he could be wearing a mask… but he's in front of her. Charley's following. There's no threat, no force. She's choosing to leave.

I close the lid and quietly climb the stairs, heading into our bedroom. The curtains are pulled but late-evening sunlight is oozing around the edges, leaving a browny frost across the room. Charley is on the furthest side of the bed, facing away. She's on her side and the covers are rising and falling slowly as she breathes.

Should I wake her? Perhaps I should just go? There's a massive part of me that wants to know what really happened, but then there's another that simply wants to be by myself. A storm is on its way and Charley is peacefully dozing through the beginning.

Is she the person I thought I knew? The person I married?

I've always thought that whatever was in a person's past is irrelevant to a relationship. When you meet someone, that's a new starting point... and yet now I think I was probably wrong. That past is what makes a person who he or she is.

The phone Alice gave Charley is on the nightstand close to her head. I wonder if she's used it to call or text the man from the photos since she got back. Perhaps she has her old one hidden away somewhere?

I round the bed and lean against the window frame watching my wife sleep. Long, deep breaths in; slow full breaths out. I rest there for a few minutes, sometimes opening my mouth as if I'm going to speak and then closing it again.

In the end, it's not me that wakes her. The phone screen blazes bright white, the ringtone generic and annoying blaring through the dim light. Charley blinks awake and grabs the device, eyeing the screen and then putting it down again as it rings off. She plops her head back on the pillow and then notices me in front of her.

'Oh,' she says softly, her lips creasing into a smile.

I don't say anything and she pushes herself up slightly, not really sitting but not on her back either.

'How long have you been back?' she asks.

'Not long.'

'Did you have a good time with Raj?'

'Not really.'

'Oh.' She licks her lips. 'Are you coming to bed?'

'Who was calling?'

'The publicist... Pamela. It's a bit late, isn't it?' She rolls towards the clock and then back to me. 'It's earlier than I thought...'

'You should call her back,' I say.

'Why?'

'Because people know, Charley. It's out there.'

She pushes herself up, resting on her elbows, still blinking from the tiredness and lack of light.

'What's out there?' she asks.

I don't reply at first because I can see in her face that she already knows. There's a resigned acceptance that she knew this would happen sooner or later. I want her to say it, but she doesn't.

'You left our wedding voluntarily,' I say, surprised by my own calmness. 'There was no abduction, no knife. Probably no mask. Probably no shed. No escape through the woods. You made everything up.'

Even through the gloom, I can see the wideness of her dilated pupils. Puppy-dog eyes, scared and cornered.

Charley whispers a single, scared word: 'How?'

'Just call Pamela.'

She does and I go downstairs, not wanting to listen to it. I find myself back on the laptop, except, by now, the photos have all disappeared. I refresh the page but can only get 'this user's album is empty'.

Raj had cleared everything out, not that it matters, of course. It's easy enough to download a photo and save it somewhere else or take a screengrab. The damage is done.

When Charley gets into the living room, she's already dressed, shoes and all. She's pale and washed out, as if she's seen a ghost. 'I have to go out,' she says.

'No. You have to tell me what's going on.'

It wasn't that long ago that I was happy to wait for the explanation. Now I need to know.

She tilts her whole body to the side and sighs. When she offers her hand, I don't take it. 'I will,' she says. 'I'll tell you everything, I promise. But I have to go out.'

'It's after ten on a Saturday night. Where are you going?'

She bites her tongue, then turns into the kitchen and takes the car key from its hook. I get to the front door before her, standing with my arms spread across it like a giant spider.

'I want you to tell me,' I say.

'Please let me go. It's important.' She's unerringly calm.

'*I'm* important… or I thought I was.'

She reaches out and cups my chin. Her touch is delicate and soft. 'I've not forgotten that… but I have to go.'

Charley reaches for the catch and I step aside. There's a softly spoken grimness about the way she's talking that makes me think I don't know her at all. Her eyes that were once so green and vibrant are grey and lifeless. The woman I knew was only ever a stranger.

It's like she's broken. Suddenly, the anger has gone.

I step to the side.

'Can I come with you?' I ask.

She opens the door but pauses for the merest of moments. 'Yes.'

And so we're in the car. I don't know where we're going, but it's dark and the roads quickly become narrower. We've been driving for a few minutes when Charley whispers so delicately that I can barely hear her over the engine.

'They think I'm a fraud,' she says. 'That's what Pamela says they're going to say in the papers tomorrow.'

It's brutal, I know that, but what other reply can I give. 'Are you?'

Charley is quiet for a full minute. Maybe two. She stares straight ahead towards the road, continuing to drive. I'm not sure she even blinks.

And then she tells me what really happened fifteen years ago.

FORTY-THREE

15 YEARS AGO

Charley Willis, 13 years old

I burst through the front door, calling after Mama and Father, hoping they're home. When there's no reply, I call for them again, stopping in the hallway and listening as my voice echoes around the empty hall.

'Hello?'

There's no answer. It's not necessarily a surprise because one of them is often out when I get home from school. I usually make myself a sandwich and then do some homework in the reading room. If it's nice outside, I might go into the garden.

It's rare they're both gone, though.

But I'm so excited!

I move through the hallway, still listening carefully in case they're upstairs, or perhaps in the garden.

'Mama?'

Nothing.

The kitchen is empty and so is the dining room. I look through the window towards the back garden, but that's clear, too. There's nobody in the reading room, nor the TV room. I knock gently on their bedroom door upstairs, but there's no reply. There is nobody in my room, nor the ones that used to belong to Martha and Liam.

I return downstairs, my excitement starting to deflate. It's such a shame. I so wanted Mama to know what I've done.

At the bottom of the stairs, I'm about to head towards the reading room when I hear the faint sound of voices. There are two, but they sound distant. I'm not sure where else to look but follow my ears. It's like a game of hotter and colder. Ten steps towards the living room and the sound is getting colder, back towards the front door and it's warmer. Onto the driveway and it's hotter still.

My parents are in the double garage at the side of the house. There used to be two cars, but now there's only one and the other side is filled with boxes. Sometimes I wonder if we're getting ready to move out.

The regular door at the side of the large metal garage door is open and I edge inside. Mama and Father are close to the boxes, but they stop talking when they see me.

'I'm going inside,' Mama says.

'I'm not done yet!' Father shouts back.

Mama strides out of the garage back into the house. Father is a little behind, calling after her, while I trail after them both. I follow them all the way through the house to the living room. Mama looks as if she's about to start shouting at Father when she turns to me instead.

'What are you doing here?' she asks harshly.

I offer her the envelope, bouncing on my heels with bundled excitement. I know this is going to make her happy. Whatever they're arguing about will go away now.

Mama snatches the envelope and removes the card from inside. She scans the page and then hands it to Father.

'What do you think, Mama? Did I do good?'

The page is the best thing I've ever managed. It's one A after another. Maths: A. English: A. Sciences: A. I've got the clean sweep, one of only five people in my entire year. I even got an A in Information Technology and I don't particularly like that.

Father glances at the page quickly and then looks to Mama. 'What do you reckon?' he asks. 'Do you think it's worth leaking?'

Mama turns to me and then back. 'Who cares? It's not like I can phone up a producer and tell them we've got some smart-arse for a daughter, is it?'

Father spins the envelope and certificate off to the side like a Frisbee. It sails through the air, landing face down with a swish next to the sofa.

'You could tell them you're going to lose some weight,' he says, ignoring me.

Mama has both hands on her hips. 'Oh, you're one to talk. It's a good job we've got separate rooms. It's like sleeping next to a poached elephant.'

Father presses himself high onto the tips of his toes. His voice booms like thunder. 'I'm not the one they call Wide-Load Willis. You must think I don't know about all that chocolate you keep hidden at the back of the cupboard with the bedding. It's like a bloody sweet shop in there. What the hell's wrong with you?'

'Right – because downing a bottle of wine every night is *so* much better.'

I hate it when Mama and Father fight. It's been happening so much recently that it's hard to escape. I usually go and hide under the covers in my room, holding my hands over my ears and hoping it all goes away. Either that, or in the wardrobe behind the clothes hamper. I feel frozen to the spot this time. It's like they've forgotten I'm here and if I were to move they'd be angry with me.

Father is shouting as loudly as I've ever heard him. 'I'm not the one who's supposed to be a lifestyle guru, whatever the hell that means. Your whole career is supposed to be about being fit and healthy, now you waddle around like a sweaty warthog. No wonder they don't want you on television. They'd need a widescreen camera.'

'Says the man who gets through a bottle of hair dye every week. No one's convinced, you know. People laugh at you. Badger head – that's what they call you. "Look, there goes Badger Head mincing down the street. Didn't he used to be famous?"'

'At least I'm not known as a whore. Everyone knows you shagged that producer bloke with the floppy hair. Christ, he was half your age.'

Mama's laughing but it doesn't seem like she's finding this funny. 'You're just jealous,' she says. 'When was the last time you could even get it up?'

Father's fists are balled.

'STOP!'

It takes a second for me to realise I'm the one who's shouted. I've roared like a lion. Mama and Father have both turned to stare at me as if I'm something completely new they've stumbled across.

'Please stop,' I add, quieter this time. '*Please.*'

Father takes a step away, but Mama marches across the living room and bends so that we're eye to eye. Hers are the same colour as mine, but they're furious.

'You listen to me,' she says. 'The *only* reason you exist is so we could sell the story to those idiots out there who lap it all up. I had a book coming out. Your father was in line for a few panel shows. A new child nine years after the last one. What a story.'

She takes a small step back, but her eyeline doesn't change.

'You're nothing. Do you hear me? You're numbers on a bank statement, you're the worst mistake we ever made. And after all that – after everything we've done for you – all you can do is think of yourself. You piss in corners. You mess all over your bed. You invade *our* conversation because your teachers can't see you for what you are. None of this is about you. You are *nothing* – and that's all you'll ever be.'

Mama straightens herself, smooths her top and steps away. There are tears in my eyes and, even though she hasn't touched me, it feels as if she's slapped me in the face. My whole body is tingling.

I look up to Father, hoping he'll say something. My bottom lip bobs and I almost beg him. He stares down at me and it's with such disdain that I know he doesn't love me. He never has. I'm the worst mistake they ever made.

Mama turns back to Father. 'What shall I do?' she asks. 'Do you have the number for that Greg guy? I heard he's off to Channel Four…'

It's as if the past minute hasn't happened. As if their argument before that was in my imagination. Father replies calmly to her, but I don't hear what he says. It's like there's somebody else controlling me. As if an idea has been planted into my mind and now I have to do it. I walk into the kitchen and open the drawer that's filled with cutlery. I know precisely what I'm looking for because I've washed and dried it up so many times. It's on the left-hand side, sheathed in a plastic case.

I slide out the thick knife with the pointy end that Mama uses to dice beef. It glimmers in the lights. So, so shiny. So, so sharp.

Then I go back into the living room.

FORTY-FOUR

SETH. NOW

I don't know what to say. Charley has spoken so calmly, so assur-edly of the horrors to which she was subjected that I don't have the words. It's so awful that I'm shaking with rage on her behalf. I feel sick. It actually hurts.

'I should've told you before,' she whispers at the end.

I want to hug her, to hold her close and stroke her hair, but, because she's driving, all I can do is touch her shoulder. It's a pathetic, nothing gesture, but I don't know what else to do.

'Are you okay?' she croaks.

It makes me splutter with a humourless laugh. 'Me? It's you this happened to.'

'I've done my crying. I did it all when I was thirteen.'

She sounds so unruffled that it sends a shiver along my spine.

'How did it never get out that your parents were treating you like that?' I ask.

'It probably would have done eventually. Martha didn't realise how bad it was until I went to live with her. They were worse with me than they were with her. Afterwards, everyone wanted to say how brilliant they were. What was the point in arguing?'

Charley glances up to her mirror, indicates and then takes a turn off the motorway.

'My feelings for you have never changed,' she says. 'Never.'

'Then why leave the hotel after our wedding and tell everyone you'd been taken?'

Another glance to the mirror. 'In time. We're nearly there. If he's seen those pictures, then everyone's in danger.'

'Is that where we're going?' I ask. 'Liam's house? I recognised his baseball cap in Raj's photos. I did wonder where he got my phone number from.'

Charley doesn't seem surprised that I know. She's as calm as she has been since we left the house. 'I didn't give it to him,' she says. 'Not directly. He must've stolen it from my phone. I didn't know he was going to call you. I didn't know he was going to meet you or leave my dress in some bush, either.'

She sounds particularly spiky about that – but then I have no clue what actually happened between them in the days after she walked away.

'But you never got on,' I say, 'and then you left *our* wedding to go with him.'

'I'll explain. I promise.'

She's still cool and emotionless and I'm not sure if I should be scared for her or myself.

Charley turns off the road and the car bumps into a pothole and then over the kerb until we're on the driveway of Liam's house. When we were here before, I was stunned at how big it was. Pillars and big bay windows on the outside, everything sparkly and new on the inside. Everything is dark now. None of the lights are on, upstairs or down. The driveway is clear. No cars.

'Looks like no one's home,' I say.

Charley ignores me, stopping the car abruptly with a squeaky skid. She gets out quickly and races to the front door, ringing the bell and pounding it with her hand.

'Liam?!'

I follow her, but there's not a lot I can do. Charley crouches and jabs at the letter box, getting a mouthful of dark bristles for her trouble. 'Try the window,' she says.

The house is symmetrical on the outside. One arching window on either side of the front door. Charley goes one way; I head the other. The curtains or blinds seem to be open, but the glare from the moon makes it hard to see much of anything. I press my face to the glass, cupping my eyes with my hands as a shield. There's a television in the corner, a fireplace, a sofa… grim, dark shadows licking the corners of the room.

It's only as I shift around the window that I see what I missed first time round.

Oh, no.

FORTY-FIVE

15 YEARS AGO

Charley Willis, 13 years old

I'm sitting in the kitchen hugging my knees to my chest when there's a knock on the front door. The knife is at my side, glistening with thick crimson. There's a trail of red from the living room to the kitchen.

Whoever it is knocks again, louder this time, but I don't move. I'm not sure I'll ever move. I just want to sit here by myself.

The letter box clatters and then a voice echoes through the house. 'Is there anyone in? I can't find my key.'

Martha.

The letter box snaps back into place with a clang and then there's a scrabbling. A minute or two passes and then the door bangs open.

'What the hell is it with this family?'

Martha's voice echoes through the house. She slams the door and then her feet clip-clop across the hallway. It's only a moment and then she's in the kitchen.

'Char? What's wrong?'

I'm not looking at her, but I somehow know exactly what she's doing. Her rucksack hits the floor and then she follows the drips of blood into the living room. It takes her a while to return and, when she does, she's walking very slowly. She's on tiptoes, in fact. Martha is suddenly on the floor next to me, hugging her knees as well.

'I want you to listen to me very carefully,' she says. 'Are you listening?'

I don't move. My whole body feels floppy and useless, as if I want to lie down and never get up.

'Will you nod if you can hear me, Char? It's really important.'

I nod. Only a little.

'This is what we're going to do, okay? I'm going to go into the garage and get a couple of those big blue rubble sacks that are in there. You're going to take off everything you're wearing and put it all – including your shoes – into the sack. All right?'

'But then I'll be naked.'

'Don't worry about that for now. Nobody can see. You need to be really still though. Don't make any more footprints around the kitchen and don't touch anything. Don't go back into the living room. I'll lift you out and then you need to go upstairs and get into the shower. You need to wash everything away from your face, your arms, your legs.' She stops for a moment. 'It's okay if there's a bit of blood on your hands. Do you understand?'

I blink for what feels like the first time in a long time. Martha places a hand on mine, rests her head on my shoulder.

'I never should have left home,' she whispers.

'Are they…?'

I feel Martha gulp. 'Don't worry about them for now,' she says.

'I'm going to go to jail, aren't I?'

My sister squeezes me. 'No you're not, honey. No you're not.'

'But I—'

'No you didn't. You didn't *do* anything.' She looks at her watch. 'You got home from school, you did your homework, then you went to bed. It was a perfectly normal evening.' A pause. 'Nobody else has come round, have they?'

'No.'

'Good. People saw you getting off the bus from school, didn't they?'

'Yes.'

'So that's what happened.'

'But—'

Shhhhh.

We sit together for a little while and I can feel Martha's heart beating through her top. It's really fast, like a train racing over a bumpy set of rails.

'What are we going to say?' I whisper.

'I'm going to raid Mum's jewellery box and then bury some things deep in the garden. It's dark and the sun's not coming up for hours. I'll smash a window at the back of the house later on.'

'Why?'

'Because this was a break-in, Char. You heard noises and hid in your wardrobe. That's it. You didn't see anything, all you heard was voices down here.' She pushes away from the cabinet and stands. 'This wasn't you. Okay?'

I don't reply and she bends over, wrapping her arms underneath my pits and lifting me up.

'Clothes,' she says.

When I lean against the sink, Martha tuts.

'You can't do that,' she says. 'We're going to have to scrub the kitchen clean later.'

I move myself away, standing freely. My legs feel wobbly because I've been curled up for so long. Martha holds my hand.

'You remember when that reporter came over a couple of years ago?' Martha asks.

'Yes.'

'You remember how you told me that Mum made you run through the questions over and over until you knew the answers?'

'Yes.'

'We're going to have to do that. The police will want to talk to you, maybe other people, too – like social workers. We're going to have a really simple story that's easy to remember – but you have to get it right every time. *Every* time. You can't slip, not ever.'

'People won't believe me.'

'They will, Char. You're thirteen. No one's going to believe the alternative. You were scared, you were hiding. That's it. It's not complicated. If anyone keeps on at you, say you can't remember.' She bites her tongue, showing me the stud. 'Wanna know another trick?'

'What?'

'Cry. Say you can't remember and cry. Fake it if you need to. Nobody's going to continue asking you things after that. It's all you need to do.'

Martha peels off her cardigan and tosses it towards the counter on the far side. She rubs her arms.

'You're smart,' she says, 'and I know you'll get it, but we don't have long. We've got to get moving.'

'Okay.'

'Clothes off then.'

I start to peel off my top, but that's all I manage when Martha stops me, kneeling so she's at my height. We're eye to eye just like I was with Mama — with *Mum*. We all have those same green eyes.

'You know this isn't your fault, don't you?' Martha repeats. '*None* of this is your fault. You didn't ask to be born into this damned family.' She wraps her arms through mine and, for the first time, I hug her properly.

'She said I was the worst mistake she ever made,' I say.

'That's not true, honey. You're not a mistake.'

'She said I was numbers on a bank statement.'

Martha squeezes me, hands pressed into the middle of my back. For a moment it feels as if everything is going to be all right.

'You'll always have me,' she says. '*Always.*'

A NATION IN SHOCK

by SAMANTHA BAILEY
(Archived 15 years ago)

Among the field of flowers and messages, there is a single teddy bear sitting atop a heart-shaped wreath of lilies. There is a small card on top, pristine felt-tip letters clear to read across the driveway.

'Everyone's mum and dad,' it reads.

The police officer stationed at the front gate gives me the kind of smile officers do when they have orders to follow. I'm not allowed onto the Willis property, which isn't a surprise. The surprise comes with the officer's reaction when I tell him why I'm there.

He nods, gulps and then glances off into the distance. 'I grew up watching them,' he says. 'My mum used to have Annie's show on every morning and then my dad would watch *Wheel Of Fortune* in the evening. It was like you knew them even though you didn't.'

It is thirteen years since I first sat in the reading room of this house with Annie Willis. She told me how much she was enjoying being a mother to a newborn, saying how her daughter Charlotte had started smiling at three weeks. For a couple who built a career on being parents to the nation, it is beyond shocking that everything should end in such gruesome fashion.

Details are sketchy for now, but the basics seem to be thus: at some point on Friday evening, a person unknown broke into the Willis home on the outskirts of Langton. What happened after that is a mystery – but the outcome was that both Annie and

Paul Willis were left dead in their own living room. It might have been a robbery gone wrong, perhaps someone looking for money, or an obsessed fan. Theories abound, especially given the lack of information from the investigating team.

Central to the whole appalling incident is that Charlotte Willis, just 13, was hiding in her wardrobe upstairs.

The one question being asked by the locals, not to mention the nation, is why? Why would a couple so beloved come to such a grisly end? What robbery could possibly be worth this?

The chief inspector of the local force, Dean Dixon, tells me they're examining all angles. 'It's senseless,' he says. 'Hard to get your head around.'

Mr Dixon adds that he can't say a lot more than that, given this is an ongoing investigation.

Despite the scene being off limits, that hasn't stopped well-wishers coming from all around the country to lay flowers and, indeed, that teddy bear. A part of the Willis garden close to the road was set aside for people to leave their tributes, though the patch was filled within four hours. Police later opened up another part of the garden. Mourners can come to the house and leave their tribute with an officer, who will place it with the others. This has a created a striking rainbow carpet of sorrow. It is beautiful and moving.

For many, Annie and Paul Willis, along with their children – Charlotte especially – were the perfect family. *The Willis Way* ran for almost seven years, a magazine show of parenting tips, recipes and general household help. Before that, there was breakfast yoga, prime-time quiz shows, science programmes, a *Royal Variety Performance* hosting gig. Even in recent years, there were fetes and fairs, gardening shows, festivals and conferences. As a couple, Paul and Annie Willis have created a legacy that will live long in the lives of British families.

While I'm waiting close to the gates that lead to the house, a small car pulls in and parks on the other side of the road. It's a Mini, its exhaust rattling and sputtering against the silence. A woman clambers from the driver's seat and then reaches back inside before emerging with a bouquet of roses. She looks both ways and then crosses the road before approaching one of the officers and asking him to lay the flowers for her. We both watch as the officer pads carefully around the homages already laid and then places the roses next to a small round tin.

'Someone brought cookies,' he says when he returns to the gates. 'She said it was one of Annie's recipes. We didn't know what to do with them, so…'

The woman who brought the roses offers a teary smile and then returns to her car. She never gave her name, didn't feel the need to be identified.

The officer asks me if I knew either of the Willises and all I can do is reply that I'd met them a couple of times.

'What were they like?' he asks.

I suppose it is this question that lies at the very core of who Annie and Paul Willis were. They were whatever people wanted them to be.

A guiding hand in the kitchen? Unquestionably.

A soothing voice of prime-time television when that actually meant something? Definitely.

An advocate of women's health and fitness? Of course.

An all-round entertainer who could joke and empathise in equal measure? For sure.

Or, as Charlotte Willis, then 11, told me two years ago: 'They will always be Mum and Dad to me.'

Millions of fans will feel the same. After all, that card with the teddy bear says it best.

'Everyone's mum and dad'.

FORTY-SIX

SETH. NOW

Liam's wife, Helen, is lying face down on the sofa, one arm dangling onto the floor. I bash the window but she doesn't stir. It's hard to tell, but I think her eyes are closed.

Charley dashes across and plasters herself against the glass, whacking it hard with her fist.

'How can we get inside?' she asks.

The windows are double-glazed, the type that aren't supposed to break.

Charley rushes back to the front door and tries it just in case. It's locked.

'They're weaker in the corners,' I say.

'What are?'

'Double-glazed windows. You can't smash them by hitting them in the middle.' This is where having a friend like Raj comes in handy. He's worse at football than I am. It might be one of the reasons we bonded, I suppose, that wayward shot that cannoned into the corner of the school hall's newly installed windows.

Charley seems to take this as a challenge. There's a rockery a little off the driveway. She crouches and picks up a pair of stones, then moves back to the window.

Clang!

The first rock bounces off the glass, as does the second.

Helen is still out of it on the sofa.

I follow Charley's lead, taking a rock and arching back.

Crash!

My rock connects with the corner of the window and sends a splintering, creaking trail arching up towards the opposite corner. It crinkles and ripples and then shatters onto the ground.

The second pane is a lot easier – and Charley dispatches one of her rocks through the middle. With that, I use one more stone to bash out the larger shards of glass and then reach through to open the window. There are glittering knife-like sprinkles everywhere, but Charley doesn't seem to care. Her shoes crunch across the glass as she pushes herself up and jumps inside. I'm a lot more careful than her and somehow manage to get inside while avoiding the glass outside, inside and still attached to the frame. It's more by luck than judgement.

Charley is kneeling next to her sister-in-law.

'Find the kids,' she says, flashing an arm towards the door that leads to the rest of the house. I must have frozen for a moment because she shouts 'GO!' and then I'm moving.

When I was here before, I was only in the hall and the living room. I have no idea where I'm going, dashing across the main entranceway and finding myself in the kitchen, which is empty. There's a second downstairs lounge room, but there's no one in there, nor in what I find out to be cupboards. Upstairs and the bathroom is clear, so are the bedrooms. There are a pair of cribs in a room that has been painted pink. The covers are ruffled but the beds are empty.

'Hello?' I call. 'Skye? Jasmine?'

I realise too late that they're far too young to call back. They're babies, for crying out loud.

'Liam?'

Nothing. The house is silent.

I race back downstairs into the living room. Charley is still on the floor and turns to face me. 'Are they here?'

'No.'

'There's a basement under the stairs. Try there.'

I wonder how she knows this. We've only visited once and I'm pretty sure she didn't spend any time there then.

There's no time for questions now though. As I shift my weight to race out of the room, there's a grumble from the sofa and then Helen groans and rolls over. Charley quickly glances between us but doesn't have to shout at me a second time.

I run across the tiled hallway, sliding to a stop by the stairs. I missed the door to the basement first time round – it's one of those that looks like a wall, where the handle is embedded in the raised decorations.

The inside is dark and I'm only a centimetre or two from stumbling down a set of wooden steps before I catch myself on the frame. There's a dangling cord, which I pull, sparking a bulb to life.

The basement is cold and damp. There are boxes in one corner, a fire extinguisher in another. Apart from a folded camp bed, that's it. No children, no Liam.

Helen is swaying from side to side when I get back to the living room. She's sitting up, but her eyes are almost closed.

Charley spins, but I hold my hands up. 'They're not here.'

Back to Helen: 'Look at me,' Charley says, part gentle, part urgent. 'Helen, look at me. It's Charley. You need to wake up.'

Helen flops backwards, head on the rest at the back of the sofa. Charley moves onto the seat herself, trying to support her sister-in-law's head.

'Come on,' Charley says. 'I need you to tell me what happened.'

Charley manages to manoeuvre Helen into a position where she's more or less sitting by her own volition. Helen still looks like she could fall asleep at any moment.

'We were going to watch TV,' she mumbles.

Charley is rubbing the other woman's arm. 'You and Liam?'

'Yeah.'

'What then?'

'He made us tea.'

'Where were the girls, Helen? Where were Jasmine and Skye?'

'Upstairs.'

'And what happened?'

'When?' Helen slumps to the side but then rights herself, rubbing her eyes. She blinks and blinks and blinks, trying to clear her thoughts.

'There's no one here,' Charley says. 'What's the last thing you remember?'

'Tea,' Helen says. 'I remember tea. Liam made it.'

FORTY-SEVEN

6 WEEKS AGO

Charley Willis, 28 years old

Liam stops pacing, looks me dead in the eye, and then he says the words he can't possibly say: 'I know about Mum and Dad.'

I stare at him, mouth open. One of the twins starts crying from the living room, the high-pitched yet somehow gentle whine echoing through the rest of the house. The kitchen suddenly feels very small.

'What do you mean?' I reply.

He leans in. The anger has been replaced by a cocky, sneering amusement. The type of smug arrogance when a person knows something others don't and wants to boast about it without actually saying what they know.

'I know what you did,' he says.

It feels as if I've been dropped in an ice bath. My whole body has chills. No way.

'I don't know what you're talking about,' I reply.

'You do. I know it was you who killed Mum and Dad.'

He's so close to me that I can see the veins of his eyes. I can *feel* his words, the air brushing across me.

'How…?'

'Martha. She couldn't live with it.'

I push myself away from him, but the eye contact is unwavering. 'I don't believe you. There's no way she'd have told anyone. Especially not you.'

I shouldn't have said that. His eye twitches with anger and volcanic fire. 'So how do I know, little sister? How else would I know?'

'No...'

'Martha had to tell someone. She couldn't believe what her little sister had done.' A pause. 'What *our* little sister had done. She was ashamed. Embarrassed.'

I'm shaking my head. 'No...'

I don't want to believe him. There's no way Martha could have said that. It feels like Liam can read my mind as I'm trying to analyse it all. The problem is that he's right. I've never told a soul what happened fifteen years ago. The only way he could know is if Martha told him.

'You know I'm telling you the truth...' he says.

He doesn't seem to be gloating any more. He's already won.

'I don't understand...'

'There's a lot I don't understand either, sis – like why you'd do it.' He holds up a hand before I can say anything. 'I'm not asking. This isn't some heart-to-heart.'

'What do you want?'

'I told you.'

'I don't have money, Liam. It doesn't matter what you say – we don't have anything like what you need.'

'Then I'll go to the police. Simple as that.'

We are interrupted by another cry from the other side of the house. I turn, thinking that someone might be there. Helen with one of the babies, or Seth wondering where I am.

There's no one there, only us.

'What do you get out of that?' I say. 'It's not going to get you any money, is it?'

He steps backwards, further into the kitchen and finally giving me some space. Whatever he might be, Liam must know it's true.

He clicks his fingers and then points at me.

'What?' I say.

'I've got an idea.'

'No.'

'You can't say no, Charlotte. I'll tell the police what I know.'

As I glare back at him, I wonder how we're related. Then I realise it is me who's the odd one out. I can see how he's an amalgam of Mum and Dad. He has their overwhelming desire but none of their talent. He's also got our mother's cruel streak.

I must have come out wrong. Martha's somewhere in between all of us. I loved her so much. I *love* her. I love those kids of hers.

And yet she betrayed me.

I still can't believe it.

'Tell them,' I reply.

'What?'

'Tell the police. Tell anyone you want. Who's going to believe you? What proof have you got?'

It's awful, it's scary and yet I still get that buzz when I see the confusion on his face. He's not even considered this.

'They'll believe it,' he says – but his voice falters halfway through.

'I'm going home,' I reply.

I'm almost out of the kitchen when Liam lunges, grabbing my arm and pulling me roughly back into the room with him.

'If I go down, if I lose this house, everyone's coming down with me. You, Helen, those girls, *everyone.*'

The chills are back. His teeth are clenched, spit flecking between them.

'What do you mean?' I reply.

His eyes are wild. 'That inheritance should've been for Martha and me. You were thirteen, for God's sake. What were they thinking? How could they leave us all the same?'

The strange thing is that I've always wondered about this, too. Liam's furious about this – but it was always money with him. If he'd had one million or ten million, he'd have found a way to blow it. That's who he is.

I'll never know why Mum and Dad decided to split everything equally between us. Martha said she thought it was the fear of shame. Whether they died when they did, or if they lived until they were in their nineties, they had a legacy. People remembered them fondly and if it had come out that they'd done something odd with their will – leaving me out, for instance; or giving everything to a dog sanctuary or something – then it would have affected how they were viewed.

She was probably right. Mum and Dad were thinking about keeping up appearances even when dead. That's their real legacy, I suppose.

'Don't you dare touch those girls,' I say – and in doing so, my brother knows my weakness. If I'm honest, if I were *really* put on the spot, it's hard to care about Liam. We've never known each other and we share nothing in common.

But those girls…

I love Dillon and Daisy like they're my own. Every time I see them, I remember those evenings alone with Martha in the flat. The fun and the jokes. The way we made time pass through doing so little. And when I saw Jasmine and Skye for the first time, the feeling was there, too. I'm not even sure why.

Liam smirks and shows all the nastiness in him. He really is our mother's child.

'Or what?' he scorns. 'What will you do? Go to the police? Do it – you tell them your story and I'll tell them mine.'

Those poor girls. Poor Helen. I don't know how this keeps happening. How my parents somehow fooled so many people for so many years. Child entertainers who were heroes to millions, only they weren't.

'What do you want?' I ask.

My question brings perhaps the first genuine smile of our exchange. I'm shattered.

'All I want is about a hundred grand,' Liam says. 'That'll help me settle a few bills and then I'll leave you alone – that's if you want. You can see the girls. It's all up to you.'

'I don't have a hundred grand, Liam.'

'I've got an idea for that. Mum and Dad used to do it all the time. They were the masters at it. Now it's our turn.'

FORTY-EIGHT

SETH. NOW

'Call the police.'

Charley's instruction is terrifying in its simplicity. I think she's talking to me, but she's not. Helen is still swaying on the sofa, but her eyes are wider and she's starting to sit straighter. Charley pushes herself up from the sofa and strides towards me. She stops in the doorway.

'Call them now,' Charley says.

'Tell them what?' Helen replies, then: 'Where are you going?'

'My parents' house in Langton. Send the police there. Tell them it's urgent. Call now.'

Charley waits until Helen picks up the phone and then rushes past me towards the front door. By the time I catch her, she is almost back at the car.

'Hey, I'm coming, too,' I say.

'Fine.'

I'm not sure if her driving is impressive or reckless. It's probably both. It's definitely frightening. All the while, she's staring unwaveringly in front. Her parents' old house is only six or seven miles from Liam's place – although it's all country lanes.

'How do you know he's gone to your parents'?' I ask.

'Where else is he going to go? It's all about the story for him.'

There's little point in arguing. He's her brother, after all.

'Were you at his house the whole time you were missing? Is that why you knew about the basement?'

'Yes.'

As simple as that. No expansion – one word.

'What about Helen and the girls?' I ask.

'He said they were staying at her mum's. I don't know.'

'You were with him the whole time?'

'Yes.'

I pause as Charley takes a corner on the wrong side of the road. I know I should tell her to stop. If she has a death wish, that's one thing – but there might be other drivers out as well.

When we're back on course, I wait a few moments before asking the other thing. 'What about the black eye?'

'He said he wanted it to look good.'

Liam. Her own brother said that.

'But why?'

Charley finally shows some emotion: a long, loud sigh. Regret? Who knows.

'Money,' she says. 'It's what it's always about with my family.'

She takes another corner and then brakes sharply, tyres squealing on the road. Thank goodness it's dry.

This is ridiculous, but I have a feeling that if I were to say something, she'd screech to a halt and tell me I'm free to get out.

The gates to the Willises' old house are open and Liam's 4x4 is parked where Mason stopped when we visited. The headlights of our car flash across the building site and Charley leaves them on as she slams on the brakes and opens her door. The car's buzzer whines in annoyance at the headlights still being on.

As if the battery matters much right now.

I'm slow off the mark, dazed by the evening. It's late and everything has gone wrong.

Liam is here, precisely as Charley said. It feels as if he's been waiting for her. He's in jeans and a plaid shirt as if he works on the site, standing with his back to the pit. He's on the edge and as Charley races towards him, he holds up a hand.

'Steady there, sis,' he says. 'Don't come too close.'

She stops four or five metres short.

There are two lumpy blankets at his feet and it takes me a second to realise those are his daughters.

They're not moving.

I approach slower, arms out to my side, trying to be unthreatening. Liam acknowledges me with a sideways glance, but he only has eyes for Charley.

'What have you done to them?' she asks. Her voice is calm, but I know her too well. Or thought I did.

She's scared.

I am, too.

'Bit of this sleeping agent,' he says. 'Got it on prescription. Helen seemed to enjoy hers.'

'Those things are dangerous for children.'

'Bit late now.'

Charley takes a half step forward, but Liam growls at her. His feet are right by the blanket balls and he is so close to the edge that it would only take a flick and they'd both be over the top and into the pit. The fall would be five metres, or so. Perhaps enough that an adult might break a bone or two and survive. *Perhaps*. A baby, though…

Liam crouches and nudges the blankets to the side. His eyes don't leave Charley, but he uncovers one twin after the other. There are wispy bits of blonde on top of their heads. They're five months old now, definitely bigger than when we last saw them. They're wearing matching yellow all-in-one romper suits, bottoms bulked from a nappy.

'They're heavier than they look,' he says before standing again. 'I thought you might turn up.'

'Have they been outside this whole time?'

Liam doesn't reply.

'Are they still breathing?' Charley sounds like she might cry.

Liam smirks and there's something awful there. When it comes to Charley's family, her parents specifically, I only knew what everyone else did, until this evening. If her mother was even half as cruel as Charley says, then I can see where it comes from. He's actually amused by all this.

'They're not going to pay you, are they?' he says. 'We're never going to get that money for your interviews.'

Charley is cool again, cooler than me, that's for sure. I'm a little behind her, off to her left, not daring to go any closer in case her psycho brother flips one of those poor girls off the edge. That's if they're still breathing, of course.

'*We* never wanted the money,' Charley replies. 'I didn't want it before and I don't want it now. *You* wanted it. *You* made me do all this. It's always about the money. You really are our parents' son.'

I want to say her name, to tell her to shut up. The bloke is literally on the edge – that's not a time to start pushing.

I say nothing.

'What's wrong with that?' Liam replies. 'It's the world we live in.'

'Your world,' Charley says.

Another smirk. 'Not any more, Charlotte. You were a natural on TV.'

Charley edges a centimetre or two forward. 'Let me take the girls,' she says.

'Uh-uh. Get back.'

His foot hovers over one of the bundles. I'm not sure which twin is which.

'This is murder,' Charley says. 'What do you think's going to happen? How will you explain this?'

'You're the one who knows about murder.' He glances to me. 'Do you know about the monster you married?'

'I, um…'

'Don't talk to him.' Charley speaks over me and her brother grins.

'No one needs to know about this.' He nudges one of the twins with his foot. There's a horrifying fraction of a second where I think he's going to keep pushing, but he doesn't.

'No one needs to know about us being here?' Charley asks.

'Right. We can forget all this.'

'What about the other stuff?'

'They don't know I was with you,' Liam says. 'I've seen the pictures online – it's only the back of my head. You could make up anything. Say it's anyone. You're having an affair, or whatever. Tell them you're still a wreck after what happened to Mum and Dad and Martha. You ran off with someone else and then changed your mind. You made up all that stuff about being abducted because you're mental, or whatever. No one will care in a few weeks.'

'What about the money? I only did all this – *said* all this – because of you. I can do what you say, but it's not going to get you the money.'

'I know. I've thought of that.'

It's not a cold evening. Long-sleeved top and shorts or jeans. No jacket needed – but it feels cold now. There's a slight breeze tickling across the pit but it's more like a hurricane.

Liam nudges one of his daughters with the toe of his boot again. 'This will be the killer,' he says. 'The one from fifteen years ago. He came back and took the girls, threw them into the hole where the house used to be. Cursed house, cursed family. *That's* the story, isn't it? That's what they'll pay to read. This will get us back in the spotlight. Another tragedy. It's all there: Mum, Martha, the girls…'

He tails off as if this is all a straightforward plan that makes perfect sense. As if there aren't people involved. As if his baby daughters aren't at his feet, either dead, doped or both.

'This isn't going to work,' Charley says. Her voice is cold, a tickle on the breeze.

'Why? This is the next thing. My turn, I guess. Mum, dad, sister, now my girls. This is my story, isn't it?'

'Don't do this.'

'You have to keep giving people more, don't you? Mum and Dad knew that. It's why they had you. People were forgetting them, so they had another baby and then they were famous again.'

I'm staring sideways at Charley and I want to hold her so badly. How can anyone live their life knowing this? That a person – an actual human – is window dressing for their egomaniac parents.

'Don't say that, Liam.'

'But it's true, isn't it? I knew it as soon as Mum said she was pregnant. You spent all those years with Martha, thinking you were better than me, but, really, I'm the original. You were there to sell books and make a TV show. You're a prop.'

I take a small step ahead, but I'm still a little behind Charley. I want to tell her she's not a prop to me, she never will be – but this isn't my place. I'm not even sure I should be here.

'People demand more stories,' Liam says. 'More pictures. More access. More everything. The strange thing is, even though you killed Mum and Dad, it completed their story, didn't it? It made them more famous than they could have ever hoped. If they'd stayed alive, they'd have drifted away and, five years later, no one would know who they were. You made them in the end. You know that, don't you?'

I've not had anywhere near enough time to process what Charley told me about her parents – but Liam is right. Charley knows it, too. I can see it in her expression. It's a stunned state of bewilderment, like he's actually struck her.

'I—'

Liam cuts her off. 'That's what gave me the idea. I should've thought of it before. When Helen had twins, I thought people would care. Continuing the Willis legacy and all that – but that isn't what they want. They want tragedy. There is no curse, no killer – but it's only us who knows that. People will believe what they want. They believed it with Mum and Dad, they believed it with Martha.'

It's as if everything has frozen. Charley stares at Liam and he stares back at her.

'There's no way Martha told you what happened,' Charley says. He smiles.

'How could you know?' she adds.

Then Charley's expression changes from measured anger to outright horror.

'Tell me you didn't…'

FORTY-NINE

4 YEARS AGO

Martha Willis, 33 years old

I don't recognise the number that calls my phone. It's a mobile, probably some random who used to know the person that had my number before I did.

'Hello?'

'Martha.'

I recognise his voice straight away, even though I can't remember when we last spoke. Liam.

'How are you doing?' he asks.

The thing is, it doesn't matter how my brother greets me or whatever I say to him, he'll always bring the conversation back to money. It's what he does.

Dillon is busy trying to eat a Duplo block, while Daisy is sleeping in her crib. Mason's busy in the garden, but I pull the living room door closed in case he comes back inside.

'What do you want?' I say quietly.

'All right, sis. Bloody hell. What sort of greeting is that?'

'Just tell me what you want.'

'Fine. I've got news about what happened to Mum and Dad. Can you come to the house?'

I was ready for him to ask for money, primed to tell him to get lost. What I didn't expect was this. How can he know about

Mum and Dad? He can't. Surely he can't? Charley wouldn't have told him and it's only us who know.

'Martha?'

'I'm still here.'

'Can you come? I'll meet you at their house. Don't tell anyone. I'll be there in twenty minutes. It's important.'

I'm about to tell him that it's going to take me at least forty to get there, but he's already gone.

I spend a good minute staring at my phone, wondering if he'll call back or text, wondering if I should.

What the hell?

How could he know? It's impossible.

'Mummy…' Dillon is tugging on my leg, but I didn't even realise he'd crossed the room.

'What, sweetie?'

'Will you come play? I'm making a fire engine.'

There's a mound of red bricks on the carpet that have been bashed together. A fire engine is probably pushing it a bit. If my house was on fire, his concoction of randomly slapped together bricks is not what I'd want rolling up. Not that it *could* roll up. It's only got three wheels and two of them are square.

'That's really smart,' I say. 'I'll see if Daddy can help you.'

'Want you.'

I smooth his hair. 'I know you do, honey – but Mummy has to go out.'

He frowns up at me and it's hard to know if he's actually annoyed. Either way, I pick him up, make a quick check on a still sleeping Daisy, and then head through to the garden.

Mason is busy doing his man stuff. Grrr and all that. He's been digging a hole because, presumably, that's what men do. I want to make fun, but he's all sweaty and the muscles in his upper arms are bulging. Yeah. Grrr and all that.

'I need to go out for a bit,' I say. It's our little code when either of us want a short break from the kids. An hour here, ninety minutes there.

He wipes his brow and puts down the spade. 'Can you give me a couple of minutes to clean up – then I'll come in.'

'Sure.'

It's a long two minutes as I sit in the living room, watching as Dillon puts wings on his fire engine. I can barely focus on him, all I can think of is Liam and what he knows. Or *thinks* he knows.

There's no way I'll let him harm Charley. That girl's been through enough already. None of it was ever her fault.

Mason comes into the living room, wiping his wet hands on his trousers. He grins and places his clammy palms on my cheeks, growling as he gives me a quick kiss.

'Love you,' he says.

'So you should.'

He smiles and laughs as I pass him. We brush hands and there's an electric spark of a tingle between us.

I stop in the doorway and half turn back to him. 'I love you, too.'

Mason has not heard me – because Dillon has launched himself across the room. He's on his back, our son lifted high above him for aeroplanes. I have to go, but I take a second or two to watch them, just that moment in time, to listen to my son giggling his little head off. I want to stay longer, watch them play. This is what it's all about. What everything's about. You want the meaning of life? It's there. A father and son playing aeroplanes on the floor.

But I have to go.

I know the route to my parents' house instinctively, even though I've never driven there from the house where I now live. Uncle David's solicitors keep firing through letters about who knows what. I don't read them any longer. One day the house, or what's left of it, will be sold – but, until then, David can keep whistling for his money.

Money.

This damned family.

When I get to the house, I expect to see Liam's car on the driveway. The gates are open – not that there's anyone to lock them nowadays – but the drive is clear. I park and then head for the front door.

No obvious sign of Liam and I wonder if I should call him. Perhaps this is some stupid joke of his? It's the sort of thing he might do.

I don't even know how we're related. We've never got on, even when we were both living at home. Or *technically* living at home. We were at different boarding schools, back when Mum and Dad could afford it. Not like poor Charley. She was stuck with Mum every day when she got home.

The thing that nobody seems to know, certainly that nobody's asked about in the past ten years or so, is that I have a key for the house. All the toing and froing over who owns what and I could have come and let myself in at any time. I thought the solicitors or whoever would have at least asked – but they never have.

The door creaks noisily inwards as I let myself into the house. As I step inside, I find myself short of breath – and it's not because so many of the surfaces are coated with dust.

I've not been here since that night with Charley and our parents. The time I walked out of this hellhole into the arms of the police is that last time I *ever* walked out of here.

Hardly anything has been moved. The dresser is still off to the side, with the lamps and telephone on top. Mum used to tell people the dresser was an antique, but I was there when she found it among a pile of abandoned furniture on the side of the road. It wasn't an antique; it was someone's cast-off. She got someone to re-varnish it and that was that. She had a story. It was always about the illusion with her.

Liam is in the kitchen, resting against the sink where Charley left a smear of our parents' blood. I scrubbed that area like I've never cleaned anything before – then I dribbled a few drops of tea over it – and the floor. I learned about illusions from my mother.

'You've got a key, too,' Liam says and there's a fraction of a second where I forget everything he's done. He smiles and we're brother and sister.

I hold mine up and he nods.

The kitchen is covered in the same veneer of dust as the rest of the house. I wonder if anything works. I can't believe anyone's been paying the bills, so the electricity and gas must have surely been cut off. Probably the water, too.

Liam holds a hand up, indicating the house. 'Can you believe Uncle David's still arguing over this damned place? They should just knock it down.'

He's skinnier than I remember and I wonder if he's on something. I've seen that rapid weight loss before, although that's perhaps more of a testament to the type of people with whom I was hanging around at the time. The illusion from a moment ago has gone. He's pale and looks less like me than he ever did.

'Why am I here?' I ask.

He tilts his head slightly, doesn't reply.

'What have you found out about Mum and Dad?' I add.

A shake of the head. 'Nothing really… just that life is rubbish. Uncle David's still being a knob about selling this place.'

I almost gasp with relief. Of *course* he doesn't know about Charley. How could he? It was all about getting me here. He's going to ask about money. Why didn't I see that?

'So what?' I reply.

'I'm out of money, sis. I could do with my third of the house.'

And there it is.

'If this place ever gets sold – and that's a big *if* – there's not going to be any money left. The solicitors will take it all.'

He shrugs, but his eyes are unfocused. 'It's been eleven years,' he says.

'I can count.'

'No one cares,' he says. 'Not any more. Everyone's moved on. They did that ten-year thing about Mum and Dad, but that's the end.'

'What did you expect?'

He shuffles on the spot, not even bothering to shrug this time. 'How much have you got left?'

'Nothing for you. Get a job. Find something else to do. Stop living off Mum and Dad's memory – you're the one who said it. It's been eleven years.'

We stand in silence for a few moments.

'I'm going,' I say. 'I've got kids to get back to. You need to sort yourself out.'

'Don't go.'

'Why?'

'I've been thinking. They never caught the person who killed Mum and Dad, did they?'

I stop where I am and then creep back into the kitchen. Is he talking about Charley? Does he *actually* know and this is some strange set-up?

'What are you talking about?'

From nowhere, he seems to focus on me, as if he's in the room properly for the first time. 'What if there *is* a Willis killer?' he says. 'What if there's some sort of family curse? What if whoever killed Mum and Dad comes back all these years later?'

'What are you on about?'

I don't know how it happens, but it suddenly feels as if he's staring through me, as if he can read my mind.

His eyes narrow and he takes a step forward, standing taller, more confident. 'You know who killed them, don't you?'

He's surprised and I know he isn't faking. He didn't know anything – but now he does. I've given the game away.

'Why did you bring me here?' I ask.

It's as if a cloud passes him. There's darkness in his eyes. His very soul. Before I can get out of the kitchen, he's on top of me. I'm on the hard floor of the hallway, his forearm squeezing down hard on my chest. I've stood up to plenty of men in my time, especially when I was younger. Blokes with wandering eyes or, worse, wandering hands. I'd fancy my chances against Liam – but not now. Not when he's like this.

Besides, I've gone soft.

I try to push back against him, but he's too strong – and he's enjoying it too much.

'Who was it?' Liam demands.

He eases off a tiny amount, enough to let me breathe but not even close enough to let me fight back.

'Was it you?' he adds.

'Yes,' I say.

He eases off even more, clamping my arms to my sides with his knees and rocking back. He shakes his head slowly.

'No it wasn't.'

'It was.'

He's still shaking his head. 'It was her, wasn't it? The prop.'

'Don't call her that.'

He grins and there's evil there. The worst of Mum and the worst of Dad, all rolled into one. 'But it was, wasn't it? She finally snapped. I didn't know the little bitch had it in her.'

He actually seems impressed.

'It was me,' I say. 'I did it. Mum slapped me and I lost it.'

'You're a terrible liar.'

I try to wriggle from side to side but can barely move my hands, let alone my legs. It's as if I can see his mind whirring behind those eyes.

'No one else knows this, do they? Just you and the prop… and me. The killer *could* be back. It *could* be a family curse.'

'What are you on about?'

'This is what people want, isn't it? They might have forgotten Mum and Dad, but this is how they'll remember.'

'How?'

Then he punches me in the face.

FIFTY

SETH. NOW

'Tell me you didn't...'

I'm not sure what Charley's talking about. Brother and sister continue to stare at each other and then, finally, Liam speaks.

'I killed her for us.'

I'm the third wheel of all third wheels. Killed who?

Charley is trembling. Her knees wobble and there's a moment in which I think she might crumble to the floor.

'I made us known again,' he says.

Charley's reply is a broken, sorry whimper. 'I didn't want to be known...'

'But it worked, didn't it? If Martha hadn't have died, then everyone would have forgotten. There's a cycle. People forget, so you make them remember again. Look what happened with you last week. We should've been smarter.'

It's then I get it. I blab before I can stop myself. 'You killed Martha?'

Liam sneers at me. 'You're a right Sherlock Holmes, you are.'

Charley hasn't moved. 'Don't do this, Liam.'

'Go home, Charlotte. Get your story straight. Figure out who it was you went off with last week. You were having an affair. So what? You were confused and emotional because of Mum, Dad and Martha. Make it sound good when you say sorry. People will forgive you anything if you convince them. Mum knew that. Tell them what they want to hear. We've all got it in us.'

'I'm not like you.'

He winks. 'Perhaps you should be.'

'Let me take the girls, Liam.'

'No.'

'What are you going to do?'

He glances backwards towards the pit. 'I'm not sure. At first I thought I might just bury them or something. Or throw them in a river? I'd get back to Helen and then we'd both wake up in bed. What do you know, the kids have gone. That's worth a bit, isn't it? People will pay to hear that story.'

'Helen's awake. This is never going to work. Never.'

'I'll think of something. You can help.' He looks to me. 'Both of you. We're family, aren't we?'

In a flash, he bends and sweeps one of his children into his arms in a single movement. He bobs the twin on his shoulder, cooing gently in her ear. I have no idea if she's breathing – or whether it's Skye or Jasmine. Neither of the infants seem to be awake.

Charley steps forward but there's still a good three metres between them.

'Don't,' Liam says. He glances back and there is barely a couple of centimetres between him and the edge. A gust of wind, a slight misjudgement, and he'd be over the edge – twin and all.

Charley moves forward once more. 'You're a maniac,' she says. '*You're* the Willis curse.'

I didn't think there was anywhere to go, but Liam somehow manages to edge back even further. There's a gentle pitter-patter as a crumble of dirt and stones slide down the bank to the pit below. I feel helpless.

'Don't think I won't,' he says. 'Go home.'

'No.'

I take a couple of steps forward, if only to keep up with Charley. 'C'mon, Liam, mate. We can work something out if you need money. I've got savings. There's no need for all this.'

'It's too late now,' Liam says.

If he was manic, I'd expect wide eyes and wild limbs – but he isn't. He's calm and measured – and, if anything, that's even scarier.

There's a pause in time. Everything stops and then: 'Just one,' he says. 'One twin without the other is more of a story, isn't it?'

And then he spins and holds his arm out at full length, daughter extended out over the pit.

FIFTY-ONE

A swirling spectral of red and blue floods the building site as a police car blasts onto the Willis property. A second car is close behind – and a third. The mix of the spiralling lights, the headlights of our car, the moon and the darkness itself creates a dazzling, disorientating disco ball of light. Perhaps it's that, or maybe it's because I blink at the crucial moment. It might even be that I don't want to see what's in front of me – but everything happens at once.

Charley lunges before Liam can figure out what's happening. He doesn't get a chance to resist before she snatches the child from his grasp. There's a moment, the length of time it takes to blink, and then Liam wobbles backwards over the precipice, flailing into the pit below. I don't hear him hit the bottom.

He was on the edge and became disorientated when Charley grabbed the baby. He lost his balance and fell.

Or…

Charley pushed him and then turned away.

I saw what happened, but even I'm not sure. It's almost as if my left eye saw one thing and my right eye saw another. Both versions are equally true and equally false.

Charley kneels on the ground, hugging one twin to her chest and checking on the other. The spiral of red and blue continues as I dash towards her and pick up the bundle of blankets.

'I've got Skye,' Charley says.

'Is she breathing?'

'Yes.'

I place a finger underneath Jasmine's nose – but I don't need to do that. I can see her tiny little chest rising rhythmically and then fall again. Her eyes are closed and she's out like a light.

'We need an ambulance,' Charley says – and I know she's not requesting one for her brother.

Police officers are now out of their cars, edging towards us. I don't recognise any of them, but they seem more confused than aggressive. One of them calls for us to step away from the hole – and we don't need telling twice. Charley moves first, not bothering to look backwards as she walks towards the cars.

I don't get any closer to the edge, but I do glance down. Liam is at the bottom, his left knee at a right angle to the rest of his body.

That's far from the worst thing.

There is a trail of blood dribbling along the concrete pillar lined with spiralled wire that's wedged into the ground. Liam must have hit his head on the way down and, from the unnatural angle at which his neck has contorted, I think he has finally proved the existence of the Willis curse.

FIFTY-TWO

The posters at the police station haven't got any better – but there are a couple of fresh additions. The most obvious newcomer has a picture of a pair of typical stoners. Long coats, backwards baseball caps, marijuana leaf on T-shirts in case the message isn't enough of a sledgehammer.

'You can talk to your kids about drugs, or THEY CAN,' the poster booms.

Subtle.

A second has some bloke with a gormless smile handing his mobile to a random stranger. 'Be SMART with your PHONE,' it reads.

Someone was paid for this.

The police station's waiting room is silent except for the buzzing vending machines. I treat myself to a Double Decker because it's the only chocolate bar that hasn't sold out. The coffee from the machine is like licking a toilet bowl, but I have two anyway. It's the only thing keeping me awake.

I gave my statement about everything that happened, even though I'm not entirely sure of it all. We went to Liam's house where we broke in to find an unconscious and probably drugged Helen, then we drove to Charley's childhood home. There, Liam threatened to drop Skye into the giant hole and then... Charley saved her.

When it comes to why, I tell them what I know – even though it is all second-hand information. Charley wasn't abducted, she was hiding at her brother's because he wanted her to extort money from media interviews. He's skint. When it came out that she'd lied, she was worried about what he might do. I don't know why she did it. You'll have to ask her and all that.

They act like I'm the victim, all sympathy and thanks for your time.

I wasn't sure what to say about the rest. I don't tell anyone what Charley told me about her parents, nor what Liam said about Martha. They don't ask specifically anyway – why would they? It's Charley's secret to share.

When I'm led back to the waiting area, I ask about Jan Astley. He was never officially identified by the police, simply 'a 51-year-old man helping with inquiries' – but that didn't stop his name being mentioned online this morning. Or yesterday morning. It still feels like Saturday, even though it's the early hours of Sunday.

The officer says there is no one currently in custody – but that doesn't change the fact that someone who'd done nothing wrong was dragged in for interview and then named on the internet. There's no one to blame for that other than Charley. Telling the police it wasn't him was never going to be enough.

My wife has been giving her statement for a lot longer than I did and it is now exactly a week since I was scrabbling around the bushes and trees at the back of the hotel looking for her.

Someone had said something about putting off her interview until morning, but I think Charley wanted to talk. Besides, I don't know if she's merely a witness, under arrest, or anything else. She called a solicitor to be at her side and he drove down from London. Someone she used to know through Martha, apparently. I'm not that sure of the details. I was by myself.

It's hard to fight back the yawns as the sun starts to come up again. It's not simply the length of time I've been awake, it's the sheer number of things that have emerged in the recent hours.

My wife is a murderer.

She admitted as much to me. It's not that I don't understand the reasons why, but it's hard to get my head around. Will I ever look at her the same?

It's all I can think about and yet it doesn't feel as if I *can* process any of it. Time passes: a blink and yet an age. Charley eventually emerges from one of the interview rooms along the hall.

The officers take her to the counter at the front of the station and they talk about something I don't catch. The solicitor leaves and then they bring her over to the area where I've been waiting. She yawns but smiles wearily through it. Her hair is limp but there's a curly bit at the front from where she must have been twiddling it.

'Morning,' she whispers, linking her arm into mine. I don't resist.

The officer asks if she understands when she has to return to answer bail and, after Charley says she does, she is officially free to go.

Our car is still at the Willis family house – evidence, apparently – though I'm not exactly sure for what. We're in Langton, the place closest to where Charley lived as a child. There are no buses at this time on a Sunday, no obvious way to get back except for a taxi perhaps.

'Do you want a walk?' Charley asks.

I'd rather sleep but we have a lot to discuss.

'Yes,' I reply.

Charley squeezes my hand and interlocks her fingers with mine. I let her but don't press back. 'You waited,' she says.

'You're my wife.'

She squishes my fingers again as we head onto the pavement and set off in the vague direction of… I'm not even sure. It's much too far to walk home, but the sun is on its way up. The sky is a smoky wash of red and orange and it's already warm.

'Are you in trouble?' I ask.

'Maybe. My solicitor says there are plenty of mitigating circumstances.'

I wait and then it comes.

'...For going missing,' she adds. 'They're looking at wasting police time, but they can find out that Liam was in financial trouble. They know he took his daughters to the house, that he had problems.' She pauses. 'And it's my word against someone who can't claim any differently.'

I would tell her that it's *our* word. I've told the police pretty much what I would imagine she has. Given the police will take some sort of statement from Helen, plus there will be toxicity tests on her and the twins to find out whatever it was Liam doped them with, that will be a pretty powerful picture painted against him.

'Jasmine and Skye are at the hospital,' Charley says. 'An officer said they were going to pick up Helen and take her there – but that was hours ago. I should call her. The officer said he'd spoken to a paramedic who thought they were going to be fine.'

She doesn't mention Liam.

'Did you tell the police about Martha?' I ask.

There's a long pause, only the sound of our footsteps interrupting the morning quiet.

'Didn't seem much point,' Charley says eventually. 'Not now. What are they going to do? No one can prove anything. I'll tell Mason. He's been through enough.'

'What about your parents?'

Charley is silent. She points over towards an elaborate building that has a spire on top. 'That's the town hall,' she says. 'There's a plaque for Mum and Dad out front. There's another in the park behind, too. People lay flowers every year.'

We continue walking and I can't believe how loud the birds are. From nowhere, it's like they've all got up early to do their absolute best to annoy the town. C'mon, fellas, it's a Sunday.

'That wasn't me with my parents,' she says after a long break. 'I mean, it was. But not me as I am now. I was thirteen. That was Charlotte. I'm not like that any longer. Martha saved me.'

I think about that blink at the Willis house. The push or the stumble. I told the officers I didn't see what happened, that I was distracted by the spinning red and blue lights. If they'd seen properly, they wouldn't be asking. Besides, she saved a baby, didn't she?

'I'm sorry,' Charley says quietly. 'I'm sorry for leaving. I'm sorry for lying. I'm sorry for not telling you about everything else with my parents.' A pause and then: 'I think the Willis curse is real.'

I don't reply. I'm not sure I can.

'I don't mean a curse like a horror-movie thing, I mean I think my family is broken. Mum and Dad never wanted me. Liam was right – I was a prop to them. I did something awful. Martha helped cover it up. Liam did something terrible to her – and now look at him. Everyone's gone. It's only me left – but look at what I did to you. Look what I let Liam talk me into. Look at what he was going to do to his own daughters. We *are* cursed, or perhaps it's just me…?'

She leaves it there and I know she probably wants me to refute it. To say that she's not a jinx at all. Then I wonder what Jan Astley might think of it all.

I wonder if I still believe what I thought before. When you meet a person, if that *is* a new starting point, if you can forgive everything that went before, then you surely can't have a *second* starting point. How many lines can a person draw?

Thirteen-year-old Charlotte Willis was a different person than the Charley Willis I know and so, perhaps, the past *is* the past. She didn't tell me about her parents and she had a reason for that.

The problem is that blink. The push or the accidental fall. Left eye. Right eye. A killer. A saviour.

We're not holding hands any longer. I'm not sure if it was me who let go, or her.

I need to sleep; we need to go to the hospital. At some point we'll be back at the police station. Pamela will probably call. Charley's a liar, a rescuer, or both together.

Her brother's descent into madness, the kidnapping of his daughters and subsequent death is even bigger than what happened last week, which has left us back at the beginning. Liam got so much wrong, but he was right about this: tragedy sells. Misery sells – and, my word, if there are two things that the Willis family does well, it's tragedy and misery.

They say you can't choose your family, but I chose mine a week ago.

The problem is that I have no idea what I picked.

AUTHOR'S NOTE

I've written a fair few books over the past years. Within them all are different characters and scenarios. Good people and bad. Ones that came easily, others that didn't. In among the hundreds of creations who've been scattered among those pages, nobody has had the effect on me that Martha Willis did.

After I finished writing this book, Martha was stuck in my head like nobody I've ever written about before. I ended up writing another novel entirely – *Two Sisters* – because I couldn't get past the relationship between Martha and Charley here. (I realise *Two Sisters* came out before this – but I wrote it afterwards.)

In literary terms, what happened to Martha here is probably the worst thing I've ever done to a character. I still can't quite believe it. I knew her fate before I started writing and the closer I got to her end, the more it felt like I couldn't quite write the words. She didn't deserve what happened to her.

This is the end of Charley and Seth's story. There is no sequel, but that doesn't stop me from thinking about poor Charley from time to time. She's the best and the worst of me. The light and the darkness. The thing I like most about this job and the thing I could live without.

I hope you enjoyed reading this as much as I enjoyed building Charley's world. If you did, please do leave a review on your platform of choice. It'll mean a lot.

Cheers,
Kerry Wilkinson, May 2018